"I'm leaving the magazine, Max."

Sara stared at him defiantly. "First you take my work apart, then you criticize my appearance, and now you try a little sexual therapy because you think I need it. Well, I don't. And I'm quitting. I never want to see you again."

His eyes were blazing with pain and anger. "All right, Sara," he said finally. "If that's what you want. Live in your little frozen fantasy world for the rest of your life. Why should I care?"

He strode to the bedroom door and turned, his features drawn and bitter.

"Just remember this. When you finally grow up, don't come running to me. I've had enough of your ice-maiden act. As far as I'm concerned, we're finished!"

Books by Vanessa James

HARLEQUIN PRESENTS
784—THE FIRE AND THE ICE
793—THE DEVIL'S ADVOCATE

These books may be available at your local bookseller.

Don't miss any of our special offers. Write to us at the
following address for information on our newest releases.

Harlequin Reader Service
P.O. Box 52040, Phoenix, AZ   85072-2040
Canadian address: P.O. Box 2800, Postal Station A,
5170 Yonge St., Willowdale, Ont.   M2N 6J3

VANESSA JAMES

the fire and the ice

Harlequin Books

TORONTO • NEW YORK • LONDON
AMSTERDAM • PARIS • SYDNEY • HAMBURG
STOCKHOLM • ATHENS • TOKYO • MILAN

Harlequin Presents first edition May 1985
ISBN 0-373-10784-6

Second printing July 1985

Original hardcover edition published in 1982
by Mills & Boon Limited

CHAPTER ONE

'Am I late?'

Still out of breath from her race from the bus stop, Sara swung the foyer doors behind her and came to a halt at the reception desk. Mr Jones, commissionaire, messenger, and general factotum, gave her a broad wink. She saw his eyes take in what she was wearing—all of which had been put on in haste, because she had overslept. Tight jeans, a crumpled blouse, and somewhat scuffed shoes. Mr Jones consulted his watch with an oracular air.

'Two minutes past, love,' he said. 'You're O.K., I'd say. He's been in since eight-thirty, mind. Flipping great Jag too, blocking the whole car park. . . .'

Having got her breath, Sara began to take in Mr Jones's appearance. She stared at him in fascination. His normal attire was a natty three-piece suit, with, in summer, invariably a red carnation. It was eccentric, but it suited him. Today . . . she gazed in disbelief at an appearance of military majesty. He was wearing a dark blue serge uniform, complete with epaulettes, and on top of the desk rested a cap with a badge and a shiny sergeant-major peak.

Mr Jones grinned.

'Like it? I do. Takes me back to the war, this does.'

'I think I preferred the suit.'

'Oh, I don't know . . .' Mr Jones put the cap on and adjusted it to a rakish angle, so Sara had to laugh. He tapped his nose in a gesture indicating he was sussing the lie of the land.

'There's going to be a few changes, I'd say, love, and this is just the start of it. Oh yes, one month from now I'd say this magazine was going to be a *very* different kettle of fish. *Very* different. Wait till you see what's happened upstairs on editorial . . . All done in three days too, *and* to Mr Christian's personal specifications.'

'Has he made a lot of changes?'

Mr Jones gave her another broad wink.

'Just you go on up, Sara. Wouldn't want to spoil the surprise, now would I?'

Sara stared at him.

'But the office has only been shut for three days,' she said weakly. 'Just Friday to Sunday. They can't have done much.'

'Oh no?' he gestured towards the lift. 'You go up and take a rain check, love. Why, I'd lay evens that Miss Sara Ford will be coming in here in a skirt pretty soon—and that's not a bet I'd have taken on before.'

Sara stared at him weakly. 'A skirt—me?'

'That's right, love. Got the paper for me, have you?'

Hastily Sara rummaged in her bag and found the copy of the *Daily Mirror* she always brought in with her for Mr Jones. He took it from her, and instead of opening it at the racing page as usual, tucked it away under the desk.

'Have to save it for the lunch hour now,' he said. 'Now, you go up. Wish I could see your face when you get there!'

Hastily Sara hurried into the lifts, and pressed the button for the fifth floor. Even the lift looked different, she noted. Its floor had been cleaned, the mahogany shone, someone had polished all the brass handles. When she reached the editorial floor she hauled back its heavy gates and stared around her. The corridors smelled of new paint. Gone was the linoleum and the shabby cream walls she had grown so fond of. Instead everything was white; posters of *London Now* covers framed in expensive steel lined the walls. A new beige carpet had been laid . . . She flung back the door of her old cubbyhole of an office and stared in disbelief.

'Oh *hell*!' she said finally. 'Where's my desk?'

Before the weekend, the offices of *London Now* had consisted of a comfortable clutter of small rooms, all partitioned off from each other, all somewhat messy, a warren of desks and ancient filing cabinets, of books and back issues of the magazine, of superannuated typewriters and coffee cups and giant tins of Nescafé. Now . . . Sara could hardly believe her eyes.

The partitions were gone. As far as she could make out, the entire staff of the magazine was congregated in one giant room that ran the length of the building. The whole room was pristine, glaring white. The desks were new, the secretaries were perched in front of the most expensive golf-ball typewriters; one end of the room was banked with brilliant red filing cabinets in front of which a cluster of girls from the typing pool was bent over piles of papers, obviously rearranging the entire filing system. There was a typing pool, she realised, down at one end, and from there the staff were carefully arranged in serried ranks. First the sub-editors, with her flatmate, Jennifer, the senior sub, sitting at the largest desk; then the editorial staff— Mark Shand, the Arts Editor, Harry Wallace, the Features Editor, Deirdre Neal, the Home Editor, who was responsible for the kind of stories Sara most disliked, all about interior design, wretched wallpapers and curtains, and fancy cookery . . . Then, at the far end of the room, were, she realised, what must now be the desks for staff writers. She recognised her own at last, but only by the stacks of papers piled on its top, and the wilting rubber plant that had been a present from Jennifer. She took a deep breath. She had expected changes, yes, but this was worse than anything she had ever imagined. In three days, the new editor had managed to erase everything about the offices she had most liked. The place looked chic, and expensive—and also unfriendly. It was like a factory, she thought rebelliously. A word factory.

'Jeans, dear? Aren't we bold!'

Deirdre Neal, who was sitting nearest the door, gave her an acid smile.

Sara ignored her. From the far end of the room she could see Jennifer making signals towards the door of the ladies' cloakroom, and she followed her there, grinning at the chorus of catcalls and ribald remarks that greeted her appearance as she walked the length of the room. She must talk to Jennifer, and it was impossible in here now. Every word, every phone call would be audible to about forty other people . . . In the cloakroom she dumped her overflowing bag on the basins, and leaned against the cool tiled walls. At least the new broom hadn't reached this far! Jennifer came in and gave her a grin.

'Quite a transformation, isn't it?'

'It looks ghastly.' Sara rummaged in her untidy bag for her hairbrush and stared gloomily at her own reflection in the glass. Her face stared back at her, heart-shaped, pale, dusted with gold freckles. No matter how she tried to discipline it, her long hair continued to curl in soft tendrils around her face. She looked nervous, she thought irritably, and—as usual—boyish. Not that she minded *that*, but she looked about fifteen rather than twenty-three. Not the kind of woman who'd be able to stand up to Max Christian.

'Was anyone consulted about all that?' She gestured to the room next door where the telephones had begun to shrill.

Jennifer laughed. 'Consulted? Don't be stupid. Of course not. Max Christian apparently believes that open-plan offices create a greater sense of work intimacy. They stimulate the exchange of ideas or something. And he wasn't particularly interested in his own staff's views on the subject.'

'He wouldn't be.' Sara abandoned the desultory attempt to tidy her own appearance, and pushed the brush back in her bag. She gave Jennifer a wan smile. 'And where's his place in this new scheme of things? He's going to be in there with us, is he, madly exchanging ideas?'

'Wrong again.' Jennifer lit a cigarette and leaned wearily against the basins. 'He has Geoffrey's old office: unchanged in structure, but rumoured to be redecorated. Four soundproof walls, and three secretaries to guard the door.'

'Three secretaries?' Sara's eyebrows rose. The amiable Geoffrey, to whom she owed so much, had managed with one plus the typing pool.

'It seems Mr Christian expects to be generating a great deal more work from his office, so he's brought his *Bystander* secretaries with him. The word is, you don't get past the door without a prior appointment.'

'An *appointment*?' Sara stared at Jennifer in horror. To see Geoffrey Fletcher at any time of the day had involved no formality. If a problem had come up, one had simply taken it straight to him, and he had dealt with it. No fuss, no pomposity. Oh, *why* had Geoffrey retired? she thought. Why, of all people, did the new editor have to be Max Christian? She sighed.

'He's in already, I gather.'

Jennifer giggled. 'Certainly. One brown Jaguar XJ6, latest registration, blocking the entrance where everyone used to park illegally. *Not* popular with the parking attendant!'

'And has anyone seen the miracle man yet?'

Jennifer shook her head.

'Absolutely not. He's been closeted away in his office. We're all scheduled to see him today at precisely timed intervals. A bit like the animals going into the Ark, except we have to face him on our own. Pity it's not two by two. I'm not looking forward to it. Still, I'm not till after lunch, so I intend to fortify myself first. Just a bit. What time are you?'

Sara fumbled in her bag and eventually found the dog-eared memorandum she had received the previous week.

'Not until six,' she said.

'*Six?*' Jennifer looked surprised. 'You know what that means? It means he's left you till last—the latest other appointment is five-thirty.'

Sara considered this piece of information. It did not exactly increase her confidence.

'It doesn't surprise me,' she said miserably. 'In the circumstances. He's probably saving me for the last so he has plenty of time to haul me over the coals. I'm sure he's looking forward to it.'

'Bound to be,' said Jennifer, cheerfully and unsympathetically. 'And it's your own fault. Serves you right for being such a bitchy writer. This is where you get your come-uppance, Sara Ford.'

Sara stared at her friend.

'Bitchy?' she said slowly. 'Do you really think that?'

Jennifer hesitated. 'Well,' she said finally, obviously trying to be more gentle, 'you can be a bit . . . well, harsh sometimes. And what you wrote about him . . .' She broke off, seeing the expression on Sara's face. 'All right, all right,' she said hastily. 'I know what you think about him. I can remember what you wrote. So can he, I expect! But I shouldn't worry. It was two years ago—and anyway, he can't have a very long lecture in mind. The party's at seven, remember?'

'Oh no! I'd forgotten.' Sara groaned.

'Sara! You're impossible! How can you forget something like that? I reminded you last night . . .'

'I was writing last night.'

'I know you were. But still . . .' Jennifer looked at her critically. 'You have brought something to change into, haven't you? I can't think why you wore those wretched jeans today anyway. I told you not to. You were the one who quoted all those remarks of his about women in trousers, remember?'

Sara looked away. She did remember, only too well. She felt herself blushing, and felt furious with herself.

'He's bound to think it was a calculated insult.'

'And so it was,' Sara said, with bravado. But Jennifer was not to be fooled.

'Rubbish,' she said crisply. 'It's probably just that you don't possess a skirt, and if you do, it's crumpled under a pile of ironing waiting for the magic moment when you haven't got something to write and feel domesticated.'

Sara laughed.

'O.K.', she said, 'I admit it. But I had honestly forgotten about the party. Do we have to go?'

'Nothing would make me miss it.' Jennifer grinned. 'It's at his house, so champagne and caviare, I should think. I can't wait! The whole staff's going, anyway, so you can't duck it.'

Sara picked up her bag. The prospect of the day ahead, and then the party, filled her with gloom. If only she could get a job somewhere else, she thought. Anywhere would do, just so she didn't have to work for Max Christian.

'Oh well,' she shrugged, 'I'd better go and do some work, I suppose.' She made for the door, and Jennifer caught her sleeve.

'One more thing.' She lowered her voice to a whisper. 'Have you seen where your desk is?'

'Sure,' said Sara miserably. 'In the most cramped corner of that beastly room, so my elbow will be sticking into the Xerox machine. Very cosy!'

'Worse than that. Have you seen who's been given the desk next to yours?'

Sara stopped in her tracks. 'No, who?'

'Delia Waterlow.'

Sara groaned in disbelief. '*Delia?* But she's fashion. She was on another floor altogether. Why should she be that end of the room?'

'Malice, I would imagine,' Jennifer said simply. 'He may not know how much you dislike her, but it's a pretty safe guess that you two wouldn't get on. Quite a lot of thought's gone into the arrangement of that room, I'd say.'

Sara backed away from the door and slumped against the wall. All this was proving much worse than she had imagined. Of all the staff, it was Delia she most loathed. To have Delia, of all people, at the next desk, quacking away in her Belgravia voice, Darling this and Darling that. Sara felt ill at the prospect. It was not just, she thought angrily, that Delia represented everything she most disapproved of, it was that she was no good at her silly job anyway. The pictures were good—if you liked anorexic models swathed in furs leaning against Rolls-Royces, Sara thought sourly. But Delia was hopelessly disorganised. She was always messing things up, double-booking photographers for photo-sessions, muddling credits for clothes, and then having to be extricated by her own underpaid and anonymous assistants. She wouldn't even *have* the wretched job, Sara thought, if her father, the rarely glimpsed Sir Andrew, didn't own *London Now* and the rest of the group of newspapers and magazines that made up one of the last great Fleet Street empires.

'I think I'll go home now.' She gave Jennifer a smile. 'That just about puts the lid on it. I don't think I can bear it. The very thought of having to sit next to . . .'

She broke off as the door swung back.

On a waft of Patou's *Joy*, Delia came in, stopped, and gave both girls a dazzling smile. Even by her own standards, which were exacting, Delia had obviously made a considerable effort with her appearance that day. Her long mane of blonde hair was newly streaked. Her high cheekbones gleamed with a bronzy-pink blusher; she was wearing the famous false eyelashes, which took a make-up artist friend of hers an hour to apply. Her slender figure was swathed in a stunningly pretty mauve suede dress, she wore amethyst earrings, and an amethyst ring the size of a pigeon's egg on her right hand. Her nails, Sara noted, matched the colour of the dress exactly.

'Darlings,' she said, adjusting her thick hair in the glass. '*What* are you lurking in here for? You'll have to face him sooner or later, you know.'

'The later the better, I'd say,' Sara muttered.

Delia smiled sweetly. Her voice had a quite extraordinary ability to inflect from a quack to a coo, as Sara had noticed in the past. Now she cooed.

'Listen,' she said, turning to Jennifer, and ignoring Sara completely. 'He was round to dinner with Daddy last night . . .' Sara snorted at the word 'Daddy', which Delia, who was at least twenty-six, used without embarrassment, but Delia took no notice. 'He was closeted away with him for *hours*. But honestly, when we did all finally have dinner, I was totally won over. He may *seem* a bit supercilious,' here she glanced at Sara, 'but that's only if he takes a dislike to someone. He doesn't suffer fools gladly. That's all. Daddy thinks he's amazing. He thinks he's going to transform this magazine. After all, look what he did for *Bystander* when he was there . . .'

'Oh, I can well imagine,' Sara said drily, ignoring Jennifer's warning looks. 'How terrific for you, Delia. I mean, I'm sure you always hankered to work for *Bystander*, that fascinating chronicle of jet set life. Now you'll be able to. Without even changing jobs.'

'Just desks,' Jennifer said demurely.

Delia's blue eyes, which no amount of make-up could render other than slightly small and steely—rather as if she were constantly calculating the number of carats in a diamond from a distance—narrowed.

'Not at all,' she said sharply. 'He doesn't want to change this magazine. He admires its tradition of investigative reporting. He said so last night. He said it just needed re-focusing, that's all. And livening up a bit, of course, which poor old Geoffrey could never understand.' She smiled complacently at her own reflection in the glass. '*I'm* going to have *much* more space for a start. At *least* a fortnightly four-page spread, he said yesterday.'

She let this piece of information sink in, and then, with a final adjustment of her hair, swung out. Sara and Jennifer looked at one another, and Jennifer grimaced.

'I know what *that* means,' she said.

'So do I. It'll begin with fashion, and before we know where we are, it'll be features on luncheon at the Ritz, London's top hostesses and where's the really in place to go skiing. Kiss goodbye to hard news, I'd say. Roll on an up-market gossip sheet.'

'Oh well, ours not to reason why,' Jennifer said gloomily.

'Well, I don't agree with *that* for a start,' said Sara, and picking up her bag she marched defiantly back to her desk.

'*Darling!*' Delia was in mid-quack down a telephone twelve inches from Sara's elbow. With a gesture of convincing carelessness, Sara managed to knock over her rubber plant. It crashed on to the next desk, scattering dry earth all over Delia Waterlow's unimpressive in-tray. She shouldn't have done it, Sara thought. But it made her feel a whole lot better.

'Drink, Sara?'

Sara looked up from her lunch-time plate of cottage pie, to find Mark Shand at her elbow.

'It's O.K., thank you, Mark,' she said quickly, 'I'll get one in a minute—when the bar's less crowded.'

'No, you won't. Dry white wine?' He smiled at her. 'Forget your principles for once, Sara. Men are very useful when it comes to fighting their way through for a drink.'

Sara smiled. She liked Mark, and she liked his teasing.

If only he wouldn't keep asking her out it would all be fine, she thought. 'All right. Thank you, Mark.'

He disappeared in the throng of journalists at the bar, and then returned balancing glasses, with impressive speed.

'Cheers!' He raised his glass, settled himself beside her and gave her a sideways glance. Sara pushed the plate of cottage pie away, half uneaten.

'Nervous?' Mark Shand's glance was keen. Sara shook her head.

'Not at all,' she said firmly. 'I'm just not hungry, that's all.'

'You needn't be, you know. I've seen him already. I didn't think he was quite the ogre you painted.'

'You didn't?' Sara looked at him curiously. In spite of herself, she was interested to hear Mark's impressions. He was a nice man, and astute. She couldn't believe he would like Max Christian any more than she had done two years ago. But two years ago was quite a long time. It was possible he might have changed.

'No.' Mark lit a cigarette and stared at it thoughtfully. 'After what you wrote about him, I went in expecting the worst. Vanity, conceit, pride, a full catalogue of the seven deadly sins, in fact. With a few other qualities such as total intolerance, intransigence, thrown in for good measure.'

'And you found?'

'I found someone I rather liked.'

Sara stared at him.

'You *liked* him?'

Mark laughed at the disbelief in her face.

'As a matter of fact, yes. I'm not a woman, of course, let alone a liberated lady journalist like you, so I couldn't speak for his male chauvinist tendencies. But I liked him. He made me laugh. He listened to what I had to say, which I didn't expect. And he gave me the impression he'd do something about it. Which is more than Geoffrey ever did.'

'He'll never be like Geoffrey,' Sara said quickly. Mark smiled.

'Sara,' he said gently, 'You don't have to leap to

Geoffrey's defence. We all liked him. But you shouldn't blind yourself to his faults, and he did have them, you know. We all do.'

'If it wasn't for Geoffrey, I'd still be a secretary,' Sara said obstinately. 'It was he who gave me my first chance. I owe everything to him.'

'I know that, Sara.' Mark leaned across and looked at her intently. 'Geoffrey had an instinct for finding writers. It was a talent he never lost—like his nose for a story. But he wasn't young any more, you know. He was nearly sixty-five, and in poor health. It was he who suggested Max Christian to succeed him—you ought to remember that. Geoffrey knew as we'll as anyone that the magazine needed new blood, fresh ideas . . .'

Sara looked away. For some reason she felt almost close to tears. She had been so fond of Geoffrey, with his pipe and his funny old-fashioned tweed suits; his kindness and his gentleness. He'd been almost like a father to her . . .

'Sara.' Mark rested his hand gently on hers, and, as he felt her flinch, quickly removed it. 'Give Max Christian a chance. After all, it was two years ago, you know. He's probably forgiven you for all that, even if he hasn't forgotten it.'

'Oh, he won't have forgotten it,' Sara said quickly.

'No, I don't suppose he will have,' Mark spoke quietly, and Sara could hear something like reproach in his voice. She turned to him.

'You mean you think I got it all wrong?'

Mark shrugged and looked away. 'Who knows?' he said lightly. 'You do have a few prejudices of your own, Sara, as far as the opposite sex is concerned.'

'That's not true, Mark,' Sara said hotly. 'It was just him, the way he spoke to me. The way he treated his secretaries at *Bystander* as if . . . as if he were some kind of sultan in a harem!'

Mark laughed. 'They've all come with him to *London Now*,' he said drily, 'so they can't have minded all that much.'

'And anyway,' Sara ran on, hardly hearing his interruption, 'there was nothing generalised about my reaction to him. It was absolutely specific, it was because he . . .'

'Then have dinner with me tonight, after the party, Sara.'

Sara stopped in mid-sentence, feeling her cheeks flush with colour.

'Mark——' she hesitated. 'I can't . . . I have to get home. I have a piece I have to finish writing.'

Mark Shand smiled. .

'Last time of asking,' he said lightly. 'You've always got a deadline, Sara. What are you writing, *War and Peace?*'

In spite of herself, Sara smiled, and Mark rose to his feet.

'Never mind, Sara,' he said. 'Forget I asked. I'll see you at the party anyway. And—good luck this afternoon. Just remember. Forget his pride and think of your own prejudices. No one stays the same after two years. Not even Max Christian.'

Before she could bring out the quick retort that had risen to her lips, he was gone, and Sara was left staring miserably after him. So, she thought. Even Mark thought she had been unfair to Max Christian in that wretched piece she'd written about him. Well, let them wait she thought stubbornly, lifting her chin. She was right, she was sure of it. Give it a few weeks, until the honeymoon period was over. Then they'd all see what kind of man Max Christian was.

Back at the office the afternoon seemed to drag interminably. Feeling on edge and frustrated, Sara got on with routine work. One by one she watched the other members of staff disappear in the direction of the new editor's office, and return looking noticeably more cheerful. Deirdre Neal went in at four, and came out beaming.

'*What* a charmer,' she said to Delia, and the two of them whispered and giggled together.

'Like Robert Redford, I thought,' Sara heard.

'Or Clint Eastwood . . .'

'Stewart Granger in his prime?'

'Better than any of them, I'd say,' and the rest was drowned in laughter. Sara tried not to listen. She banged her typewriter keys. The hands of the clock seemed to stick, they moved so slowly. By the time six was approaching, most people were beginning to pack up. The party was ahead of them all, and Sara could feel the room pulsing with an odd sense of excitement. The light outside was beginning to fade when Jennifer came over to her desk.

'I'm going back to the flat—I've decided to change.'

Sara looked up. Even Jennifer, she noted, had been infected by the atmosphere.

'Well, I'll have to see you there,' Sara said flatly. 'I haven't time to go back now.'

'You're going like that?'

'What else can I do? I haven't even had the Big Interview yet.'

Jennifer sighed.

'Sara, you're impossible! How are you getting to Kensington?'

Sara shrugged. 'Tube, I suppose.'

'Then you'll be late, as well as underdressed. Still, it's your funeral. See you there, idiot.'

Jennifer grinned and dropped a quick kiss on her friend's head.

'Here you are,' she said. She dropped a small packet on to Sara's desk. 'For you. I knew this would happen, so I went out specially and got it at lunchtime.'

'What is it?' Sara stared in surprise at the small packet.

'It's a kit—one packet eyeshadow, one lipstick, one tube mascara. Not Estée Lauder, but better than nothing. If you have to go in jeans, you could make an effort on your face.'

Sara slowly unwrapped the paper. In spite of herself, she could feel the excitement suppressed in the room beginning to reach her. It was years since she'd worn make-up. Ages since she'd been to a party . . .

Jennifer turned.

'Don't thank me,' she said drily. 'Just wear it. Then even in jeans you might turn out to be the belle of the ball. With your natural advantages, that is.' She grinned. 'Go on, promise. I did it specially to put Delia's nose out of joint. She left at four-thirty to get ready, in case you didn't notice.'

Sara hesitated. 'Well, maybe the lipstick,' she said weakly.

'All of it. Otherwise I'll be offended. See you!'

When she had gone, Sara looked for the millionth time at the clock. It was five to six. Should she do as Jennifer suggested? Suddenly she felt lighthearted. Why not? Quickly she ducked into the cloakroom and applied the make-up. She didn't do it very well, she thought wryly, because she was so out of practice, but it did produce quite a transformation. Her own eyes, suddenly enormous, and ringed with dark lashes startlingly dark against the soft honey of her hair, stared back at her, wide with anxiety. She looked at her watch, and hurriedly stowed the make-up in her bag. It was six. Quickly she went down the corridor to the door of Geoffrey's old office. It was firmly shut. Three new desks flanked its entrance, two of them with their in-trays empty, their typewriters neatly covered. At the third a girl Sara recognised from the *Bystander* offices was typing fast. She looked up coolly as Sara approached.

'Miss Ford? I'm afraid Mr Christian is not free yet. I'll call you when he's ready.'

Feeling doubly nervous, and irritated, Sara returned to her desk. The minutes ticked by. Phrases from the article she had written about Max Christian filtered through her mind. How she had disliked him! She'd had plenty of ammunition even before she saw him, of course. All that information the paper's gossip column had given her about his partying, his long chain of ex-girl-friends, about the special tailor where he bought his suits, the hand-made silk shirts from Jermyn Street, especially made up for him in blue silk that matched the somewhat perturbing colour of his eyes . . . And then he'd given her plenty of ammunition as soon as she'd met him. All those remarks about Fleet Street feminists, about career women. Still, she thought, that was only to be expected from someone like Max Christian. In his world women were there to be decorative, to be assets to a man's career. He had been born with a silver spoon in his mouth. What did he know about people who had had to struggle to find the work they wanted, to make ends meet?

She'd been to this house where the party would be held. He'd insisted she went back there for a drink after their interview, and—curious—she had accepted. It had been just as she expected, of course—a rich bachelor's house. 'A bit far from Harrods,' he had said, as he opened the door, and she'd used *that* quote against him, of course, though afterwards, the way in which he had said it had worried her. Almost sarcastically, as if he had known what she would do with it, and it amused him to give her all the ammunition she was so carefully storing in her memory.

The internal telephone on her desk shrilled, and Sara jumped.

'This is Beverley. Mr Christian will see you now, Miss Ford.'

Sara got up quickly, feeling her heart starting to race. Her palms felt damp with nervousness. She might have been wearing jeans to work for the past year, but in spite of herself, she wished heartily she had bothered to find something else that morning.

The secretary looked up coolly as Sara reached her desk. 'Do go in.'

Tentatively Sara tapped at the door and pushed it open.

The room was in semi-darkness, but one glance told her that it had been transformed as swiftly and irrevocably as the rest of the offices. It was dominated now by an enormous antique desk, lit only by the beam of an anglepoise lamp, as if by a stage spotlight. The top was thick with papers; it was flanked by a rank of telephones. In the beam of light she saw Max Christian clearly. He was in shirt-sleeves, with the tie loosened and the shirt open at the neck. His dark head was bent over the papers in front of him, and as she came in he did not look up.

There was a silence, and Sara stood there awkwardly. There was a chair in front of the desk. Should she sit down? She was just about to move forward, when he looked up.

With a shock she saw again the face she remembered so

well. She had seen it constantly in newspaper photographs, of course, in the two years since they had met,
but no photograph quite conveyed its power, though they
caught something of its beauty. It was a harsh face,
narrow and tanned, the thick black hair falling forward
over straight strongly marked brows. The mouth lacked
all humour, she thought, as she had thought before. It
had a bitterness about it, and also a sensuality that she
disliked. But it was the eyes which were so arresting, so
disconcerting. They were a vivid dark blue, quite at odds
with the colouring of his hair, and their direct gaze never
faltered.

'Yes?'

'You wanted to see me, I think.' Sara could hear her
own voice shake, and cursed herself silently. 'We had an
appointment for six.'

'We did?' With irritating casualness he glanced at his
watch, then down at a typewritten list on his desk. 'And
you are . . .?'

Sara stared at him in disbelief. Maybe she hadn't
expected him to recognise her, not after two years. But he
must know she was on the staff; he must remember who
she was.

'I'm Sara Ford,' she said quietly.

'Oh yes. Miss Ford.' He looked down at the list again.
'Do sit down.' He said offhandedly, and gestured towards
the chair. 'I'll be with you in a moment.'

Awkwardly Sara sat down. The clock in the corner
ticked, and the minutes passed by. Max Christian had
returned to his papers. Finally, with a gesture of annoyance, he pushed them to one side and looked again at his
watch.

He smiled. The smile curved his lips momentarily, and
did not reach his eyes.

'You must forgive me,' he said. 'I've had to see a lot of
people today, and I haven't much time now. You've been
here three years, I think, and you—er—write?'

Unmistakably, and insultingly, it was a question. Sara
felt her lips tighten.

'Yes,' she said coldly, 'I write. There are two resident

staff writers and I am one of them.'

'You're not freelance?'

'No,' said Sara, seething with irritation, 'I'm not.'

He was playing cat and mouse games with her, she thought angrily. There was no way an editor of his calibre would be unfamiliar with the work of staff writers on a magazine he was about to edit.

'I see.' He had a gold fountain pen in his hand, and he was now doodling idly on the list in front of him. 'Do tell me, Miss Ford, what kind of stories do you write?'

Sara gazed at him with dislike. He knew perfectly well, she was sure of it. He must be trying to make her lose her temper, or something.

'I write profiles mainly,' she said coolly, keeping her voice level with difficulty. 'Interviews.'

'Oh, really?' The dark blue eyes lifted for a moment from the papers and met hers. She could see, she thought, something like mockery in them.

'Yes. I interviewed you once, as it happens, Mr Christian.'

She smiled sweetly at him as she said it, but the reaction she had hoped for was not there. He looked at her with an expression of infuriating blankness.

'You interviewed me?'

'Two years ago. For this magazine. When you were still at *Bystander*.'

'How extraordinary. It's entirely slipped my memory.' He favoured her with another of the curt smiles. 'A favourable article, I hope?'

'Not exactly.'

'What a shame. Still, I don't think we should consider such things now, do you? Not when we're about to embark on a new relationship. A new working relationship.' He stood up, the speed and grace of his movement taking Sara by surprise. 'Can I get you a drink? I have to change first, and then I'll drive you to this party.'

'What?' Sara felt the colour surge into her cheeks, and she stood up quickly. Max Christian watched her reaction, standing on the far side of his desk, the dark blue eyes intent upon her face.

'Whisky? Brandy? Gin?'

He gestured behind him, and Sara saw that a new cabinet had been installed, its shelves lined with bottles and glasses.

'No, thank you,' she said stiffly, feeling suddenly totally confused, so unexpected was his reaction. 'And I don't need a lift, thank you. I can take the tube.'

'You'd be late.' He smiled. 'I won't hear of it. You're ready, I take it? You don't need to change or anything?'

Insultingly his eyes lazily raked over her, from head to foot. They lingered—intentionally, Sara felt sure—just a little longer than was strictly decorous.

'No,' she said, 'but please, I really don't think . . .'

'But I do.'

He reached forward and flipped one of the intercom switches on his desk, so he could speak to his secretary.

'Beverley,' he said, his eyes never leaving Sara's face, 'fetch Miss Ford a drink, will you? I just have to change, then I'm giving her a lift to the party. You have transport, don't you?'

For a moment, Sara's hopes lifted. If Beverley was in the car as well, it wouldn't be quite so awful. But Beverley had her car, it seemed. Sara felt her heart sink.

'Do sit down, I shan't be long.'

Without a backward glance, he disappeared through a door in the rear of his office that had led, in Geoffrey's day, to an old fashioned complex of rooms—a dining room for writers at editorial lunches, a small bathroom and kitchen. The door was closed firmly behind him. As he left, Beverley came in, and weakly Sara accepted a glass of sherry.

It was on her lips to ask Beverley for a lift, anything to get out of this situation, but Beverley was so efficient, so distant, and Sara felt so disconcerted and nervous that she did not dare. Beverley disappeared, having presented Sara with a lead crystal glass, and with gin and tonic and ice and lemon left on the desk for Max Christian. Sara sat alone in the semi-darkness trying to recover her nerve. Craning her neck to see the list that lay upside down on his desk, she saw indeed her own name at the bottom of the list. Someone, she saw, had neatly circled it in black ink.

The door opened, and Max Christian stood silhouetted against the light, his tall athletic figure framed in the doorway. He had changed into a dark suit, Sara saw, and with an expression on his face she did not like was engaged in adjusting the already perfect knot of his tie. He gave her plenty of time to take in the fact that the shirt was the very same as those she had mocked in her article. Just as she had written, its dark blue silk exactly matched his eyes.

Sara said nothing, and he strolled across to his desk, standing there sipping the drink, his eyes watching her intently with that expression of lazy mockery.

'Do you know,' he said finally, 'I think it's beginning to come back to me. Your article. You didn't like me very much, did you, Miss Ford?'

He said it casually enough, but there was something dangerous in his voice, that Sara sensed as a warning. Could it be, she wondered, that he was deliberately trying to provoke her? Perhaps he wanted to fire her, she thought suddenly, and this was just a pretext to snare her into some kind of rudeness or insubordination . . .

She lowered her gaze.

'I think you remember what I wrote perfectly well, Mr Christian,' she said softly. 'You're right of course. The piece was not very complimentary.'

'I thought not. I never remember these things very well. They're of no great importance. Except as regards your capabilities as an interviewer, of course . . .'

Sara looked up quickly, but his face again wore the humourless smile, and the words had been said silkily, almost dismissively. It would be better to ignore them.

He paused for a fraction of a second, as if he had expected something from her—an apology, perhaps, she thought crossly. Well, in that case he would have to wait.

'Now, if you're quite ready?'

Sara stood up, and to her alarm he crossed round the desk and took her arm in a firm and ungentle grasp, leading her towards the door.

They went down in the lift without speaking, and Max Christian opened the gates for her with over-elaborate courtesy. Mr Jones was still on duty, and Sara saw his expression change fleetingly as he saw who was with his new boss. Max Christian gave him a warmer smile than Sara had yet witnessed, and opened the doors for her into the car park.

'Did you try that horse in the three-five at Cheltenham, Fred?' he called over his shoulder, and paused in the doorway. Sara froze with astonishment. She had never heard anyone call Mr Jones by his Christian name—not even Geoffrey.

'I did, sir.' She heard him chuckle. 'Romped in at thirty to one.'

'Then you can buy me a drink some time, Fred.'

'Just say the word, Sir.'

Max Christian came round to the side of the brown Jaguar where Sara was waiting, and opened the door. She moved quickly, but not quickly enough to prevent his helping her inside it.

As he switched on the ignition, and the powerful engine roared into life, she turned to him curiously.

'Do you follow the horses, then?' she asked. 'That's the first time I've ever known Mr Jones to have a win. His ill luck is famous.'

Max Christian smiled briefly.

'It was one of my mother's horses,' he said quickly, and then let in the gears.

'Oh, I see,' Sara said dully. Of course. She had forgotten his mother—her racing stud was world-famous. As she was herself. That was how Max Christian had inherited those strange eyes of his, from his mother's family. And his mother had a curious name: Sara wrinkled her brow trying to remember it. Ishbel, that was it. Ishbel MacLeod she had been once, but she had been married so many times since there was no knowing what she was called now.

'My mother told me to back it, as a matter of fact,' he added.

'And did you?'

Momentarily he took his eyes off the road, and that glance, like dark ice, met hers.

'No,' he said coldly. 'I never gamble.'

'You don't like taking risks?'

He turned his face back to the road, and she saw his lips tighten.

'You're not interviewing me now, Miss Ford,' he said, 'but since you ask, you're wrong. I like taking risks—very much. But not on horses.'

Sara felt her cheeks go crimson, and was glad for the darkness in the car which hid it. Why hadn't she kept her mouth shut? she thought impatiently. She should have remembered, from two years before, how chillingly he could snub anything approaching a personal question.

The car sped on through the dark streets, its tyres hissing softly on the wet winter roads. Once Max Christian lit a cigarette. At each traffic light his fingers drummed on the steering wheel with impatience, and once away he drove fast—too fast; he was certainly exceeding the speed limits. He made no attempt at conversation, and Sara did not feel like risking any further remarks or questions. To her own annoyance, she felt tongue-tied and gauche. As quickly as a remark came into her mind she rejected it, though she felt desperate to break the long and embarrassing silence.

To her surprise he turned off the road she had been expecting him to take, and drove further north, towards Holland Park.

'Have you moved?' she asked finally.

'Moved?'

'Yes. Your last house was nearer Knightsbridge. I . . . I went there after our interview.'

'Did you?' He stubbed out the cigarette in the ash-tray. 'I'd forgotten. I took that house to be near the *Bystander* offices. I wasn't there long. It was rented.'

'Oh.' Sara drew in her breath, feeling suddenly ashamed. She remembered her long description of the house and the mocking catalogue she had made of its sumptuous contents. And it hadn't even been his. How could she have made such an appalling error?

She half turned, an apology rising to her lips, and then she bit it off. No, she thought. What was the point? If what he said was true, he'd forgotten what she'd written anyway. There was no point in resurrecting it now.

Abruptly Max Christian braked, and pulled the car into a space by a tall house in a wide leafy street. All its windows were lit, and even from the road she could hear the sound of conversation and laughter. The party had clearly already begun. Before she could move, Max Christian was round to her side of the car, and had the door open. His strong fingers gripped her arm and helped her out, and for a moment, on the cold damp autumn air, she found herself encircled by his arm. Quickly she moved back, and he slammed and locked the car door.

'Do come in, I suspect we're the last.'

She followed him across the paved courtyard garden, and up a flight of steps to a wide pillared doorway. At the top of the steps he paused, reaching for his keys.

'It sounds as if people are enjoying themelves,' Sara said nervously.

'Oh, didn't you know?' He straightened, so the shaft of light from the fanlight above the door shone full on those cold blue eyes. 'I'm famous for my parties. Or so someone once wrote, in one of those hatchet jobs on me.'

He swung the door wide, and stepped in ahead of her, all pretence at courtesy gone. 'Oh, and don't bother to annotate the contents this time, Miss Ford. Last time you confused a Delaunay in the hall with a Braque in the drawing room, neither of which were mine. There were other mistakes too, but we won't ennumerate them now.'

'But I . . .'

The icy smile was even more perfunctory, and this time did not mask the anger in his eyes.

'Please,' he said. 'Never apologise. Never explain. I hope you have a good evening.'

With that, he left her, disappearing into a crowded room to the right of the hall without a backward glance. Sara stood where he had left her. Laughter reached her from the next room, and above the babble of voices she heard Delia's.

'Max darling, where *have* you been? We'd given up on you!'

His reply was inaudible, but whatever it was, it provoked more laughter. Sara leaned back against the door. She felt more than embarrassed, she felt sick, and appalled at her own conceit. She had been proud of that wretched article, that 'hatchet job'. She thought of all the fulsome praise, the malicious laughter at Max Christian's expense which it had provoked. Most of it coming from old enemies of his, of course, and there were plenty of those in Fleet Street. If she had got those things wrong, she thought, what other mistakes had she made? What a great way to start that 'new working relationship'!

She was still standing in the hall, undecided whether to leave now or brazen it out, when Jennifer found her some five minutes later. Seeing the expression on Sara's face, she crossed quickly to her.

'Whatever's happened?' she said warmly, putting an arm around Sara's shoulders. 'Didn't it go well?'

'Not exactly, no.'

Jennifer hesitated, then drew Sara towards the living room.

'Come on in,' she said quickly. 'Forget it. So—he hates you and you hate him. So what? It's not the end of the world. It's only a job, Sara.'

Across the room Sara saw Max Christian as soon as she entered. He was standing at the far end, a drink in his hand, with Delia Waterlow, clad in a tight, low-cut black dress, talking animatedly to him. For a second, those cold blue eyes met hers; then, ostentatiously, he turned his back on her. The gesture was not lost, either on Delia, or on other members of staff standing nearby. Sara saw their curious looks, and set her mouth. Her chin tilted with obstinate pride. So; that was how it was to be. Fine. Jennifer was right. She could live with it. Max Christian had declared war. However wrong she had been in the past, she wasn't going to back down now.

CHAPTER TWO

UNEXPECTEDLY, as time passed, the shock began to wear off, and Sara began to enjoy herself. Three white-coated waiters were circulating with champagne, and after three glasses Sara began to feel much more confident. The house was beautiful, the tall walls lined with books and with some beautiful paintings. It was very different from the somewhat pretentious house where she had been with Max Christian two years before—but it was still unmistakably the house of a very rich man. She might have got some of the details wrong, Sara thought defensively as she looked around her, but still her basic premise was right. Max Christian came from a rich, powerful family, and his career had been a smooth and predictable progression. True, he worked hard—even his worst enemies admitted that, but he'd never really had to fight. It had all been handed to him on a plate. And if he worked hard, he obviously also found plenty of time to enjoy himself. His parties and his party-going *were* famous, she told herself. Why, even now—and covertly she glanced at him across the room—he hadn't spoken to a single man. There he was, she thought crossly, predictably surrounded by a circle of sycophantic women, all fluttering their eyelashes and trying to get his attention. She wondered who, of all the chic women there, would win. Though his attention, once captured, was rumoured to be held only shortly.

'Miss Ford?'

Sara turned to find Beverley standing beside her. She smiled, suddenly looking much friendlier than she had in the offices earlier.

'Can I call you Sara—it is Sara, isn't it?'

Sara nodded absently, her mind still elsewhere. Beverley followed her glance and laughed.

'Did Max give you a bad time?' she asked. 'I feared he

might—he's got a terrible temper, you know, and he's never forgotten that piece you wrote about him.'

Sara turned. 'Yes, well, he did make that rather clear,' she said wryly.

Beverley touched her arm.

'I wouldn't let it worry you,' she said quickly. 'I've never known him to hold a grudge. Usually there's a terrible row, and then he calms down and apologises to everyone. And what you wrote was a bit hard.'

'Was it?'

Beverley looked away. 'Well, I suppose it's very difficult,' she said, 'when you meet someone for an interview— I mean, you can't really get a very accurate impression of them, can you? But now you're working for Max, I'm sure you'll change your mind. You wait—he's a marvellous man, really. I certainly wouldn't work for anyone else, though he's been known to throw a telephone directory at me when he was in one of his really furious rages.'

'A telephone directory?'

Beverley laughed. 'He's a very exacting man, Sara. He always knows what he wants, and he always gets it. If there's any delay, there's trouble. But don't let it worry you. He sent me red roses every day for a month afterwards.'

'And that made up?'

Beverley shrugged. 'It helped. But I don't mind his rages now anyway, I'm used to them. I just shout back at him. He prefers that. He can't bear people who toady or defer to him. He's rather like his mother, you know. Have you met her:'

'Ishbel MacLeod?'

'Ishbel MacLeod that was. Ishbel Fitzherbert at the moment, though that probably won't last any longer than the others. She's a bit frightening, just like Max. And very beautiful. You ought to meet her—it's quite an experience, I can tell you. She's coming tonight, so keep an eye open.'

Beverley drifted away, and Sara edged around the corner of the room. While they had been talking, she had glimpsed Max Christian staring haughtily in their direction, and the last thing she wanted was to have to encounter him again that evening.

Carefully she positioned herself by the table laid out with a sumptuous buffet supper. Now he had his back to her, and she felt much safer. The food looked wonderful—lobster and smoked salmon, delicately arranged salads and a huge rack of cold fillet of beef. Suddenly Sara realised how hungry she was—she had hardly eaten anything all day. Perhaps she might just have something to eat, and then slip away. She was just helping herself to some food, when she found Delia beside her. She looked more animated than usual, as if something had happened that particularly pleased her, and to Sara's surprise she greeted her with a kiss—one of Delia's social pecks on the cheek, bestowed generously around the office when Delia was in a good mood, but never before upon Sara.

'Darling,' she said, 'you're looking rather super. What have you done to yourself? Make-up? Is this in dear Max's honour?'

'Hardly at all, Delia. Jennifer bought it for me at Boots in her lunch-hour. It's to distract attention from the jeans—or that was her theory.'

Delia cast a professional eye over Sara's tall, slender figure.

'Oh, I don't know,' she said, 'with your figure you look terrific in jeans—why not?'

Sara glanced at her in surprise. Delia was not generally given to complimenting other women.

'Tell me,' she went on, drawing Sara to one side, 'did you and Max have a terrible row? He was so late, and he came in looking like thunder . . .'

Sara shrugged. 'He had just been settling a few old scores, Delia, that's all. I don't blame him really.'

Delia's sharp blue eyes narrowed.

'Oh, so *that* was it. We all wondered. I rather thought he might do that, you know—in fact, I meant to warn you. He mentioned you to my father when he first agreed to become editor, and they went through the *London Now* staff lists. Of course, *I* don't know exactly what was said, but I put in some good words for you.'

Sara stared at her, feeling suddenly cold. She found the idea of Delia's defending her unlikely to say the least— but why had it been necessary? As if she had said too much, Delia put one exquisitely manicured finger to her lips.

'Mustn't say any more,' she smiled. 'Just a friendly hint. If I were you, Sara, I'd stay out of Max's way. Just don't give him any ammunition against you. You know, always be on time, that sort of thing. Don't let him provoke you into being rude ... One thing I do know—he said to Daddy that *London Now* was ridiculously overstaffed ...' She broke off again, and smiled. 'I'll see you tomorrow, Sara. Have a lovely evening.'

Before Sara could stay her, she dodged away, leaving Sara staring after her bared shoulders as she snaked her way expertly through the crowded room. Sara put down her champagne glass, and the plate of food, half touched.

Suddenly she didn't want anything to eat any longer. Across the room, she saw Max Christian suddenly break off from a conversation with a tall blonde woman whose face Sara recognised from *Vogue* covers. To her horror, he seemed to be moving in her direction. Quickly she dodged behind the backs of Deirdre Neal and Harry Wallace, who were deep in office gossip, and made for the door. If she could only find Jennifer, she thought, and go home. But Jennifer was right across the other side of the room, deep in conversation with Mark Shand, and clearly enjoying herself. If she went over there, she might bump into Max.

Seeing her chance, she dodged into the hall, and into the room opposite. It too was opened up for the party, but all the guests were now congregating by the buffet table, and it was welcomingly empty.

A huge fire burned in the grate, and in front of it was a high-backed velvet sofa. Gratefully Sara made for its protection, for somewhere quiet to sit and gather her thoughts. Then she stopped short.

Lying on the sofa at full length, and shielded from view by its back, was a woman of about fifty. She was wearing a long white evening dress, and her feet were bare. Beside her, two thin gold strapped sandals had been kicked off on the carpet. A bottle of champagne and a glass were by her side, and she was smoking a cigarette in a short jade holder. She and Sara stared at each other for a moment, and then the woman laughed.

'So, I'm discovered,' she said. 'Or are you escaping from all that too? Why don't you join me?' She swung her legs on to the floor, and patted the velvet cushions beside her. 'Come on, do,' she said. 'It's impossible in there. I've never met so many boring men in my life! I can't think why Max allows them in the door. And I got buttonholed by a frightful woman in a cerise dress who would talk of nothing but wallpapers . . .'

Sara smiled: Deirdre Neal.

'Tell me, my dear,' the woman said, as Sara sat down beside her, 'do you work for this magazine too?'

'I'm afraid so. I'm Sara Ford. I write for it.'

'Oh no!' The woman turned and stared. 'You're not! Why did you tell me? Just when I thought I was going to enjoy myself for the first time this evening. How wretched!'

Her expression was one of such undisguised horror that Sara had to laugh.

'I'm sorry,' she said, 'but I am. We can pretend I'm someone else if you like.'

The woman shook her head. She put out her cigarette, and at once lit another.

'No, my dear, we can't,' she said. 'You see, I'm Max's mother.'

Of course. Sara cursed herself for her own stupidity. They were so alike. Ishbel had fair hair, but the same strong features, the same extraordinary eyes, though, in her case, they were lit with a warmth and humour that Sara had never seen in her son's. They were looking into Sara's now with an expression of bemusement close to laughter that they should both find themselves in such a ridiculous position.

'Oh dear,' Sara said carefully. 'How awful. And just when I thought I was going to enjoy myself for the first time this evening!'

It worked; there was a moment's hesitation, and then the woman laughed, a deep, throaty chuckle that was totally at odds with her elegant appearance.

'Well,' she said, 'at least you've got a sense of humour. But then I knew that already. So, why don't we get this over with and then we can have some champagne together? After all, I've rather wanted to meet *you*, for a long time, my dear. Now, tell me, whatever possessed you to write those simply terrible things about my son? They were so bad I nearly wrote you a very cross letter—and I never put pen to paper if I can possibly help it.'

Sara paused. 'There's no very easy answer to that,' she said slowly. 'And if it makes it any better, you're about the fifth person today to tell me I got it all wrong. Including your son.'

'Max? I can imagine, my dear. He was simply *livid* when it came out. I've never seen him so furious. And some of it was quite near the truth, of course, which made it worse. I mean, Max is quite impossible in hundreds of ways. Probably because I was such an appalling mother—who knows? But you made him sound so *vile*. I thought something dreadful must have happened when you went to interview him. Tell me, he didn't make a pass at you or anything, did he?'

Sara felt herself go crimson. 'Certainly not!'

'Well, there's no need to be so prim about it, my dear. Why ever shouldn't he? Max adores women—particularly beautiful women.'

'So I gathered.'

'The trouble is, it's always the wrong women. What Max needs is a woman with a mind of her own. But he's so maddeningly *willful*. He's absolutely terrified of being involved, of course. He's always been exactly the same. Do you know, my dear, I remember when he was about five years old, he was standing in the middle of the nursery, with this poor nanny—she must have been about the *tenth*, they never stayed longer than six months, when . . .'

'Miss Ford.'

Sara started and swung round. Max Christian was

standing immediately behind them, his face pale with anger.

'I thought I told you,' he said. 'I thought I made it perfectly clear. I don't want you prying into my affairs a second time. And I certainly don't expect one of my employees to come to my house and deliberately go round picking up gossip about me!'

'Max, *really*!' His mother stood up, and the two of them glared at each other across the sofa. 'This girl was doing no such thing. *I* began this conversation, and you have absolutely no right to . . .'

'Please.' Sara stood up. She knew she had gone pale too, and her hands were shaking. So that was why he had been watching her all evening; that was what he thought. Suddenly she felt all the tension of the day explode in her, and anger surged up. 'Obviously I'm not the only one who should check their facts,' she said, her voice tight, her eyes blazing at him. 'But I'll leave you to do your checking after I've gone. I'm leaving.'

Before Max or his mother could move, she went swiftly to the door. Out of the corner of her eye she saw Max Christian move to come after her, and his mother restrain him. As she shut the door quickly behind her, she could hear them both, voices raised, starting on a furious argument.

Luckily, there was no one in the hall, and no one to see her leave. Outside it was cold, and it had begun to drizzle, but she scarcely noticed. She turned blindly out of the gate and walked along the streets, looking to neither right nor left, going in no particular direction. As she walked, all the events of the evening gradually began to fall into place, and suddenly what Delia had said earlier made total sense. Obviously, Max Christian was looking for a chance to fire her—he'd probably made up his mind to do it before he even came to the magazine. It was a mean kind of thing to do, she thought angrily, but it was a kind of rough justice, a revenge—and he was just the sort of man who would be revengeful if he were angered enough.

Well, she wouldn't give him the chance, she thought, setting her mouth. Maybe he hoped to provoke her into resignation as an easy way out—but he wouldn't succeed in that either. She loved the magazine, loved her work. It was the most important thing in her life—the only thing really, and had been for three years now, ever since Geoffrey had first helped her. And besides, it would be difficult to get as good a job elsewhere. She needed the money; there was the cheque she sent her mother each month . . .

But she pushed that thought away, as she always did. It was meeting *his* mother, hearing her talk so casually about her own past, that has brought it all back, the endless rows, the fights of her childhood. Near the park, she finally caught a bus going northwards, and sat alone on the top deck, looking out unseeingly at the grey London streets, smoky yellow with neon.

Jennifer was not home when she got back. She made herself something to eat, then left it. By the time she went to bed she felt calmer. She had an article to finish in the morning. She would get on with that first thing.

In bed, she lay awake, tired but unable to sleep, staring at the light that filtered through the curtains and patterned the ceiling. When she finally slept, she had her worst dream, the one she most dreaded: a bedtime kiss, and breath smelling of whisky; a door banging in the night, suddenly two bowls, not three, at the breakfast table.

She couldn't remember her father, of course; no matter how hard she tried to conjure him up, he was shadowy. She could remember his jackets, which were rough, and smelled of tobacco. And being tossed up in the air and caught again, laughing. But she couldn't remember his face. Just his eyes. He had rather pale eyes, of a clear blue, and they never looked directly towards you. She had always disliked men with blue eyes. It was one of the first things that had made her distrust Max Christian.

Next morning she was awake early, and—for once—ready before Jennifer. As she padded into the kitchen in bare feet to make coffee, Sara was getting ready to leave. Jennifer stared at her in surprise.

'You're early!' she said with a yawn. 'Where on earth are you going?'

'I'm going to work.'

'At this time?' Jennifer looked at her watch.

'I have a piece I have to finish writing.'

Jennifer sighed. 'Oh, Sara,' she said, 'when didn't you?'

'Why have you dragged me to this pub, Sara?'

Geoffrey Fletcher stood in the doorway of the Cross Keys, puffing at his pipe, and looking towards the crush at the bar.

'It's not the usual one, is it?'

'I wanted to talk.' Sara took his arm. 'Come on, you sit down. I'll get us something to eat.'

'All right, my dear, I won't argue, not at my advanced age. But you'll let me pay . . .'

He pushed a note into her hand, and Sara tried to avoid it.

'Come on now,' he laughed. 'I know all about you and all that Women's Lib stuff. But I'm old-fashioned about these things. Now, don't upset me. You get the food—I'll bag the seats, all right with you?'

'All right, Geoffrey. Bargain.'

Sara took the note, pushed through the throng at the bar, and eventually fought her way back to the corner where Geoffrey had found a space on a high red velvet banquette. He was looking around him with interest.

'Well,' he said, 'can't say I approve of your taste in pubs, my dear. This place looks like a Victorian bordello. Is this what they call a sandwich?'

He looked with disdain at the flabby white bread and greasy cheese slices that Sara had set down before him.

'I'm sorry,' she said. 'And the wine's worse. But no one from the magazine comes here, and I wanted to have a talk.'

'That bad, is it?' He chuckled. 'I've heard the odd rumour, I must admit. You and Max don't see exactly eye to eye, is that it?'

'More or less.'

'And you want a bit of fatherly advice?' He tasted the

wine and grimaced. 'You're right about that anyway. Quite disgusting. Why didn't you let me take you out for a proper lunch?'

Sara sighed. 'I hadn't time—I would have loved that, you know I would. But I'm late with an article—as usual.'

'As usual?' He looked at her keenly. 'In my day your pieces were always on time.'

'That was in your time.' Sara couldn't keep the bitterness out of her voice, and she knew he heard it.

'So what's changed?'

'The editor's changed.'

'I see.'

Sara saw him look quickly around the pub, as if checking its clientele, and she smiled to herself. Geoffrey was discreet, but she had chosen this place well. It was near Fleet Street, but it was patronised almost exclusively by barristers from the Inns of Court nearby.

'Well,' he said finally, 'you'd better tell me what the problem is. See if I can help.'

'It's quite simple, really.' She took a deep breath. 'I think I want to leave. And I thought you might be able to advise me about—well, about where I could find another job.'

'Another job?' Geoffrey stared at her. 'You mean you want to leave the magazine?'

'Yes.' She looked away.

Geoffrey abandoned the cheese sandwich and returned to his pipe. He took, as he always did, an immense time filling it and lighting it, not answering her. Sara watched him closely. His illness showed now, she thought. He had aged noticeably since he had left, he was much thinner. She felt her heart turn over with affection and anxiety for him as she watched him go through the familiar ritual—his hands were now a little shaky.

'How long since Max took over?' he asked finally, abruptly.

'About a month.'

'Not very long.'

'Long enough.' Sara sighed. 'I have tried, Geoffrey, really I have. But I can't work with that man.'

'Dislike him that much, do you? That surprises me. Thought you two would get on.'

'After what I wrote about him?' Sara laughed.

Geoffrey chuckled. 'Oh that! That's ancient history.'

'Not to Max, it isn't.'

Geoffrey puffed tranquilly at his pipe, his hands clasped on the table before them.

'He's a fine editor,' he said meditatively. 'Recommended him for the job myself.'

Sara looked away. That was true, she thought. However much she disliked Max Christian, she couldn't deny his ability. And he had improved the magazine. She hated to admit it to herself, and would never have said so out loud to anyone, but he had. In one month, *London Now* had been transformed. The stories were sharper, the design much harder-hitting; the deadlines were much tighter, so everyone had to work twice as hard, but several times the magazine had broken stories before they even reached the papers. Max Christian drove everyone hard, himself hardest of all.

'So why leave now?' It was as if Geoffrey had read her thoughts. Sara sighed. She had been bottling all this up for so many weeks now that she knew once she started, it would all spill out, and would probably sound warped and disloyal. But if she couldn't talk to Geoffrey, who could she talk to? She had tried to discuss it with Jennifer, but she had been impatient—what was it she had said— oh yes, that Sara was becoming obsessed with him, and he with her, that all this hostility did no one any good.

'It's quite simple.' She smiled at Geoffrey. 'We just loathe each other—we have from the first moment we laid eyes on each other. I find him so intolerant, so high-handed. I . . .'

'Nothing else?'

Sara laughed. 'All right, I know I can exaggerate. But it's reciprocated—with interest. And he obviously loathes my writing.'

'You've done some very good pieces since I left.'

'Not the kind I like doing—no interviews, all hard reporting. Any minute he's going to send me off to cover funerals and fires—I can see it now. I've done just one interview in the past month—the one I'm writing up now, and he's got me so nervous I can't write any more. Everything I do has to be done and re-done. He's forever coming out of his office and reading my work over my shoulder, forever making changes . . .'

She broke off. She was sounding petulant, and she knew it. Geoffrey patted her hand.

'Well, my dear,' he said gently, 'my advice is—try and stick it out a bit longer. If Max is doing all that then he probably has a good reason. And it never did any journalist any harm to do some leg-work, or to do some re-writes. Tell you what——' he stood up, 'would you like me to have a word with Max, see if I can find out what the problem is?'

'Oh no, please don't do that!' Sara stood up quickly. 'I shouldn't have bothered you with all this in the first place. I couldn't bear it if Max knew that I . . .'

'Say no more, my dear. Not a word. Now, this is what I suggest. I'll walk back to your office with you now, and then I'll see you again—in a month or two's time, shall we say? If you still feel the same way then, I'll see what I can do. All right?'

Impulsively, Sara reached up and kissed his cheek. Geoffrey gave her an awkward hug, and for a moment Sara thought she saw something in his eyes which she did not understand, some pain, or perhaps regret. But it was gone as quickly as she glimpsed it, and he steered her gently away from the table.

'How's young Mark getting on?' he asked. 'Seeing much of him, are you?'

'Mark Shand? No—just in the office. He's fine. He and Max get on very well.'

'So—who's the boyfriend at the moment, then?'

He was being maddeningly slow, checking he had all his belongings, his pipe, his tobacco pouch. Suddenly Sara wished she had never begun this conversation. Just talking about Max Christian made her nervous and uneasy; she should have stayed in the office to finish her article.

'There isn't one,' she said shortly.

'Then there ought to be. Doesn't do to think about work all the time. Not at your age.'

'I don't.'

'Yes, you do, my dear. Always did. Just like Max. Now . . .' He had finally satisfied himself that he had left nothing behind. 'Let's go back through the churchyard, shall we? I always liked walking through there at lunch time . . .'

Back at the office Sara began typing straight away. But the piece was going badly. No matter how much she re-wrote and changed it, it remained obstinately dull and unconvincing. Desperately she looked up at the clock, then back at the page. She was never going to finish it in time. Damn Max Christian, she thought crossly. It was he that was responsible for all this: a month ago she would have written the piece straight off, with no problems.

She was so absorbed in what she was doing that it was some time before she realised that someone was standing directly behind her. Then, no sound, but some sixth sense warned her. She swung round to find Max immediately behind her chair, reading her copy as she typed. She flinched away, and looking up, saw that his mouth as usual was unsmiling, and he was frowning.

'You haven't finished?' he said curtly. 'That piece is late. It has to go to the printers this afternoon, and I need to read it first.'

'It's nearly done,' she muttered. 'I was held up this morning. I just have one paragraph to complete.'

'Then you should have finished it at lunchtime, instead of going out to gossip with your friends.'

Sara stared at him. How had he known that? She felt herself blushing, the more so because she knew it was true.

'Have you got the other pages?'

He reached a lean muscular arm over her chair for the typescript that lay on her desk.

'I'll take these now, and read them,' he said. 'When you've finished just bring in the last page, will you?'

'No, please!'

Sara put out her hand to stop him. She hated her work being read before it was complete. Her hand reached the pages before his, and his hand came down over hers. It rested there for slightly longer than was necessary, rather as if it would have given him considerable pleasure to crush it. Then he removed it.

'I'd like the pages, please, Sara,' he said sharply. 'And hurry up with the rest, will you? This is a weekly magazine, or haven't you noticed?'

And before she could stop him, the pages had been scooped up and were gone. Sara stared at the typewriter in front of her in despair. She wasn't pleased with the piece and she foresaw trouble. She hadn't wanted to do the wretched piece in the first place, she thought defensively. It was one of a series on the wives of famous men, the idea being to find out what kind of role they had played in their husbands' lives, how they had contributed to their achievements. 'Why can't we do a series about women who've achieved something in their own right?' she had argued at the editorial meeting. Max Christian had overruled her—and then assigned her the interview. And it had been interesting, Sara thought. Ellen Ellis was the wife of a leading publisher, her own career long abandoned in favour of her family. She had radiated a contentment and calm that to Sara had been totally unexpected. None of which made the article any easier to write.

It didn't help matters that Delia was on the telephone at her elbow, constantly quacking away. She appeared to be arranging a dinner party of some sort, because she was going on and on about canapés and cuts of beef and the choice of wine. Sara ripped another page out of her typewriter and screwed it impatiently into a ball.

'Damn it, Delia,' she snapped finally, 'I'm trying to finish this piece! I wish you'd shut up. If you want to fix a dinner party, why can't you do it from home?'

Delia gave her a steely glance, and merely reduced the level of quacking by a couple of decibels. At half past four, however, her internal telephone rang. Quickly she hung up on the other line. 'What? To see me? Now? Oh— I'd forgotten. I'll be in straight away . . .'

Hurriedly she got up from her desk, and disappeared in

the direction of the editor's office. Sara sighed with relief. Now perhaps she could concentrate. Twenty minutes discussing how she wanted the *contrefilet* rolled indeed!

But even in comparative silence, the end of the article went no better. Delia seemed to be away for hours, and Sara wondered what could have happened. Wrenching her mind back, she re-read what she had written. It was rubbish, she thought irritably. Whatever was the matter with her?

By five-thirty, she had finally finished, having re-written the lumpen last page several times. Delia still hadn't re-appeared. She took it over to the subs' desk, and Jennifer shook her head.

'It's no good, Sara,' she said. 'I'm sending the copy off now, and yours can't go until Max has finished reading it. There's a late messenger coming at seven—he's taking some stuff of Delia's that had to be completely re-written. Yours will have to go with that. You'll have to stay.'

Sara sighed and went back to her desk. Deirdre Neal gave her a tight little smile. Deirdre was about fifty, divorced, and—as far as Sara could make out—had disliked her from the moment she set foot in the office.

'Finished it at last, have you, dear?'

'Yes,' said Sara.

'Poor Delia's a long time, isn't she? Being hauled over the coals for her copy again, I gather. Still, I think Max has a soft spot for her, so she'll be all right.'

Sara said nothing, and Deirdre Neal took out mirror, comb, powder and lipstick, the application of which was an unvarying part of her going home procedure. Sara watched, fascinated, as Deirdre outlined her thin lips in thick crimson paint, and her glance registered.

Deirdre gave her a sweet smile over the top of her compact.

'Well, dear,' she said, 'we're not all twenty-three with a skin like a peach, are we? At my age we have to repair the ravages of time a bit. Tell me . . .' she leaned forward confidentially, lowering her voice, 'did I hear Max asking you out to lunch the other day? I did, didn't I?'

Sara blushed crimson.

'You hear lots of things, Deirdre,' she said sharply.

The older woman's mouth tightened.

'Yes, well ... And I heard you refuse too. *Not* very politely. But that's nothing new, is it? Still, not to worry. He took Delia instead.'

She obviously thought that a good parting shot, because she made a quick exit, leaving Sara wondering why that piece of information should have annoyed her.

By six the office was beginning to empty. At ten past, Jennifer left with a wave, leaving Sara alone in the huge room, sitting gloomily at her desk. Why couldn't anyone understand what she felt about Max Christian? she thought. Even Geoffrey had not seemed to understand. Even being under the same roof as the man put her on edge. Maybe Jennifer was right, and she was allowing all this to develop into an obsession. Certainly his presence produced a most curious effect, one she had never experienced before, one she could only define as threat. The way he looked at her sometimes, and that way he had of standing just behind her, as if at any moment he might reach down and touch her. She hated it, she thought. With all the other men in the office she could relax, forget she was a woman. But not with him.

And now she would have to sit next to him and go over her article and watch him take it to pieces in front of her eyes ... Well, if they were going to do that, she thought impatiently, he would have to hurry. Delia was still in his office, and the last messenger was coming at seven ...

At twenty past, she heard the bang of a door, the corridor light went on, and Delia burst into the room. She saw Sara and stopped, then with an odd gesture that looked like despair, she came over to her and slumped in the chair at her desk. Sara stared at her in horror. She had never seen Delia look such a mess. Her hair was tousled, her make-up streaked. She was crying and obviously had been for some time. Mascara had formed twin puddles under her eyes, which were red and swollen. For the first time in her life, Sara felt sorry for her.

'Oh, God!' she sobbed. 'Sara, you've no idea. That man is such a swine. God, I hate him! I'm going to leave. I can't work for him any longer.'

'Hey, Delia!' Sara found some Kleenex on her desk and handed them to her. 'Come on, cheer up. You know what he's like, you know his tempers. I'm sure it doesn't mean a thing. He'll have forgotten the whole thing in the morning.' It was true, she thought. However much you disliked him, you could never say he sulked. His rages were quick, over and then forgotten. Until the next time. Delia sniffed.

'He may forget it, but I shan't,' she wailed. 'I've never been so humiliated in my life!' Another torrent of sobs shook her, and a large tear fell with a plop on to her desk. 'Why are you still here, anyway?' she turned. 'I thought everyone would have gone.'

'I'm next in the firing-line,' Sara replied, sounding more cheerful than she felt. 'My copy's late, and it's not much good. I've had to wait so he can read it.'

Delia looked at her for a moment, and Sara noticed the tears had almost stopped.

'It's a bit late to go in now, isn't it?' she said, rather suspiciously. 'The messenger has gone.'

'I know. It's going by the late messenger. I can't go till he's read it, though.'

Delia gave another wail.

'Oh, don't *talk* about copy! Don't *mention* the man to me—I can't bear it. Sara, you wouldn't be a darling, would you, and come to the ladies' loo with me? I must get myself cleaned up, and I do so want to talk to somebody.'

Sara was rather surprised that Delia should pick her to be confessor, but then she seemed to be seeing a new side to Delia altogether, a vulnerable side that made her feel she might have been unfair to the girl in the past.

'O.K.,' she said, and helped Delia up. 'Now stop crying. Come and put some cold water on your face—you'll feel much better.'

But in the cloakroom, Delia did not calm down. Far from it. To Sara's horror, she got more and more hysterical, as if she were deliberately working herself up. A torrent of words poured out.

'It wouldn't matter so much,' she said, 'if we didn't get on so well normally. I mean, he's been so sweet to me, and so patient—and now this. All that happened was that my stupid fashion copy was a bit late—well, two days late, actually, but I've had this wretched dinner party to organise, and after all, *he's* coming to it, so you'd think he'd understand. Then—well, I never pretended to be a writer—it wasn't terribly clear and he made me re-do it twice, and I had an appointment with Freddie to do my hair and I had to cancel it. Then he tore it up—just like that, in my face! Jennifer had to re-do the whole thing for me—well, I asked her if she'd mind, and she didn't, and then when he found out she'd written it, he went mad, he just yelled at me. He said the cruellest things, he said I only got this job because of Daddy, which is totally untrue. He said I hadn't the first idea how to write and that I made it worse by being lazy . . . ' Her mouth distorted into a moan of such misery that Sara had to suppress a smile.

Everything he had said was perfectly true, she thought, and her estimation of Max Christian went up a few points for having had the guts to say it to the Chairman's daughter. Geoffrey never had. Still, Delia might be an idiot, but she was genuinely upset, she thought, and she—Sara—had probably been wrong to dislike her so much. It wasn't her fault she had a quacking voice. Something Jennifer had once said sprang suddenly into mind: 'Really, Sara,' she'd said, 'for a self-professed Women's Libber, you're terribly intolerant of your own sex. Have you realised how many of them you dislike?' So, now, she made a real attempt to soothe Delia. She splashed water on a tissue and helped her wash her eyes; she put her arm round her, and listened as sympathetically as she could to Delia's continued outpourings, she murmured bland encouragements, and eventually it all worked: Delia began to calm down. When she started putting on her make-up again, Sara reckoned she had recovered. She was just about to go when the door opened, and Beverley, Max Christian's senior secretary, stood in the doorway.

'Oh, Sara,' she said, with relief, 'there you are. Have you forgotten the time? Max has been looking everywhere for you—the messenger's here and he needs to go over your article. We thought you must have gone home.'

Horrified, Sara looked at her watch. It was gone seven. As she looked up, she caught Delia's face in the glass as she powdered her face. Delia gave her a look of warm sympathy. With a sinking heart, Sara hurried after Beverley.

CHAPTER THREE

THE door to Max Christian's office was open, and Sara could hear his voice from the far end of the corridor. Beverley interjected something which she couldn't quite catch, and she heard his voice rise.

'Oh, has she? Well, get her in here now. This minute, do you hear me?'

Beverley came out looking shaken, and Sara, trembling with nervousness, knocked and went in. Max was pacing up and down the room like a tiger in a cage, but he stopped dead when he saw her.

'Just what the hell do you think you're playing at?' he shouted. 'Your copy's late, and what's more, it's lousy. I've had to send the messenger away, and I'll have to drop it into the printers myself later on.'

'I'm sorry, Max,' Sara said stiffly, partly through nerves, partly because although everyone in the office now used Christian names, she found it particularly difficult to say his. 'I ... I finished it earlier. I'm sorry ... I was waiting to go over it with you and then ...'

She broke off. She couldn't exactly explain to Max Christian the scene in the ladies' cloakroom, it wouldn't be fair to Delia. He probably knew anyway, she thought, that was what Beverley would have told him.

'I've been free since six-thirty,' he said angrily. 'You meanwhile were nowhere to be found. Where the hell have you been?'

'I—er—I've been in the ladies' loo,' Sara said desperately. 'I didn't feel terribly well.'

And actually, she thought, that wasn't far from the truth. All she'd eaten all day was half that horrible cheese sandwich, and the conversation with Delia had upset her. To her surprise, his manner suddenly and totally changed. He stopped shouting, and when he next spoke his voice had a gentleness she had never heard before.

'What's wrong?' he asked. 'Do you feel faint? Here, you'd better sit down.'

Before she could speak he was at her side, and his arm came round her shoulders protectively. She felt the power of his arms, and the warmth of his body, and his proximity had a most curious effect upon her. Suddenly she did feel lightheaded, and she swayed a little. He caught her, holding her closely, and helped her into the chair by his desk. For some reason she could not fathom she wanted to stay in his arms, to be enclosed in that extraordinary feeling of safeness and protection he had suddenly given her. But he moved away.

'You look very pale,' he said. 'You'd better have some brandy.'

'Please,' she said quickly. 'I'm perfectly all right. I've never fainted in my life—really.'

He ignored her, and poured a finger of brandy into a large tumbler.

'Now,' he ordered, 'drink that. Come on, it'll make you feel much better.' His arm went around her shoulders again, and he held the glass to her lips. She sipped, and then nearly choked. He smiled, looking up at her, and his face was totally transformed. It was not the smile she usually saw, the professional smile that hardly lifted his lips and never reached those cold appraising eyes. It lit up and lightened his whole face.

'You're obviously not used to spirits,' he said. 'Come on, sip it gently. It's not like red wine, you know. Not like the wine you get at the Cross Keys, anyhow.'

Something in his voice made Sara look at him intently. That was the second time he had made an oblique reference to the place where she and Geoffrey had spent their lunch hour, and a horrible suspicion was dawning on her.

'The Cross Keys?' she echoed weakly.

'Yes,' he said, 'the pub on the corner. Where I have my lunch when I'm not in the office, or——' he paused, 'taking someone out to discuss work.'

She stared at him, her dark eyes wide.

'You were there, weren't you?' she said. 'Today at lunchtime?'

'Today?' He smiled. 'Now let me think, was I? Yes, I was. I go there, you see, to avoid the rest of the staff, so I have time to think in peace. I usually see no one from the magazine there.'

'But you saw us?'

'Not exactly. Do have some more brandy, it's bringing the colour back into your cheeks already. No, I didn't see you. I did hear you, however. You must have been sitting just the other side of my banquette.'

Sara stared at him, letting the full awfulness of this sink in. Her mind raced back over the meeting, desperately trying to recall what she had said. She could recall parts of it only too well. Oh, how humiliating! The pub had been so crowded, no one from *London Now* ever went there, and of course there were those high-backed bench seats. Someone could be sitting right behind you, and you'd never see them . . .

'You . . . you were eavesdropping!' she exclaimed accusingly.

'Hardly at all. I was sitting there having lunch and a conversation intruded upon me. I didn't intend to over-hear it, it just happened that way.'

'But I was talking about you!'

'I know you were. It was terribly interesting. When all that started I couldn't bear to leave.'

Sara felt the anger rise in her, fuelled by shame and embarrassment.

'I think that's the most horrible thing to have done!' she said hotly. 'You could have left. You could have let us know you were there.'

He smiled at her mockingly, but she could see the anger and dislike in those cold dark eyes.

'Oh, but why?' he said flippantly. 'I can't pretend that

what I heard was particularly pleasant—or particularly loyal. But it was something of a revelation. I knew you disliked me, of course. I just hadn't realised how much.'

Sara said nothing. What could she say? She could hardly deny her own words, or pretend now she hadn't meant it. Had she said one single complimentary thing about him? No, she realised, and felt sick, she had not. She hadn't even admitted out loud how much he had improved the magazine. But then she could hardly say that to Geoffrey . . .

'So. If you're feeling better now, perhaps you would forgive me for interfering with your work yet again, but we really need to go over this article. I think you must know it's not good enough.'

Sara stared at him sullenly. She did know, but she wished he wouldn't always treat her as if she were a pupil and he a scornful schoolmaster. She cleared her throat, and spoke with difficulty.

'I'm sorry you should have heard all that,' she said stiffly. 'But since you did, there's not very much I can say. And I'm sorry I've made you miss the messenger.'

Max shrugged and crossed back to his desk. He sat down, and picked up her pages, reading them once more in silence. As the minutes ticked by, Sara watched him, the thick hair falling carelessly over his brow; the narrow fine hands that made a few last alterations; the impenetrable face. She always felt glad when he was not looking at her, she realised. It was not just the colour of his eyes, it was the directness, the candour of them that so perturbed her.

As if he had read her thoughts, he suddenly looked up, and the cold blue eyes met hers with an expression she could not quite fathom. If it had been anyone but him she might have thought she saw pain there, as if what he had overheard at lunch had genuinely affected him. But not Max, she thought quickly. He was too assured, too confident for that: his enemies were legion anyway, why should he care about having another?

'The trouble with this is——' he tapped the pages impatiently with a silver letter knife—'that the writing's completely hollow. It has no conviction whatsoever. Why is that?'

Sara looked away irritably. Why did he always have to be so damnably right? She shrugged and looked at him sulkily.

'I told you I didn't think we should do it. I told you I didn't want to write it. One of the other people would have done it much better.'

His lips tightened. 'Oh, come on,' he said sharply. 'You're supposed to be a professional journalist, damn it. All that's irrelevant. This was your assignment and you've messed it up. It's quite simple.'

Sara said nothing, and he tossed the pages impatiently on to his desk.

'I'm not totally blind, you know, Sara. It's perfectly obvious what went wrong. You've allowed your own feelings, your own prejudices to get in the way of the interview. Ellen Ellis is an extraordinary and interesting woman, but because she represents everything you disagree with, you've sniped, quite unnecessarily. Even you couldn't manage a complete put-down, but you've come as near as you damn well could. The whole piece reeks of perversity.'

'Perversity?' Sara stared at him, feeling her quick temper starting to rise. The piece wasn't that good, she thought angrily, but it wasn't that bad either . . .

'Yes, perversity. When are you going to learn to report the facts instead of twisting everything to suit your own warped point of view?'

'Warped?' Sara stared at him in disbelief. 'I don't see it's so warped to believe a woman might want to lead her own life, have her own career, instead of forever playing second fiddle to someone else . . .'

'Typical!' He slammed his fist down on his desk, the blue eyes blazing at her angrily. 'That's exactly the sort of irrelevant trite generalisation I'd have expected you to come up with. I suppose that's how you see yourself, is it, Sara? Sacrificing everything else for the sake of a so-called career. God! It's hopeless . . . Here.'

He tossed the pages contemptuously across the desk, so

that Sara could see for the first time the web of changes, cuts and alterations that now covered her writing.

'There's no point in arguing about it. Unfortunately, we have to run the piece, I've no other option. Just look at that, will you, and tell me if you agree.'

Sara picked up the pages, her hands trembling. She felt close to tears, but she was determined not to let him see it. He might reduce Delia to crying, she thought angrily, but he was not going to do it to her. Slowly she went over what he had done. As she did so she saw him get up from the desk and fetch himself a drink, taking a long time over it, and keeping his back to her. The minutes ticked by, and with difficulty, Sara tried to focus on what he had done, but she could hardly see the words, they seemed to jump about on the page.

'Well?'

Resignedly she handed them back to him.

'Fine,' she said stiffly. 'I know it's not very good, but it's better than it was.'

Her voice shook slightly as she said it, but he gave no sign of noticing it, made no acknowledgment of the tacit apology. In silence he took the pages back and marked them up for the printers, his head lowered intently.

'Tell me,' he didn't look up, 'tell me, Sara, were your own parents happily married?'

The question took her totally by surprise, so much so that she answered him almost without thinking, before all the old feeling of pain had time to surge up.

'No,' she said quietly, 'they weren't. They divorced when I was six, and I haven't seen my father since.'

'I see.' The cold blue eyes met hers. 'Well, that explains quite a lot, doesn't it?'

'*What?*' She suddenly felt something snap inside her, pain mixed with anger, fury that he should have trapped her into that admission, disbelief that he should respond so coldly to something so private, so long locked away.

He sighed. 'It's fairly obvious, don't you think? I've had to suffer innumerable so-called Women's Libbers in my time, and every single one of them had an unhappy childhood. Every single one of them had a down on men because of it. You just run true to type, Sara.'

'Oh, do I really?' Sara stood up. She could feel that she was shaking, that the blood had drained from her face, and she was rigid with anger. 'Well, you run true to type too, you know. I've heard that particular argument put forward hundreds of times by men like you.'

'Men like me?' He stood up, glaring across the desk at her.

'Yes, men like you!' she retorted fiercely. 'Men who think they can dodge the issue with half-baked Freudian analysis. Men who stand around in bars bolstering their own egos, telling one another that of course all feminists are frigid, that all they need is the right man in the right way, and they'd all turn overnight into sweet, un-complaining little women . . .'

'How right you are!' He raised his voice. 'Feminists, indeed! The very word makes me feel ill! Derivative women with derivative ideas like yours, who are dead from the neck down. There's not one of them wouldn't run a mile if she saw a man was attracted to her. They're just frightened of sex and they won't admit it.'

'Oh, of course,' Sara put all the sarcasm she could muster into her voice. 'Just as I said. You would think that! You would think that's the solution, wouldn't you? That no woman minds being condescended to, or pat-ronised. Just send them a dozen red roses, and if all else fails, whisk them off to the dubious pleasures of your . . .'

She broke off. She had been been about to say 'bed', and they both knew it. At the mention of roses, she saw his face darken with anger.

'Don't you try and turn the argument on me,' he snapped furiously. 'Why don't you take a close look at yourself for a change? You emanate hostility, do you know that? I thought it the very first time I met you, when you came into the *Bystander* offices, flaunting yourself in those ridiculous clothes. Men's jeans and no bra. Typical!'

'Ah!' Sara was triumphant. 'So. I thought you'd for-gotten all that . . .'

'Yes, I do remember.' He crossed from behind his desk and came towards her, and it took all Sara's will power not to shrink back. 'I remember perfectly, if it gives you any satisfaction. You came into that room determined to do a hatchet job, and that's predictably, boringly, what you did. Do you think I was so damned naïve I didn't know what was going on? That was two years ago, Sara, and the saddest thing is, you haven't changed one iota in that time. Not at all. You're petrified, like a piece of stone. God help us, you'll be exactly the same when you're fifty—only then perhaps it won't be quite so attractive, when you're an embittered old maid, wondering what went wrong, where life passed you by . . .'

'How dare you!' Sara's eyes blazed at him, and all restraint on her temper was gone. Let him fire her, she thought furiously. No matter what he did, she was not going to stand and take that kind of thing meekly. 'What makes you think you have a right to talk to me like that? You don't even know me! You don't know anything about me! You're the most insulting man I've ever met in my life!'

'No great distinction in that,' he snapped. 'After all, you haven't met many men, have you, Sara? Oh, you'll *work* with men, just so long as they treat you like one of the boys. But the moment that one observes that under that ridiculous camouflage you affect there's actually quite a beautiful woman, you're terrified, aren't you? All you can think about is your work. You're terrified even to go out with a man . . .'

'That's not true!'

'Isn't it? Just look at yourself, will you? Go on, take a really good look. And what do you see? A woman who wears boy's clothes all the time, a stupid schoolboy watch . . .' He grabbed her wrist tightly and shook it in front of her face. 'A woman who won't wear women's clothes, won't wear make-up, who's twenty-three and looks fifteen. A woman who won't grow up and admit she's a woman because she's scared witless of what might happen if she did. No wonder you couldn't write that article, Sara! You know nothing of marriage, and nothing of men. You've never had an affair in your life, have you? You've probably never been properly kissed. In fact, do you know what you remind me of? That princess, that ice-maiden, in the fairy stories. The trouble with you,

Sara, is you need waking up, and fast. Otherwise you'll stay the way you are now for the rest of your life, and if you think you'll make a good writer then, I'll tell you for free—you're wrong!'

He still held her wrist in an iron grip, and furiously Sara tried to free herself.

'Let go of me!' she cried. 'I don't intend to stay here and . . .'

'You see?' With an effortless strength, he tightened his hold on her, and jerked her body roughly towards him. 'It's written in every line of your body, every inch of your face! Look at you now, you're trying to get away from me . . . God damn it, if my sleeve so much as touches your arm you jump a foot in the air. Why not admit it, Sara? And tell me, just what are you afraid of?'

'I'm not afraid of anything,' she said hotly.

'Oh, but you are, aren't you, Sara? You're afraid of this.'

And before she knew what was happening, he pulled her roughly, tight against him, and bent his face towards hers.

She could feel the panic start to rise instantly, and she struggled. She felt trapped, trapped by his strength, by the unfamiliar male scent of his skin, trapped by the arousal she could feel herself producing in him. She attempted to push him back, but he held her arms behind her, so she could not move, and then, very deliberately, very slowly, ignoring her struggles, his eyes never leaving hers, he kissed her.

She tried to turn her head away, and his rough skin brushed against hers.

'No, please . . .' she pleaded, and as her lips parted, his found them. Her mind went numb, as his grip on her tightened. He drew her tight against his body, so her breasts under their thin shirt were rubbed tight against the warmth of his chest, and under the pressure of his lips, she felt suddenly an extraordinary and piercing pleasure, that shot through her body like a flame, transmitting itself from nerve-ending to nerve-ending. It stopped the fighting, the fear; she let him part her lips, surrendered herself to that long slow exploration of his mouth, and she felt all the tightness in her body relax. Her hands stopped trying to push him away, her muscles slackened, and—as if from far away—she heard her own throat make a sigh of surrender.

'My God, Sara,' his lips moved against hers, his voice thick. His hold on her grew more gentle, and slowly, insistently, he stroked her body, moulding it against his own, moving his hands slowly up to cup her full breasts. Instinctively, hardly knowing what she was doing, she sought his mouth again. But then he held her away a little, took her hand and held it against him.

'Oh, Sara,' he said softly, his lips against her cheek, 'can't you feel it, can't you feel how much I want you?'

With a low moan she arched herelf against him, knowing nothing, aware of nothing, but the surge of feelings he aroused in her, which she could not, did not want to control.

But he did not kiss her again. Instead he held her still in his arms, and when she opened her eyes his were searching her face. The fear came back. His breath was coming quickly, but he looked so cold, so unreachable . . .

'Now do you believe me?' It was said with control, despite what had happened. Suddenly the room righted itself, her mind, numb before, came sharply back into focus. She stared at him in disbelief, her body stiffening. It had all been an experiment, she thought suddenly, his way of proving to her that she did need a man, maybe that she needed him. And she had fallen for it, she had let him see . . . She felt her cheeks flame with colour, and fiercely, sharply, she pushed him away.

'Please,' she said, her voice tight and low, 'please, never do that again.'

'Why not?' Max smiled at her insolently, his eyes suddenly cold.

'Because it's no way to try and win an argument.'

'It's a pleasant way.' He said it flippantly, and the words shot pain through her body.

'Not for me.'

'You surprise me. You weren't exactly registering displeasure.'

'Under your expert tuition, you mean?'

'No, I . . .'

He reached for her again, but she stepped backwards, and his hand fell.

'I don't need that kind of therapy,' she said hotly, feeling the tears start to her eyes. 'I don't need your charitable attentions. Please. Never do that again.'

Very deliberately, fighting not to let him see the turmoil of feelings that raged in her, she picked up her bag and moved towards the door.

'Sara . . .' He made a move as if to follow her, but she cut him off.

'Thank you for your help,' she said haughtily, tilting her chin, 'with my article, that is.'

'God damn it . . .'

She was out of the room before he could stop her. As she shut the door she heard him swear violently, and then there was a crash of breaking glass, as if he had thrown something after her. Very deliberately she forced herself to go back to her office and collect her things. She went down the stairs rather than use the lift, for fear of meeting Max again, and passed Mr Jones, still on duty, without a word.

On the bus home, she used an old trick from her childhood. Her mind whirled, she felt numb with pain: she counted the shops as they passed through the dank narrow streets. None must be missed out; you had to concentrate. If you did it properly, the pain eventually went away. It didn't work as it once had done, but it calmed her somewhat. She congratulated herself on the fact that, as she turned the key in the front door of their flat, and Jennifer shouted, 'Is that you, Sara, how did you get on?' she was able to answer her in a perfectly ordinary tone.

'Oh, fine,' she said. 'It didn't take long. I'd have been back ages ago, but the buses were impossible.'

There was a looking glass on the wall by the door, and her own reflection stared back at her. Her face looked slightly paler than usual, but otherwise unaffected, unmarked. Nothing that mattered had happened, she told her face. Nothing at all. Her lips were swollen from Max's kisses; but her eyes looked as blank as she could wish, just as they had in childhood.

But it was not so easy to keep her thoughts at bay when she went to bed. Then the past always came back, replayed in an endless horrible pageant that not even sleep always stopped. The accusations and counter-accusations, drifting up the stairs to her room. Her mother's bitter charges of infidelity, her father's shabby unconvincing denials. After he went, it was as if he were dead; his name was never mentioned again, not once. For a whole year Sara had crept out of bed early each morning, and slipped silently down the stairs, convinced that each new morning would bring a letter in that familiar, irregular hand. It never did.

Then, when she was older, old enough to understand, her mother said, then came the catechisms: 'Just remember, Sara, men are out for one thing, and one thing only—their own gratification. The best thing you can do is find a man with plenty of money, so at least you won't have that to worry about. Get the wedding ring on your finger, and don't make yourself cheap, because if you do, he'll be off so fast you won't see the back of him . . .'

The words rang in her head like a litany; tiredly she tried to push them away. But they wouldn't go, they stuck, a hideous commentary running behind everything that had happened to her that evening. Maybe there was some truth in what Max had said to her, she thought, but to have behaved as she had done . . . to have been such a pushover. She smarted at the memory, at the scorn she had seen in his eyes; what she had felt, what he had seemed to feel, it had been so strong, and then . . . Suddenly she thought of one of the ex-girl-friends she had interviewed two years previously: a faded debutante, chain-smoking in a smart little flat off Sloane Square. 'Max?' The girl had laughed. 'Nobody knows Max, least of all any of his women. The man's not human, he's fire and ice—fire at the beginning, and ice a week later. Ask anyone.'

She heard the clock in the hall strike two, and buried

her face in the pillow. She would never be trapped like
that again; of that at least she could be certain. Max
would never touch her again, never come close to her. She
made the resolution, and something in her heart ached.

Next morning she was white from lack of sleep, and her
face in the glass looked pinched and drawn.

'Are you all right, Sara?' asked Jennifer, as they took
the bus in together. 'You were terribly quiet last night,
and now you look ghastly. Is it one of those migraines
again?'

Sara turned her face away.

'No, I'm all right,' she said. 'I couldn't sleep, that's all.
I was worrying about my article.'

Jennifer smiled. 'As usual,' she said. 'I wish you'd go
out occasionally, Sara. Honestly, you're turning into a
kind of hermit. All you think about is work, and how
much you hate Max. Why don't you just try avoiding
him for a couple of days?'

Sara laughed humourlessly. 'I wish I could,' she said.
'How can I? I'm no sooner sitting at my desk then he's
there, standing behind me, reading my copy. He never
leaves anyone alone to get on with anything in peace.'

Jennifer gave her a sharp glance. 'Speak for yourself,'
she said. 'He doesn't do it to me.'

They reached the office by nine-thirty, and when they
went up to the office there were few other people around,
for the magazine didn't really begin functioning much
before ten, although since Max's arrival, anyone might
have to stay until eight in the evening if need be.

In the doorway, Jennifer stopped, and nudged Sara.

'Good lord,' she muttered, 'look who's in!'

Sara followed her gaze, and saw Delia Waterlow,
already at her desk, typing. Jennifer grinned.

'She *must* have had a rocket last night! I've never even
seen her in the building before ten-fifteen at the earliest.'

Jennifer went off to the cloakroom, and when Sara went
to her desk, Delia—to her surprise—gave her a warm
smile. Obviously, since last night, she had become an ally.

'You wouldn't make me a cup of coffee, would you,
Sara?' Delia said. 'Be an angel.'

So Sara made her some coffee, and brought it over. Delia looked round to make sure they were alone, and then waved a small buff envelope at her.

'Look what I found when I got in this morning,' she said in a conspiratorial whisper. 'It's a P. & C. The beast! He must have stayed here to type it himself, last night—I can tell. It's not Beverley's typing.'

Sara looked at the small envelope. She knew—everyone knew—what a P. & C. meant. The initials stood for 'Private and Confidential', but that wasn't the point. You only received one if you were in trouble—serious trouble. It was the standard method of warning an employee, and a copy was filed in their records. Three P. & C.'s and they considered they had grounds to fire you.

'Oh, Delia,' Sara said sympathetically. 'What does he say?'

'The usual beastly things.' Delia shook her head. 'A warning about that business over Jennifer re-writing my copy, and generalised displeasure with my work. He says my clothes are too up-market, if you please. Fool! What does he know about it? Geoffrey never interfered.'

Geoffrey should have done, Sara thought, but she said nothing.

'Anyway, the point is I want to ask you a favour, Sara. In fact, two favours. I know you'll probably say "no", but I wish you wouldn't. You could really help me, and I'd be so grateful. Honestly, I know we've never got on terribly well in the past, but you were so sweet last night, I felt as if I'd made a friend.'

Sara stared at her in astonishment. This was indeed a changed Delia. Her head was lowered, and she bore every appearance of being genuinely contrite. In spite of herself, Sara warmed to her. After all, she thought, Delia was a woman, and with someone like Max Christian around, the women on the staff *ought* to stick together . . .

'Please, Sara, say you'll help me. I'm in such a mess, and last night—well, I hope you didn't have too hard a time yourself.'

'No,' Sara said quickly, 'it wasn't too bad. The usual thing.'

'Did it take long?' Delia looked inquisitive.

'No, not long. He'd done all the editing, there wasn't much to say really.'

'I see.' Delia sighed. 'Well, Sara, will you help me?'

Sara smiled. Obviously Jennifer had been right, and half the trouble was that she was too sharp with other women. Delia wasn't nearly so bad as she had thought.

'Well, if I can, I will. It depends on what it is, Delia. Just don't ask *me* to write your copy. Judging by my form, it wouldn't do you any good if you did.'

'Well, the thing is . . .' Delia hesitated, 'I'd like you to come to dinner with me.'

'To dinner?' Sara was astonished.

'Yes, you know that dinner party I was arranging yesterday—I'm so sorry that interrupted you, by the way. That one. It's next week, on Tuesday, please say you'll come. It'll be fairly formal, but there's only eight of us . . .'

Sara thought quickly. Last night Delia had said Max Christian would be going to that dinner party.

'Delia, I'm sorry,' she said, 'but I can't.'

Delia groaned.

'Oh, *please*,' she said. 'If you've got something else on, couldn't you move it?'

'It's not that, Delia . . .' Sara hesitated. 'It's just—well, you said last night that Max Christian was going. And I get on with him so badly, as you know, and the thought of seeing him socially—well, I don't think I could bear it.'

Delia's face lightened.

'Oh, that's all right,' she said happily. 'He's not coming! He got so angry last night he said he wouldn't. He said it would be better to keep our relationship on a professional level—just while we were having this bit of bother anyway, so he cried off.'

'I see.' Still Sara hesitated. It was the kind of affair she was bound to dislike, of course . . .

'I think you'll like the other people who are coming,' Delia said eagerly. 'My brother Piers is going to be there, and a girl I was at school with—old chums, you know, and some quite nice fellows. Please say yes, Sara!'

Sara laughed: 'I've got absolutely nothing to wear to an occasion like that, you know, Delia. I don't want to embarrass your friends by turning up in jeans.'

She had hoped that prospect might put Delia off, but it didn't.

'Taken care of!' she said triumphantly. 'That's my second favour I'm going to ask you. Would you model for me?'

'Would I *what*?' This time Sara nearly dropped her coffee, she was so astounded. Delia gave her somewhat tinkling girlish giggle.

'Now, don't get cross, Sara. I know your opinions about all that. Let me explain. In here,' and she waved the P. & C. buff envelope, 'darling Max has given me a list as long as your arm of fashion stories he wants me to do. He wants me to mix up-market stuff and cheaper clothes— for the working girl, you know the sort of thing. So—next week I'm going out to Montreux to do some divine furs for next winter, but before I go, he wants me to get in a piece on terrific, inexpensive clothes, mass-produced, that sort of thing. And no models—he wants them photo- graphed on an ordinary girl. In fact, he suggested you. But don't let that put you off.'

'Delia,' Sara was completely bemused, 'you must be mad! I couldn't *model*, for goodness' sake. Quite apart from the fact that I think the whole business is absolutely awful, I'd just look a mess. You'd never be able to use the pictures.'

'Nonsense, darling,' Delia cooed. 'You'd look terrific. You're very slim, which is the main thing, because anyone remotely plump looks like an elephant in fashion pictures. And we'd need to do a bit of make-up, of course—nothing much, I'd get Francine in. You've got good bones. And you can't disapprove of this. Nothing's going to cost more than fifty pounds, and most of the stuff is much less. It's the kind of straightforward ordinary clothes any woman might buy, *and* it'll be telling them how to get the best things cheapest. Now you can't disapprove of that, can you?'

'But what's that got to do with the dinner party?'

'That's the splendid thing,' Delia laughed. 'I knew you'd fuss about clothes, but the photo session is the same day as my dinner party. We're going to feature one dressy thing—you know, something pretty that you could wear out on a date. You can borrow that *after* the photo session, and wear it to my party.'

'Borrow it? Delia, don't be daft, it might get messed up or something.'

Delia laughed. 'Don't be silly, darling,' she said. 'My department does it all the time. The designers and the shops don't mind. And if anything *should* happen to the dress, we simply buy it on my department's budget. Nobody minds. Everybody does it all the time.'

Sara shook her head. 'Look, Delia, I'm sorry,' she said. 'I'd help you if I could, but really, I don't think that I . . .'

Delia's eyes welled with tears.

'Oh, Sara, *please*,' she begged. 'Honestly, I'm going to be in a terrible mess if you say no. It'll take all my time between now and Tuesday to find the clothes, and I haven't got time to find another girl to model them. There's no one else here who could do it, and I'm rushed off my feet as it is fixing the Montreux trip. It would mean some extra money for you too—I'd pay a modelling fee, of course . . . Besides, Max suggested you, and if you won't do it, he'll blame me, I know he will. I'll get another of these . . .' and she waved the buff envelope again.

Sara sighed. She thought quickly. She had no wish to get Delia into further trouble, and the extra money would be useful: she could send a little more to her mother.

'All right,' she said finally, 'I'll do the modelling for you, Delia—just this once. But I'm not wearing the dress to your party. I'd feel awful. I'll borrow something suitable to wear, and I won't shame you. O.K.?'

Delia leapt to her feet and embraced Sara warmly.

'You're an *angel*,' she smiled. 'I knew I could depend on you. Bless you, darling. You've made my day!'

After that, Sara hardly saw Delia for the rest of the day. At mid-morning, she departed on a search for clothes for the photo session, taking in tow her two assistants.

' 'Bye, Sara,' she waved. 'Don't worry, I'm going to find some divine things.'

Sara didn't doubt it. Delia might not be able to write fashion copy, but her eye for clothes was brilliant, and her fashion pictures—if over-exotic—always first class. But still Sara felt nervous. What had she let herself in for? she thought. Despite what Delia had said, she thought she'd make a hopeless model, and the thought of cavorting around in front of a camera made her feel ill. And then that dinner party! Debs and weak-chinned Guards officers—she could just imagine it. She couldn't think why Delia wanted her, of all people, to go, and she would loathe it. But Jennifer had said she ought to go out more, and perhaps she was right. So, why not? It would be a bit of an adventure, as well as a bit of a joke, and Max Christian wasn't going, so it was quite safe.

That day, to her heartfelt relief, she hardly saw him. He emerged only once from his office, and ignored her totally.

'What's up with him?' asked Jennifer at lunchtime. 'Beverley says he's been even worse than usual, finding fault with every single thing. He reduced one of the secretaries to tears this morning. *And* hardly anyone's laid eyes on him. He's only been out once, and that was to lay into Mark Shand, the rest of the time he's been shut away in there like a hermit.'

In fact, for the rest of that week Sara managed to avoid him almost completely. She was researching an interview with a politician, and had to spend most of the days in the cuttings library making notes. She deliberately prolonged the task; the article wasn't urgent, and in the library she felt safe. He wasn't likely to go marauding in there.

She was just congratulating herself that she had managed something of a record—four days without encountering Max Christian—when she got into the lift on Friday night and found herself face to face with him. She very nearly backed out again, but just stopped herself in time, although her heart gave a lurch. She didn't want him to think she was running away from him.

He nodded at her coolly, and the lift descended slowly and creakily with neither saying a word. Just as they were reaching the ground floor, and Sara was reading the fire and escape notice with fixed attention, he spoke.

'I see you're wearing a skirt,' he commented. 'Good.'

'My jeans are in the wash,' she said, looking up at the floor indicator board—one more stop. She was nearly safe.

'I'm glad to hear you're doing that fashion story with Delia,' he went on. 'Quite a change from what we've done before. I think you'll do it very well.'

His tone was surprisingly kind, but when she looked at him she saw he was merely attempting politeness.

'Yes,' she said evenly, 'I think it will be very interesting. Good evening.'

And as the doors opened she was out of the lift, across the foyer and out the swing doors. Max Christian hadn't had time to say another word. Perfect! She thought. Jennifer was right—she had found the perfect technique. Just avoid the man altogether. It was much simpler. She felt better than she had done for weeks.

Jennifer was mystified that she had agreed to go to Delia's party, even more mystified that Delia should have asked her.

'Your fault,' Sara told her. 'You said I should go out more. High society! Canapés and *contrefilet*. Anyway, I'm a reformed character. I'm trying to see the good side in all the women you said I was rude to, and Delia's top of the list. You'd just better help me find something to wear, that's all.'

The two girls spent Sunday going through Jennifer's wardrobe, trying to find a suitable dress, and eventually came up with a short black frock that had seen better days, but was passable. Sara put it on, and collapsed laughing. It was too large, and hung on her in folds. Jennifer looked at it ruefully.

'Hell! I never realised how much fatter than you I was. I'm going on a diet. We'll have to take it in a bit.'

Jennifer borrowed a friend's sewing machine, and they

did. When Sara tried it on again, plus a pair of Jennifer's shoes, it looked a bit better.

'I still look like a crow, though,' Sara laughed. 'I don't exactly look like a high-fashion model, do I?'

Jennifer giggled. 'Not exactly.'

'Ah, but you see, Francine hasn't done my face yet. And I'm standing all wrongly. Watch this!'

And Sara leaned back, pelvis forward, in a good imitation of the classic model's stance. She sucked in her cheeks, lowered her lashes, and gave Jennifer a sultry glance.

'How's that?'

Jennifer gave her a long look.

'Actually,' she said, 'and much as I hate to admit it, it's not bad. You look quite different. I see what's usually wrong with you now. You slouch. You've always got your hands in your pockets. In fact, you look like a schoolboy going unwillingly to school. Now you look . . . almost pretty.'

Sara chucked a cushion at her, and Jennifer ducked expertly. It missed.

'Mock not,' Sara grinned. 'Come Tuesday night, this will be electrifying the Hooray Henries. Just you wait!'

CHAPTER FOUR

SARA spent all day Monday at the House of Commons, watching a debate, and interviewing the M.P., who turned out to be self-important and tedious. But she didn't mind. She had clocked up another day without seeing Max. It was a dull day, but still . . . And she would escape him all the next day as well, she told herself. The photo session would last all morning and all afternoon, and then she and Delia were going straight on to the dinner party.

She arrived at the photographer's studio, which was just off the King's Road in Chelsea, at nine-thirty, feeling extremely nervous. Delia was there already, plus her two

assistants, Francine the make-up girl, Clive Paget the
photographer, and his assistant. The place was in apparent chaos. Everywhere she looked there were clothes,
shoes, hats, jewellery, tights—even wigs. Clive, who Delia
had assured her acidly could make even a witch look
beautiful, was checking his film. His assistant was setting
up the studio, unreeling great sheets of white paper, and
angling silver umbrellas.

'What's all that for?' Sara asked.

'You stand against the paper—it's to get a clear back-
ground that shows up the clothes sharply,' said Delia.
'And the umbrellas reflect light where he wants it on your
face. Now, let's get Francine to work on you. Come on.'

She plonked Sara down at a make-up table surmounted
by a huge mirror flanked with light bulbs. Francine came
over, carting a huge metal box with handles—like the
kind mechanics use to keep tools in, Sara thought with
amusement. But when Francine opened it, it was full to
the brim with make-up, pots and tubes and sticks and
pencils and brushes.

'Goodness!' exclaimed Sara. 'I thought you said there'd
only be a bit of make-up.'

'Shut up, there's a darling,' said Delia. 'Now, put this
cape on, lie back, and think of England. Did you wash
your hair last night, the way I told you?' And she ran her
fingers disdainfully through Sara's blonde soft curls. Sara
nodded.

'O.K. Freddie will be along later to do your hair. No
wigs, I think. We want it to look natural.'

Delia seemed quite different here, Sara thought, from
the way she was at the office. Here she was on her ter-
ritory, and she knew exactly what she was doing. Francine
approached, and gave Sara a wink in the mirror. Sara
tried not to be alarmed at Francine's own appearance,
which was startling to say the least, and Francine grinned
at her reflection.

'But she's *beautiful*!' she said. 'You didn't tell me,
Delia.'

'I said she was pretty.' Delia sounded huffy.

'More than pretty—beautiful. Look at those cheekbones, those eyes! No problems here. What are you wearing on your skin?' She peered at Sara closely.

'Nothing.'

'Nothing? It's fantastic. Boy, am I going to have fun! Right, love, now relax.'

Sara didn't relax, she was too fascinated to watch what was happening. Francine never stopped moving, and when the photographer's assistant put on a tape of rock music, extremely loud, she began to make little dancing movements in time to the music, as her fingers deftly sought, and found, exactly the materials she needed.

Sara stared at the mirror with growing amazement. Francine used an extraordinary amount of make-up, yet so delicate, so sure, was her touch that Sara did not look over made-up. It was just that her face seemed to come alive. Her cheeks were flushed with delicate colour, the hollows beneath them accentuated. Her lips glowed, her already large eyes seemed twice as big. It was the eye make-up that took longest.

'No lashes, I think,' Francine said critically, as Delia watched over her shoulder. 'Look, Delia—hers are almost black—with that hair, it's fantastic! She doesn't need them.'

Delia blinked her own carefully applied false ones, and walked away.

Seven colours—Sara counted them—were blended over her lids and brows. Expertly Francine highlighted and shaded. She touched the base of the lashes with kohl, applied several successive thin layers of mascara. When she had finished, she stood back and surveyed her handiwork critically.

'Look at that!' she said triumphantly. 'You can even see those glorious freckles still, and look at those eyes! Clive, come and look—you won't have any problems here.'

Clive came over and peered at her. Sara began to feel like a specimen in the zoo, but even so she couldn't help feeling pleased and excited. A totally different woman looked back at her from the glass, beautiful, young, vital. Well, she thought, I may never wear all this stuff again, but it is fun.

'A right little darlin',' Clive pronounced in his heavy cockney accent.

'Ravishing!' said a high-pitched man's voice behind him, and Freddie made his entrance. He was all in white, and as camp as a row of tents, Sara thought; he smiled at her warmly. He picked up tendrils of her hair, and turned her head this way and that.

'Have to do something here, though,' he said. '*What* have you been cutting it with, sweetie, the bread-knife?'

'Nail scissors, actually,' said Sara, and Freddie laughed.

'Naughty!' he said. 'Now *don't* get in a tizz because I'm going to snip it just a bit, then the Carmens. Oh yes, I can see it now. I might spray in just the teensiest bit of highlighter. Not pink, duckie, don't worry.'

Sara stopped worrying, and let him get on with it. It took half an hour at most, and at the end even the perfectionist Freddie was pleased.

'Clive!' he said. 'Clive, now you've just *got* to do one with the wind machine! Imagine these lovely curls, just ever so slightly disarranged—a little tendril just here, perhaps. See what I mean?'

Clive nodded. 'Yea,' he agreed, 'we could angle it a bit low—so she has to clutch her skirt a bit. *The Seven Year Itch*—the Marilyn Monroe bit, y'know what I mean? I like it. I like it.'

After that, the morning seemed to go by in a flash.

Clive's assistant produced champagne, the rock music got louder, and when she found herself on the white photographic paper, with the lights blinding her eyes, Sara found to her surprise that she wasn't nervous. She was beginning to enjoy herself.

'Now come on, darlin',' said Clive. 'No posin' now. Just move around to the music till you feel loosened up. That's it! That's lovely!' He began clicking his Pentax. 'Right, turn the head a little, arm up, towards me, give me a look, darlin', come on, right down the lens. Got it! Keep it up. We got a natural mover here, y'know that, Delia . . .'

And Sara did relax. Perhaps it was the champagne, perhaps it was the music, perhaps it was just the knowledge the mirror had given her that she'd never looked better in her life. So she moved, held it, moved again, smiled, laughed, moistened her lips, pouted and looked stern. She put on a bewildering succession of clothes—trousers, skirts, dresses, a skin-tight leotard and glittery shoes with six-inch heels. And all the time Clive never stopped talking, hypnotising her with his lens and his words. Just before lunch they tried the wind machine—a large fan—and she held down her skirts in the famous Monroe pose, and the rush of air caught her face, her hair, and she laughed.

'Terrific!' Clive gave her a quick kiss on the cheek. 'Want to know somethin'? I was dead worried when Delia told me what we were going to do. Thought you'd freeze, see? Most do, if they're not models, that is. You could make it in the modellin', you know, you're a natural . . .'

It was then that Sara realised that someone else had been watching the last shots. The room was so crowded and she'd had so many lights in her eyes that she hadn't noticed him before, but now she saw him. There was a young man, standing at the back. He had long fair hair, and was wearing an old tweed coat and a scruffy pair of jeans.

'Who's that?' she said to Delia, who seemed to be rather quiet, and a bit irritable—perhaps the strain and rush of it all, Sara thought. Delia turned.

'Oh God,' she muttered, 'it's my brother Piers. I know what *he* wants. He'll have come to borrow money. Oh, it's too bad, blast him!'

Sara stared. Delia's brother Piers! He looked like an out-of-work rock musician, not at all the smooth young man-about-town she would have imagined.

'Delia.' He was coming across.

Delia went to head him off in a hurry, and Sara could hear that a whispered—and on Delia's part cross—conversation was taking place. She saw Piers nod in her direction, and Delia made a shushing gesture

'No, you can't, Piers,' she heard. 'I've told you a billion

times I won't have you interfering with my photo sessions. Now what is it you want, for goodness' sake?'

More muffled talk, and then Sara saw Delia reach resignedly for her handbag, take something out and hand it to him. 'Now push *off*, Piers,' she heard. And Piers did. At the door, however, he turned, and—catching Sara's eye—blew her an elaborate, graceful kiss. Then he went. Delia saw the gesture and came back, lips tight.

'Baby brother,' she said grimly. 'On the scrounge as usual.'

'He's very good-looking,' commented Sara.

Delia's eyes narrowed. 'Good-looking, and good for nothing,' she said. 'He can be terribly charming when he wants something, and that's about it. He's just taken up with some frightful band, and Daddy's furious. I told him, if he turns up in that gear at my party tonight, I'll get him chucked out. I mean, did you *see* what he was wearing? If it was punk, one could at least make a joke of it—it might be quite amusing. But those jeans! And that coat! So Sixties. Half the time I think he does it just to annoy me.'

After that, the afternoon sped by even more swiftly than the morning. When they finally finished, it was gone six, and Sara could hardly believe it. Everyone had some more champagne, and she felt elated and excited.

'I'm glad we're going back to your place now,' she said to Delia. 'It might have been a bit of an anti-climax, after all this, to take the bus back to Islington.'

She saw Delia suppress a shudder at the idea of living north of the Park, and then she patted her hand.

'Well, we'll have to hurry a bit,' she said. 'People are coming at around seven-thirty, and I must get back to the flat first.'

'Well, I'll just take this make-up off,' said Sara, 'and find my clothes—don't worry, Delia, it's a dress, a perfectly respectable one. I brought it in a carrier bag—it's over there somewhere.'

But Francine was offended at the idea of her removing the make-up.

'Take it off?' she screeched. 'But you're going out!—

Delia told me. You look a million dollars. You can't take it off. Look, keep it on to please me—I'll just touch it up a bit. You look terrific, really.'

So, in the end, Sara agreed. She took off the clothes she'd been wearing, and searched around for her carrier bag. It was nowhere to be found. While she was scrabbling about under a great pile of clothes, Delia came over.

'Do hurry, Sara,' she said. 'We'll have to go soon.'

'I'm sorry, Delia,' Sara said. 'I just can't find that stupid carrier bag—I know I left it here somewhere.'

So Delia helped her look, and one of her assistants joined in. They searched high and low, but it had totally disappeared.

'Oh, damn!' said Sara. 'Well, it looks as if you've got a straight choice, Delia. Either I don't come, or I come in the jeans and tee-shirt I wore here.'

The prospect clearly horrified Delia, because she began searching with renewed energy. Suddenly she stopped.

'I know what's happened,' she said. 'Jacinth, my assistant. She took all the clothes we'd finished with back to the office, to start working out all the merchandising details. She must have taken that as well. That's it.' She looked at her watch. 'She'll have left the office now, we can't get it back.'

Sara shrugged. 'Well,' she said, 'it doesn't matter as long as it's safe—it's not mine, it's Jennifer's, you see. But I'm afraid that either spoils your *placements*, Delia, or you get me in jeans. Take your pick.'

'Wait—I know just the thing!' Delia darted away to a different part of the studio, and came back. Folds of silk and lace spilled over her arms. 'You can wear this!' She smiled at Sara happily. 'It's one I brought along for the session and didn't use. It's lovely, it's your size, and it's just the thing for this evening.'

Sara stared at the dress doubtfully, as Delia held it up before her. It was exquisite. She had never worn anything like it in her life. It was of heavy black silk taffeta, with a huge collar of antique lace. It had long sleeves, a tiny waist, and a full skirt. At the neckline the collar was fastened with a beige silk rose.

'Delia!' she protested. 'I couldn't possibly wear that! It must have cost a fortune!'

'It didn't, darling. This is the cheap clothes feature, right? I found it in a little shop over by Portobello market. There's a girl designer there who's just starting, and she makes these divine dresses with old materials she buys up very cheap. Two years from now when she's made her name they'll be five hundred a throw. But not yet. It was thirty-five pounds, and the only reason I didn't use it was time—we had more than enough pictures for two spreads anyway. Go on, Sara, try it on—it'll look fantastic.'

Sara felt embarrassed. She wanted to try it on—she even wanted to wear it, because she felt gay and elated, and she wasn't likely ever to wear anything like that again . . .

'Delia, I can't,' she said miserably. 'I told you. It's not mine, and if anything happened to it . . .'

Delia began to look impatient.

'Sara,' she said crossly, 'I *told* you. People borrow session clothes all the time. If it was Yves St. Laurent, I might hesitate, but it's thirty-five quid. Now don't be silly. Put it on and hurry up. I'm *not* having you there in jeans, and I don't intend having my numbers at dinner messed up. Come *on*, Sara.'

In the end, Sara agreed. She put it on, and it did indeed look very beautiful. She smoothed her hand down over the full skirt, and stared at her reflection in the glass. If Max Christian could see you now, she thought ironically. But she put that thought from her as quickly as it came. He might find her unfeminine, but *she* didn't need clothes to convince herself she was a woman. And when Susie, Delia's other assistant, came over, and whispered that it looked smashing, and that Delia was right, people *did* often borrow session clothes, she felt better. Just this once, she thought. Why not?

It was gone six-thirty by the time they left the studio, and it took them ages to find a cab. Sara was rather surprised that Delia hadn't ordered one, as she usually never set foot outside without a car of some kind being at the ready, and her favourite boast was that she hadn't taken public transport since she was five. But having been in such a rush at the studio, Delia now seemed to be less in a hurry.

'I think everything will be O.K.,' she said. 'I've borrowed some of Daddy's servants for tonight, including Sergio, who's a sweetie—so I should think everything will be in hand. But I've got to have a bath and get changed. You won't mind waiting, will you, Sara? I'll be down before any people arrive, don't worry.'

Delia's house turned out to be in a tiny mews, not far from Brompton Oratory.

'Isn't it sweet?' she said, as the taxi pulled up. 'It's just a workman's cottage really, attached to the old stables, but it cost Daddy a fortune, not to mention what he spent doing it up for me.'

Sara looked at the house. It was small, and in the kind of street where small houses cost close to a hundred thousand. It was painted pink, had the predictable bay trees outside the door, and burglar-proof iron gates over all the windows. Yes, she supposed you could call it sweet.

Before Delia could even reach for her keys, the door swung open to reveal a manservant in striped trousers and black jacket, who made a slight bow.

'Sergio!' Delia cooed. 'I'm frightfully late, I know. Have you and Maria got everything in hand?'

'Everything is ready, Miss Delia,' he answered. 'And Anna is running your bath, I believe.'

He took their coats, and led them through a small hallway, where he opened a door.

Delia gave Sara a peck of a kiss on her cheek.

'Now, darling,' she said, 'you go and rest by the fire, you must be exhausted. Don't be intimidated by Sergio—he'll bring you a drink.'

Sergio offered champagne, and Sara, who had vaguely read somewhere that you could never get drunk on champagne, provided you mixed it with no other drinks later, accepted. It arrived on a silver salver, in a long fluted glass.

Sergio withdrew, and Sara looked curiously around her. So, she thought, this is how the other half lives! The

drawing room was unexpectedly large, and a fire was
burning in the grate. The armchairs were soft, and
covered in pink and green chintz. The lighting was flat-
tering, and there were several little tables covered with
floor-length cloths, and scattered with *bibelots*, silver snuff-
boxes, and a great many photographs—all of Delia, and
in silver frames. It was a pretty room, but curiously anonymous, and Sara guessed it had been planned by a
decorator rather than Delia herself.

The chair was comfortable, the champagne ice-cold and
delicious. She sipped it, and began to relax. The evening
might be fun, she thought. She just hoped Delia kept her
word, and didn't take so long getting dressed that Sara
was faced with a whole lot of guests, none of whom she
knew.

At seven-thirty Delia still hadn't reappeared, and Sara
heard a car pull up and the front door-bell ring.

'Bother Delia,' she thought. 'How typical! Now what
am I going to do?'

She heard muffled voices in the hall, and tensed. For a
moment she had thought she recognised that voice ...
but no, it was impossible. Then Sergio threw back the
door, and she knew it wasn't. Framed in the doorway,
immaculately dressed in a dark suit and a dark blue silk
shirt, and regarding her with considerable surprise, was
the one person she had been sure she would *not* meet:
Max Christian.

Typically, and predictably (Sara thought), Max Christian
recovered himself before she did.

'Sara,' he drawled, 'what a delightful surprise!'

And to her absolute fury, he advanced across the room
with total self-composure, took her hand and kissed her
lightly on the cheek. She could not even back away, because she was hemmed in by the armchair, and in any
case, Sergio was still hovering in the doorway.

But the kiss, if graceful, was perfunctory, although Sara
felt as if her cheek had been branded. He turned away
almost immediately.

'No, no champagne, thank you, Sergio. I loathe the

stuff. I'll have a glass of Glenmorangie, if you have it. Water, no ice.'

Sergio went to fetch the drink, and Max Christian warmed his hands at the fire, and then with total composure sat down in the chair opposite her, and stared at Sara. He continued to stare while Sergio fetched the whisky and added the water, offered canapés, and withdrew. Sara could not meet his gaze, and lowered her own defensively. Her brain was a seething mass of contradictions. Her first reaction had been fury—with Delia, who had clearly lied to her. Her second was a kind of odd triumph that if the hateful man had to turn up, he was seeing her, at least, as he'd never seen her before. Her third, that perhaps she could leave. But clearly that was impossible. Somehow she had to get through the evening, and not let him see that she was affected by his presence in the least.

'Astonishing,' he said finally.

Sara looked up. 'I'm sorry?'

'Astonishing,' he repeated. 'You are totally transformed. You look . . .' he hesitated. 'It's a very beautiful dress. This isn't due to anything I said to you the other evening, by any chance, is it?'

'If you mean my dress and my make-up, no,' said Sara quickly. 'It's just that I happen to have come from the photo session.'

'What a shame.' He smiled lazily. 'I thought it might be in my honour.'

'I'm afraid not,' she said sweetly. 'Sorry to disappoint you, but I didn't even know you were coming. Did you wear the blue shirt on my behalf?'

His tones were equally sweet. 'No,' he said, 'I wore it for Delia. It's her favourite colour.'

He had won *that* round, she thought. Never mind, there was the rest of the evening, and he wouldn't out-spar her every time. But at that prospect, she felt suddenly panicked. The dress and the make-up were making her desperately selfconscious, and besides, she didn't at all understand what was going on. Why had Delia lied to her like that? What could be the reason? If she were to get through the rest of the evening, she had to find out, and quickly, before the other guests arrived. She might just have time to find Delia . . .

'Will you excuse me a moment?' she said stiffly, and he rose with alacrity and opened the door. She went through it without giving him a second glance. Luckily none of the servants was in sight, and she made for the stairs. She had no difficulty in finding Delia, for there proved to be only one bedroom, and the door was open. Delia was clearly visible, sitting at an enormous dressing table, and fluffing powder on her face. She turned as Sara came in.

'Sara darling,' she said, 'was that someone arriving? I'm awfully sorry. Hey, you look a bit white—do you want the loo or something?'

Sara marched straight in.

'O.K., Delia,' she said fiercely, 'just tell me what you're playing at. You swore to me that Max wasn't coming. Well, he's downstairs now.'

Delia had the grace to blush, and she opened her china blue eyes wide.

'Oh, Sara!' she breathed. 'I didn't realise it was him, I'd have been downstairs in a flash. I didn't dare tell you before, because I thought if I did you wouldn't come, and I did so want you here. He changed his mind. We . . . we had a little reconciliation.' She smiled demurely. 'He apologised, and I forgave him, and frankly things are going rather well between us at the moment, so I hadn't the heart to refuse. You're not really cross, are you? Do you hate him so much?'

But as she prattled on, Sara's eyes were mesmerised by a large heart-shaped silver frame on Delia's dressing table. In it was a photograph of Max Christian, wearing a deep blue shirt. Some words in his illegible writing were scrawled across it.

Sara felt suddenly sick, and exhausted. Clearly things *were* going well between them, and not just, as Delia had put it, on a 'professional' level, either. She felt her heart contract—with sympathy for Delia, she told herself. Clearly Delia was infatuated with him; maybe he loved

Delia. Sara looked at her. She was wearing a dress of deep blue, with a narrow band of sapphires around her neck, and she looked very lovely . . . why not?

'Sara, please, do forgive me. Say something! I didn't think it would upset you this much, honestly. I so wanted you to come, you see. You're the first friend I've ever made at work, you know . . .'

Delia's voice had taken on a plaintive note, and with an effort Sara roused herself. Well, she thought, it's not Delia's fault, not really. I'd probably do the same myself if I were head over heels about some man. And it *was* true Delia had made no friends at the office, perhaps she *had* felt cut off. She forced herself to smile.

'O.K.,' she said. 'I just wish you'd warned me, Delia. I got a shock, that's all. However, I promise to control my anti-social instincts. But you know Max and I don't get on, so if you'd keep us apart as much as you can, I would be terribly grateful.'

'Of course I will, darling.' Delia was wreathed in smiles. 'Did you like the look of brother Piers? Well, I'll rearrange the *placements*; it'll mean one husband and wife sitting next to each other, but never mind. I'll put you next to him at dinner. He can be very amusing, and he was *frightfully* taken with you . . .' She put her arm around Sara's waist and the two descended the stairs with Delia in high good humour.

As they came down, other guests began arriving, of whom the first was Piers, transformed from earlier in the day, and resplendent in a claret-coloured velvet suit. He was followed by Delia's old school friend Charlotte and her husband, a tall thin young man wearing a grey suit and an old Etonian tie. The last couple, who arrived late, proved to be Gordon Ellis, the publisher, and his wife Ellen, whom Sara had interviewed a few weeks before. As soon as she saw Sara, she came straight across to her.

'Sara!' she smiled. 'How lovely you're here, and what a surprise. I meant to write and thank you for your piece, and I haven't had a moment. Even Gordon liked it, which surprised me, because he hated the idea of my seeing a journalist. Gordon . . .' she beckoned to her husband, 'come and meet Sara Ford, from *London Now*. The one who did the interview. Sara, my dear, you're looking absolutely lovely. What an incredible dress!'

To her delight, Sara found that without effort on her part she was well protected from Max Christian. Piers Waterlow had made straight for her elbow, both the Ellises were talking away to her animatedly. Max was left by the fire with Delia, her school friend, and the husband, both of whom, Sara thought, looked rather heavy weather.

She drank a couple more glasses of champagne, and by the time they came to go in to dinner the elation she had felt earlier in the day had returned in abundance. Piers Waterlow was very funny, and he made her laugh; she liked the Ellises. It was going to be fun after all.

'I hope my beloved sister has arranged for us to sit next to each other.' Piers was at her elbow as they went through into the candlelit dining room. 'I offered to bribe her at lunch time, so I hope it's worked.'

'Oh, I think you'll find it has,' Sara smiled up at him. 'Wait and see.'

He took her elbow. 'If it hasn't,' he said in a low voice by her ear, 'then I just might make a scene. Which would upset my dear sister terribly. I get very cross if I don't get my own way.'

Sara was conscious that Max Christian was looking at them both, his face a mask of cold displeasure. She laughed, and deliberately tilted her chin up towards Piers in a flirtatious manner.

'And do you usually get your own way?' she asked.

'Always. When it matters.' He gave her a long look from under his thick lashes, and Sara smiled to herself. He was about her own age, she thought, and terribly good-looking, although his mouth had a slightly spoilt and petulant look. She could well imagine he did make scenes, and she suspected she'd find them tiresome. But still, he was amusing, and he seemed to arouse Max's distaste, and just at the moment she could think of no better reason to favour someone.

In fact, it was clear that both men had met before, and disliked each other cordially.

'Dear old Max,' said Piers, as they seated themselves. 'How are you? I didn't get a chance to say hello earlier.'

'Don't let it bother you, Piers, you were otherwise engaged.'

Piers totally ignored the frosty tone in which this was said, a tone which might have daunted another man.

'Still grinding away at the office, Max? Though of course if you have other journalists tucked away there who are as delectable as Miss Ford, I can understand your obsession with work. Do tell me, Sara, are there any more there like you?'

'A few.' Max Christian answered for her, and looked directly at Delia as he said it. The look registered on the entire company, and Delia bridled coquettishly.

She had arranged the table, Sara thought, exactly as she had promised, and she gave Sara an encouraging smile as they sat down, as if to say—well, I was as good as my word.

At one end of the table sat Delia herself; on her right was Max Christian, on her left her brother Piers. Sara was next to Piers, who drew out her chair for her, and helped her into her place with what she felt was a slightly excessive display of good manners. On Sara's left was Charles, who turned out to work as a merchant banker in the City; opposite her were Mrs Ellis, Charlotte, Delia's 'old chum', who had a high colour and an already much canvassed interest in horses, and Gordon Ellis. It was perfect, Sara thought. She might have preferred not to be facing Max, but he was absorbed in conversation with Mrs Ellis, who was clearly an old friend, and with Delia. And the food, it was clear, was going to repay the care Delia had taken.

They began with smoked salmon, wrapped around an avocado mousse; the *contrefilet* followed, slightly rare, with duchesse potatoes, and crisp French beans with almonds. The wine was as good as the food, as carefully chosen, and as impeccably served by Sergio and a white-capped and aproned maid.

'Delicious, darling,' said Piers, as they were finishing the beef. 'Jolly clever of you to get Maria in, she's done it beautifully.'

Sara saw Delia blush crimson, and make a gesture as if to silence her brother. Max Christian turned to Delia with an air of enquiry.

'Oh, Maria's Daddy's cook,' she said hastily. 'She came in to help, but I did most of it myself.'

'Oh, come off it, Delia.' Piers waited until there was silence. 'You might have taken the strings off the beans, though I doubt it. But that's it. Delia can't boil an egg,' he said cheerfully.

'Really?' Max Christian's eyebrows arched, and Delia glowered at her brother.

'Honestly, Piers,' she snapped, 'you don't know what you're talking about. That was true once, but it's not true now. I've been taking lessons.'

'You don't say?' Piers gave her a radiant smile. 'I had no idea, you *do* surprise me. I think she must be contemplating matrimony,' he said *sotto voce* to Sara, in a whisper that managed to carry right round the table. 'It's a sure sign in a woman, you know. First they take cookery lessons, then they start cooing over babies in prams outside supermarkets, then they rush round the place dusting everything in sight and arranging flowers, and finally they start peering intently in jewellers' shop windows. Has Delia shown any of the other symptoms, Max?'

'Not so far as I'm aware,' Max said coldly.

'What about you, Sara?' Piers turned to her again. 'I've already discovered you're a terrific model, and—I hear—a fierce lady journalist. Can you add cookery to your other accomplishments? Have you thought of taking lessons?' The last words were said almost into her ear, and accompanied by a frankly admiring glance. Sara, conscious that Max was looking at them both intently, laughed.

'No,' she said. 'I'm sorry to disappoint you, Piers, but I'm totally undomesticated. I can't cook, I loathe housework, I never coo at babies, and I couldn't arrange a bunch of daisies.'

Charles, who had, Sara noted, consumed claret at twice the rate of everyone else, gave a far-back chortle.

'Oh, heck,' he groaned, 'don't say we've got one of those dreaded Women's Libbers in our midst!'

'Very much so, Charles.' And Max gave Sara a charming smile, the kind that didn't reach his eyes.

To Sara's relief, Ellen Ellis came to her rescue. She gave her a motherly smile, and Sara thought again how much she liked her.

'Charles,' she said strongly, 'you really oughtn't to use that awful hackneyed term. Women's Libber, indeed! Sara's an independent young woman, who quite naturally wants to use the talents she's been given. I was exactly like her at that age. And what's more, she gave me a lot of food for thought when she came to interview me. She asked me a perfectly horrible question—which she was quite right to ask, incidentally—she asked me if I ever felt I'd wasted my life. I worried about it for days afterwards.'

'Wasted your life? Stuff and nonsense!' said her husband.

'No, Gordon,' she went on, 'it's not as easy as that. It's a question every woman who gives up work for her family avoids asking herself all the time. I was very glad Sara asked it, it made me think a good deal.'

'That's an enormous relief.' Sara leaned across to her. 'Because afterwards, when I was discussing the interview, someone suggested to me that it was a presumptuous question. And then *I* felt terribly worried.'

Ellen Ellis laughed. 'You don't need to tell me who *that* was,' she said. 'You put it very tactfully, my dear, but it was Max here, wasn't it? Well, you don't want to take the slightest notice of *him*. He has appallingly old-fashioned ideas about women. He'd have a ball and chain round their ankles if he had his way. Come on now, Max,' she turned to him, 'you know that's true. You're a terrible male chauvinist—to use another hackneyed term. You'd have got along fine in the nineteenth century, but those views just won't do any longer.'

Max was about to protest, and Sara knew he had seen

the gleam of triumph in her own eyes, but Delia interjected.

'Well, I don't agree *at all*, Ellen,' she said. 'I think a woman should devote herself to her family, just as you've done. Look how happy you've made Gordon, look at yourself...'

'And I quite agree, Delia,' put in her friend Charlotte. 'It's totally natural for a woman to devote herself to her home and her babies. Now, if you look at brood mares...'

'Oh, my God! Brood mares! We'll be having a lecture on stallions and mating procedure in a minute...' Piers' lips were against Sara's ear again, and this time he made sure the rest of the table didn't hear him. Sara's eyes danced. From where she sat she could see the expression on Max's face very clearly, and that he was extremely angry—presumably with the turn of the conversation— was obvious. His lips were tightly compressed, he appeared to have forgotten Delia, who was trying to attract his attention, and he was fixing Sara with a cold blue-eyed stare.

'Piers, I do wish you'd stop whispering—it's frightfully rude,' Delia hissed at him. Piers drew back.

'Sorry, old thing,' he mocked the prep school parlance as he said it. 'If you don't want me to whisper, you shouldn't put me next to such tantalising guests.'

Sara thought that at any minute Max Christian was going to explode with rage, but Delia, seeming to sense a diversion was needed, pressed the bell, and Sergio appeared, carrying before him an enormous dish of fresh raspberries and a huge silver jug of cream.

'Raspberries! Delia, wherever did you get those at this time of year? You *are* clever,' said Charlotte. 'Ours all died of mould last year,' she added to Gordon Ellis, who had had a long lecture on mares and fillies from her, and looked paralysed with boredom.

'They're flown in from California,' said Delia. 'Just leave them, Sergio—I'll serve the pudding.'

Sergio was just behind Sara as she said it, and Delia moved to her feet rather hurriedly to take the tray from him. Quite what happened then Sara never knew, but evidently the tray slipped, or tilted. Sergio made an exclamation of concern, Piers was half on his feet to intercede, Delia seemed to grab the tray to stop it from falling, and the next thing Sara knew was that the whole bowl of raspberries was tipped right over her. She jumped up in horror, but it was too late. Raspberries had spilled right down the front of her dress; the lace collar was soaked, the silk rose was seeping a slow purple, the taffeta was drenched. She froze with embarrassment. As if from a great distance, she heard Delia uttering cries of concern. Piers was mopping at her with a napkin, Sergio had run to fetch cloths, everyone was on their feet except Max Christian, who was too far away to do anything, and who was watching the scene with an air of thoughtful detachment.

'Oh no!' she heard Delia cry. 'That lovely dress! Sara, what are we going to do?'

'It's all right,' said Sara, as calmly as she could, and feeling a complete fool. 'I'll have to go and change, that's all. I've got my jeans somewhere . . .'

'Inevitably,' she heard Max Christian say lightly, and she glared at him.

Fortunately, Ellen Ellis took command. 'Come upstairs with me, Sara,' she said. 'I'll help you clean yourself up. And we'd better try and soak that collar. I think it'll come out after cleaning if we do. It's lucky it wasn't blackberries,' she added to Delia, and her voice was cold.

Upstairs she was calm and efficient. She helped Sara find her clothes. She and the maid Anna soaked the lace collar in the wash basin, and to Sara's enormous relief, some of the stains came out.

'Well,' she said, coming back into Delia's bedroom as Sara finished pulling on her old clothes, 'it's better than it was. I think cleaning will get it out. What a shame for you, my dear, and you looked so lovely. Still, never mind.' She smiled warmly. 'With a face like yours, you can look just as lovely in jeans and a tee-shirt. I wouldn't worry about it.'

'It's not even my dress,' Sara told her. 'That's what's so awful. I borrowed it.'

'It wasn't your fault, dear, and these things will happen. It—well, it was just an accident, wasn't it?' Her tone was slightly odd, and Sara glanced up at her, but she was looking at the photograph on Delia's dressing table, and she said nothing more.

Sara brushed her hair, and gathered up her things, and to her surprise Ellen Ellis put an arm around her.

'Tell me, my dear,' she said, 'before we go back downstairs. Have you known Max long?'

'No,' said Sara, surprised at the question. 'Only since he became editor.'

'I thought I seemed to remember something from before that? Some article perhaps?' Ellen's shrewd dark eyes met Sara's, and Sara knew she remembered the piece perfectly well.

'Yes,' she said, 'I interviewed him once before, about two years ago. We didn't get on awfully well. Not a good beginning!'

Ellen smiled. 'Let me give you a piece of advice, my dear. You won't listen, I don't suppose, but never mind. I've known Max since he was a baby—his mother and I were at school together. I know he can be terribly demanding, and something of an ogre, and of course he has the most absurd ideas about women—or pretends to have. But underneath that façade of his, he's a very gentle, very good man. Totally straight—no compromises, no lies. He has lots of enemies who'll tell you otherwise, naturally— though in some ways I sometimes think he's his own worst enemy. He *will* pretend to be so hard, so invulnerable . . .'

'His mother said that.'

Ellen looked at her curiously. 'Of course,' she said, 'you've met Ishbel, haven't you? She was very taken with you—she told me all about it.' She dropped her gaze. 'I think Ishbel is a lot to blame,' she added slowly, 'she acknowledges it herself, of course, and she was always impossibly flighty . . . And then there was his father . . .' She broke off.

'His father?'

Ellen's eyes met hers with a look of candour, as if she had suddenly made a decision to reveal something.

'You don't know about that?'

Sara shook her head. 'I know he was in the army—that he died when M . . . when his son was young . . .'

'Max was seven,' Ellen said briskly. 'His father committed suicide, you know.'

'*What?*' Sara stared at her in horror, and Ellen looked away, beginning to gather up her things as if to distract from her words.

'Well, he gambled, you see. Unsuccessfully. He lost a lot of money, even by his standards. And then there was all the business with Ishbel—in the end he couldn't take it any more, I suppose. It happened at their country place; Ishbel wasn't even there. One of the nannies told Max.'

Sara felt herself go faint. Suddenly the conversation that first night in the car, on the way to his party, came back to her . . .

'But I didn't know,' she said weakly.

'It was hushed up, of course.' Ellen set her mouth. 'They managed to keep it out of the papers. Ishbel's cousin was the Chief Constable of the county, so the inquest was held *in camera*. The verdict was accidental death—a shooting accident. Ishbel remarried six months later, and Max . . .' She shrugged. 'One can't blame his mother. The marriage was a disaster almost from the first. But it left Max scarred. It's as well, sometimes, to remember that . . . Now.' She stood up, and took Sara's hands warmly in hers. 'I'm telling you all this, my dear, although Max would be furious, because I think it's a shame you don't understand one another better. And it's a shame that two such nice people should be at odds with each other. Particularly when I suspect that underneath they're rather alike. So—shall we go back downstairs?'

She led the way from the room, and Sara followed her, still feeling numb with shock. She felt as if her eyes had been bandaged, and someone had suddenly ripped the bandage away. Her heart turned over with pity; she had judged Max so invulnerable, so harsh, and now everything seemed changed. All the other events of the day receded into unimportance beside Ellen's disclosures. No wonder, she thought, that he often seemed so hard, so defiant, so proud. He'd had long enough, after all, to practise not showing his hurt.

CHAPTER FIVE

WHEN they went back to the drawing room, the air was electric with tension, and it was clear that the dinner party was already breaking up. Piers and Max were standing in the centre if the room, Max with an expression like thunder on his face, and his fists thrust deep into his pockets, Piers looking sulky and cross. They looked like two pugilists, sizing one another up for a fight—and if it came to one, Sara thought, she knew who would win.

Gordon Ellis was trapped in a corner by Charlotte, who had moved on from horses to labrador dogs, and his face was communicating intense distress and boredom. Only the merchant banker Charles appeared unaffected by it all. He sat in the corner, nursing a large tumbler of whisky, as Delia fluttered around trying to ease the tension. As soon as they entered the room, Sara's eyes met those of Max, and for the first time she recognised in his face not the haughtiness she had come to expect, but an uncertainty and a pain.

As soon as he glimpsed his wife, Gordon Ellis sprang to his feet.

'Ah, Ellen, there you are,' he said. 'What an age you've been! We really must be going, I'm afraid, Delia. Thank you so much—wonderful dinner . . .'

Even as he spoke he was edging towards the door, and making frantic signals at Ellen. She smiled.

'Of course, darling,' she said smoothly. 'I'm sorry, Delia, but Gordon has to be in so early in the mornings, and if he doesn't have plenty of sleep, there's no living with him . . .'

Sara smiled to herself. It was beautifully done, she thought, and would clearly brook no denial on Delia's part. Relief was writ large upon her husband's features. They said their general goodbyes, and Ellen kissed Max warmly on the cheek.

'Now, Max,' she said firmly, 'you must do something for me before I leave—yes, I'm *coming*, Gordon. Poor Sara has had a horrid shock. She's putting a brave face on it, but she's been working all day, and I can see she's exhausted. Gordon and I would take her, but we're going in completely the opposite direction, so I think the best thing for all concerned would be if you would drive her home. You will, won't you, Max?'

This was all said lightly, and with total aplomb, as if it were the most natural request in the world, but Sara thought she could see a gleam of amusement in Ellen's shrewd eyes. She must have known the reaction her words would provoke, Sara thought, and—indeed—it was instantaneous. Delia went scarlet; Piers looked annoyed, she herself tried to intercede. Only Max himself appeared totally unmoved.

'Not necessary,' Piers shouldered his way forward. 'I have my car outside. Where do you live, Sara?'

'Islington,' she said.

'Oh,' said Piers blankly, and Sara felt a slightly hysterical wish to laugh. She could see only too clearly that while Piers might be happy to flirt with her, he didn't relish the drive several miles north.

'Not at all, Piers. I wouldn't dream of it. I shall take Sara home.' Max moved across to her with a cold smile. 'In fact, I think if you'll forgive us, we should go now, Delia. It's been a long day, and a delightful evening.'

'Oh, don't go,' Delia wailed. 'I can call Sara a cab, nothing's easier . . .'

'Please,' Sara tried to evade Max's grasp and failed, 'I can perfectly well take the tube . . .'

'Shall we go?'

He was already propelling her towards the door.

'It's too *bad*!' Delia wailed. 'It's only eleven, I can't bear to see you all leave like this!'

'*We're* not in a hurry, Delia darling,' said Charlotte. 'I want to have a good talk, and there's some simply *sweet* photographs I want to show you. My bitch has just had the most *adorable* litter of puppies . . .'

Piers shrugged. 'Oh well, I'll stay too, then,' he said, giving Sara a rueful grin. 'I'll keep Charles company with the whisky, if I may, Delia. Oh, and have you any of those cigars of Pa's?'

'God, Piers, you just come here to free-load!' Sara heard, as in the hallway Max firmly helped her into her jacket, and opened the door.

Delia reappeared, looking furious, just as they were going out.

'Thank you, Delia,' said Sara, trying to convey by her expression that she too had not wanted events to take this course. 'I've left the dress to dry. I'll see you tomorrow, it's been lovely . . .'

'You might.' Delia gave her a perfunctory peck on the cheek. 'I'm off to Montreux, though, so . . . Have a safe journey, Max,' she called into the night, but she got no answer.

Reluctantly Sara climbed into the brown Jaguar, hoping that Delia would understand. She waved to the Ellises as they drove off. Then Max got in, revved the engine, and reversed out of the mews at speed.

'Islington, I think you said?'

'Yes, it's near the antique market, but really, it'd be fine if you just dropped me at the tube . . .'

'I'll drop you at the front door,' he said sharply, and slammed the powerful engine up through the gears.

He went a good two miles before he spoke, his mouth tight, his eyes never leaving the road. Sara watched him covertly, trying to piece together the man she knew, the man Ellen had spoken of, and the sad little boy parked with a succession of nannies.

'Well,' he said at last, never looking at her, 'I see I was wrong about you after all.'

'What do you mean?' she said nervously.

'I was wrong about a lot of things, I'd say. But in particular it seems I was wrong about your running away from men. Perhaps that's just at work. You certainly didn't behave that way this evening.'

Sara stared at him in surprise. He was clearly very angry. He glanced across at her, his eyes dark.

'You behaved appallingly,' he said savagely. 'You never stopped flirting with that damned useless brother of Delia's all evening!'

'I thought that was exactly what you were recommending I should do,' Sara said gently, deliberately keeping her voice light and teasing.

'I didn't mean indiscriminately, you little fool,' he said roughly, his vehemence surprising her. 'If you knew Piers as well as I do . . .'

'I thought he was very pleasant,' Sara said sweetly.

'Very pleasant! So much for your judgment.'

'Not at all.' She hesitated. 'I don't trust my judgment very much any longer, I . . .'

'Oh yes, you do. You're the most bloody obstinate woman I've ever had the ill luck to encounter!'

'That's not true,' she protested, 'I was just . . .'

'Right!' Suddenly he slammed on the brakes and swerved the car abruptly into the kerb and stopped. 'We'll have this out, once and for all. I've had enough of your prejudices. Now.' He turned and glared at her.

Sara looked at him mutely. A week ago, even a day ago she would have made some sharp taunting retort, she would have lost her temper nearly as swiftly as he; but not now.

'Everything I do, everything I say, you twist it, you misinterpret it. I can't work with someone like that. I *won't*!' He banged his fist violently on the steering wheel. 'Do you think I'd go to all this trouble if I didn't think it was worth the bother—if I despised your work? Of course not! And what do you do—you resent it. You've resented me from the first. Then you deliberately avoid me . . . what the hell is going on?'

'Max, please . . .' She spoke softly, but she managed to stop him. 'I . . . I don't want to quarrel with you.'

'What's this?' He stared at her suspiciously, her words

clearly surprising him. 'That's a new tack. What do you want to do, hate me in discreet silence?'

'I ... I don't hate you.'

'You just want to work somewhere else. As you told Geoffrey.'

Sara blushed. 'That was a week ago,' she said defensively. 'I ... I've changed my mind.'

'You change your mind pretty frequently, it seems to me.' His voice was still cold. 'And your mode of behaviour.'

She stared at him wordlessly, unwilling to risk saying anything, because whatever she did say seemed to make the situation no better. He looked into her eyes, and his face softened: for a moment it seemed as if he would relent. But he looked quickly away.

'I detest women who behave as you behaved tonight,' he said fiercely. 'Still, it was certainly something of a revelation, seeing you in that dress, seeing how well you could flirt with someone once you set your mind to it. Oh, quite a revelation.'

'I thought you said the trouble with me was that I was too cold,' she said softly.

With a muttered exclamation he turned back to her and reached for her hand. His eyes searched her face.

'But you're not cold, are you, Sara?' he said, his voice low. 'Quite the opposite.'

He said the words flatly, and she wasn't sure if he meant them to be insulting. But when she looked into his eyes, she could see only bewilderment and hurt. Her mouth felt suddenly dry, and her hand burned as he held it.

Very gently and slowly he raised it to his lips, turned it, and kissed her palm.

'Sara ...' He leaned forward towards her, his voice catching, suddenly all the anger gone. She expected the panic to start, for he was very close to her now. She could feel his breath against her skin, the tall powerful body was close beside her own. But to her surprise there was no panic, no tension. Instead she felt swamped with a sudden urgency, as if this, of all the moments of her life, was decisive, and had to come out right. Impulsively she leaned towards him, but before she could speak, with a low groan he gathered her in his arms, his mouth seeking hers. The kiss was gentle this time, and sweet, oh, so sweet, shaking her to the roots of her being, so she felt herself tremble in his arms, and her breath caught in her throat. Gently he cradled her in his arms, stroking her hair, kissing her mouth, the lids of her closed eyes. Then, very gently, he just held her in his arms, leaning her against his chest so she could hear the thudding of his heart. Then he took her hand, her left hand, and held it before them, in the dim light of the street lamps, and just held it, looking at it, for some moments in complete silence. Sara said nothing; she could not speak. Suddenly she felt suffused with an extraordinary happiness, a joyousness so intense that she felt irradiated by it. She knew it must be in her eyes, what she felt, and when finally he turned, and lightly kissed her lips again, she thought she saw something like it in those strange impenetrable blue eyes of his.

He smiled, and very gently released her, pressing one last kiss against her hand.

'I'm going to take you home now.'

Don't, she wanted to cry out. Do anything, but don't leave me, not now. But she could not bring herself to speak, didn't know, in any case, what she could possibly say if she did. So she let him disengage himself, and said nothing as he started the car engine again and eased the car out on to the road.

He drove in silence, reaching across just once to take her palm where it lay in her lap.

They reached Islington without a word being exchanged, and she directed him to the somewhat shabby street where she and Jennifer had their flat. He pulled up outside, and looked at her. She felt a pang of happiness and pleasure shoot through her, but still she did not speak.

'You will be in the office tomorrow?' he said, rather awkwardly. 'You've hardly been there for some days.'

'Yes,' she said quietly, 'I shall.'

'May I talk to you then?'

She nodded.

He came round and helped her out of the car.

'You have your keys?'

'Yes, Max. Thank you for driving me home all this way.'

'Goodnight, then.'

'Goodnight.'

Still he did not touch her, and so, awkwardly, uncertainly, she turned and went up the stairs to their door.

Max waited until she was safely inside the front door, then—as she stood in the darkness of the hallway—she heard his car's engine fire. The car pulled away, and gradually the sound of its motor disappeared into the silence of the night. She climbed the stairs slowly to their flat, and when she went in, found Jennifer still up, watching a late film on television. She switched it off when Sara came in, and jumped up excitedly to greet her friend.

'Sara!' she exclaimed. 'I'm so glad you're back. Now you can tell me all about it . . .' She broke off and stared at Sara's face.

'What's happened to you?' she asked in amazement. 'You look completely different.'

'It's the make-up,' said Sara.

'No, it's not that, it's something else, you look . . . well, happy, I suppose, but it's not just that . . . whatever happened to you? Was it a good evening? Did you meet some terrific man—*that's* what it looks like. That's it, isn't it? Sara, you look as if you've got stars in your eyes! Come on, tell me, who was it?'

Sara smiled, and shook her head.

'I'll tell you tomorrow,' she said. 'It's been a very long, very strange day.'

'But what *I* don't understand . . .' Jennifer banged the lift doors, and pressed the button for the fifth floor, 'is why you came home looking like that last night? I mean—was it the champagne that made your eyes shine, or Maria's cooking? Maybe you like having raspberries tipped all over you?'

Sara smiled and said nothing; Jennifer's mouth twitched.

'The mysterious brother Piers?'

'No.'

'Well, *something* happened, that's obvious. Tell me——' Jennifer looked at her inquisitively, 'did Delia flirt with Max all evening? According to Deirdre, *that's* all going very well. *She's* expecting the wedding invitation any moment; in fact, I should think she's already bought her hat. Cerise, probably.'

Sara felt herself colour, but Jennifer seemed not to notice. She ran on, in good imitation of Deirdre's clipped tones.

'"So suitable, my dear. Quite made for each other. And then Max would inherit the Waterlow empire from Sir Andrew . . ." Ugh!' Jennifer's brows wrinkled with distaste. 'I think he's got *far* too much sense, don't you?'

They had reached the editorial floor, and—opening the lift gates—Sara could avoid a reply. To her surprise, she saw Beverley hovering in the corridor, looking faintly embarrassed. As soon as she saw Sara, she hurried towards her.

'Oh, Sara,' she said, 'thank goodness you're in. I've been waiting for you. Max wants to see you at once.'

'Now?' Sara looked quickly at her watch, feeling her heart lift with a sudden wave of happiness. She wasn't late, she thought quickly. He had said last night that he wanted to see her.

'Why the sudden urgency?' asked Jennifer, looking curiously from Sara to Beverley. To Sara's surprise, Beverley looked away.

'I . . . I don't know,' she said evasively. 'But I think you'd better come along straight away.'

Quickly she disappeared, and Sara and Jennifer exchanged glances.

'Trouble?' Jennifer touched her friend's arm. 'Beverley looked very odd—and she always knows what's going on. You're not late with copy, are you?'

Sara shook her head. Suddenly the happiness drained away, and she felt intensely apprehensive. Quickly her mind raced over her assignments—no, nothing was late. Perhaps some job had come up . . .

'You'd better go. See you later.'

Just as Sara reached Max Christian's outer office, where the secretaries were stationed, his door opened, and Delia came hurrying out. She saw Sara, stopped, and then made as if to pass on.

'Hello, Delia,' said Sara, surprised that she should go without a greeting. 'You're in a hurry.'

'I told you last night,' Delia said shortly, 'I'm catching the plane for the Montreux story. I'm late.'

'Well, thank you for last night . . .' Delia was already moving away. 'And I'm terribly sorry about the dress. Will it be all right, do you think? You must let me know—if it is ruined, then I'll just have to pay for it.'

'Yes, well, I can't talk about that now . . . 'Bye!'

Delia disappeared without a backward glance.

Beverley had been watching this exchange, Sara noted, but as Sara looked towards her, she hastily dropped her gaze. 'You can go in now, Sara,' she muttered.

Sara's eyebrows rose. Whatever was going on? She was being treated like the office leper, yet she couldn't think of anything she'd done. Taking a deep breath, she tapped on the door and went in.

Max was seated at his desk, and he did not smile or greet her as she came in, but merely nodded curtly towards a chair.

Sara took it, feeling completely nonplussed. As she did so, his telephone rang; he didn't answer it, but threw the switch on his intercom.

'I thought I told you, Beverley,' he said sharply, 'no calls.'

The telephone was silent.

'Now,' he looked at Sara briefly, looked away. He too appeared embarrassed, she thought. Whatever was wrong? 'Perhaps you would be good enough to explain this?'

He handed her a small sheet of paper.

Now completely confused, Sara looked down at it. As she saw what was on it, she froze.

It was a bill. At the top of it was the title, and the Bond Street address, of one of the most celebrated international

fashion designers. Underneath was written, in hand:
Ensemble Caprice: Black silk taffeta with silk lining and under-
skirt. Brussels lace collar; silk rose trimming. £450.

'This will have to be paid today,' Max said coldly. 'In
fact, I've already authorised Accounts to settle it
immediately.'

Sara felt the colour drain from her face.

'But I don't understand . . .' she began weakly.

'Well now,' he said, 'it's not very complicated, is it?
You can hardly imagine that such an establishment would
accept the return of such a garment in the condition it
was in last night. Nor after cleaning. If it makes you feel
any better, we shall not, of course, tell them what really
happened to it. We shall say it was damaged at a photo
session. But that's not really the point, is it?'

Sara was silent. She was calculating how many weeks
of salary it would take her to pay off such a sum.

'You have something to say, presumably?'

She cleared her throat. 'Of course,' she said haltingly,
'you must deduct that money from my salary . . .'

'Is that all you have to suggest? I'm not interested in
further solutions at this moment, nor in ill-judged and
belated heroic gestures. I should like an explanation.'

Sara said nothing, and her mind whirled. Had Delia
lied to her about the dress—surely she couldn't have made
a mistake? But if she said anything now, she would be
getting Delia into trouble, and perhaps there was some
explanation . . . Could two similar dresses have been
confused, in the mêlée at the studio? No, she knew it was
impossible. Delia would never make a mistake like that,
and so . . .

'I'm waiting.'

She looked up at him, and saw that he was pale with
anger. The dark blue eyes blazed at her. Still she was
silent.

'Very well, then,' he said coldly, 'I have no option but
to believe the account I've already received.'

'And what is that?' she said slowly.

'I gather that at the studios yesterday, when you came
to leave, you saw this dress. What the dress was doing

there at all, at a photo session for cheap clothes, I still don't quite understand, but I gather there was some confusion among the fashion assistants, who thought their editor wanted to inspect it for another fashion story. But that's by the way. The fact is that you saw the dress, and expressed a wish to wear it that night . . .'

Sara drew in her breath sharply. So it *was* Delia. No one else could have told him that, or made up such a story. He pressed on:

'The fashion editor, quite correctly, pointed out to you that although it had been the custom in the past for fashion department personnel to "borrow" clothes used in stories, that practice had been specifically and unequivocally banned by me, since I became editor. When she pointed this out to you, a scene ensued, as a result of which, and against her better judgment, she capitulated. Naturally, in the light of what's happened, she now regrets that decision. Now——' he paused, as if waiting for Sara to say something, and when she did not, he continued. 'I have made it clear to my fashion editor that I hold her extremely culpable in this whole affair. She should not, under any circumstances, have agreed to your wearing the dress, and it was partly due to her . . . clumsiness . . . that it was subsequently damaged. I've reprimanded her on both scores. However, I'm afraid that the main share of the blame rests with you, and I cannot and will not tolerate such behaviour.'

Sara listened to the formal language of editorial reprimand in a daze. The words seemed to her to come from afar. She was stunned that anyone could be so malicious, that they could be prepared to lie to that extent. She could see no reason for Delia's having done it, unless she had been desperate to extricate herself from the whole sorry mess. It must be that, she thought. When Delia had realised the dress was ruined, and would have to be paid for, she must have panicked. She'd have known that a bill for four hundred and fifty pounds wouldn't go through unqueried. But how had there been the mix-up over the dresses in the first place? Delia had been so definite about it . . . She stared at Max Christian blankly. There was, she realised, absolutely nothing she could say, except that Delia had lied. And she wasn't prepared to do that. If Max Christian wanted to believe this farrago of lies, she was not going to try and exonerate herself, and drag Delia down into the mud with her. There must be some reason—if only she could talk to Delia before she left for Montreux . . .

'Sara.' With difficulty she turned her face to him, and focussed on what he was saying. 'Sara, I would have thought that you, of all people, would understand the seriousness of all this. I'd made it absolutely clear that this wretched practice had to stop. It placed the magazine in an impossible position; half the time the shops and designers concerned knew perfectly well what was happening to their clothes. They turned a blind eye to it, because by doing so they were able to exert a certain pressure on fashion staff to feature their clothes. The same goes for the system of large discounts to fashion staff actually purchasing clothes—which was also common in the past. I will *not* have that kind of thing going on on my magazine. It places us in disrepute, and we become vulnerable to pressure from commercial concerns who know our staff will accept perks. I will not have it, and that fact was—I gather—made abundantly clear to you.'

'I see.' Sara had gone cold, and she found her voice with difficulty. 'Then what was my alleged reason for borrowing the dress?'

'I can hardly speculate on your reasons, Sara.' He looked away. 'However, it would not surprise me in the least that the knowledge you were deliberately flouting my wishes should not be an encouragement to you. Besides,' his mouth tightened, 'I gather that Piers Waterlow put in an appearance at the photo session, and it was shortly after meeting him that you expressed the wish to borrow this dress.'

'*What?*' Sara felt her cheeks flame with colour. 'I'm supposed to have borrowed this dress to impress Piers? Why, I didn't even *speak* to him at the photo session!'

'You made up for that later.' The cold blue eyes flashed. 'In any case, your motives are not my concern. What *is* my concern is that a scene ensued that was becoming an embarrassment to my fashion staff. Outsiders, the photographer for instance, were present. And so they acceded to your request.'

Sara stared at him in silent horror.

'*They?*' Her voice sounded choked, and she fought back the tears. 'You mean Delia, don't you?'

He sighed, hesitated, and when he spoke again, his voice was more gentle.

'I'm in a very difficult position, Sara,' he explained. 'I can hardly ask junior staff to corroborate something I'm told by their direct superior. I'm asking you to corroborate it—or to give me your version of what happened.'

Sara drew a deep breath, trying to calm the pain that surged through her. It was not just that Delia should tell such appalling lies, it was that Max should believe them. Hurt twisted in her heart. So that was what he really thought of her. She tilted her chin proudly. She would *not* cry, she thought, she would not sink to Delia's level.

Suddenly, from her whirling thoughts, she plucked one. She knew what she must do.

'I'm sorry,' she said stiffly. She stood up, trying to control the trembling that shook her. 'I have nothing to say.'

'Now look, Sara, I . . .'

'Please.' She avoided his gaze, and put her hands palm down on his desk to steady herself. 'You . . . leave me no alternative. I shall give you a formal letter of resignation today.'

'What?' He stood up abruptly. 'Sara, please. This isn't necessary. Believe me, the last thing I wanted to do was . . .'

'No, please.' She could see that he was about to move towards her and she quickly backed away. All she could think was that she must find Delia, must have it out with her, before she left for Montreux.

'This isn't a sudden decision,' she said, forcing back the tears. 'But I'm sure it's the right one. And I'd rather not talk about it.' She forced herself to meet his eyes, and saw his mouth set in an obstinate line.

'I should remind you,' he said coldly, 'that you are on

two months' full notice. That means you can't leave until a month after Christmas.'

Sara caught her breath. 'But that's at your discretion,' she said quickly, her voice near to breaking. 'You can release me immediately.'

'I don't intend to do that.'

'Please, Max . . .' She looked at him pleadingly.

'No!' he said sharply. 'If you can be so goddamned obstinate, so can I.'

'Very well.' She forced herself to sound matter-of fact. 'I'm due for three weeks holiday. Would you arrange for the cost of the dress to be docked from my holiday pay? I think it will cover it.'

It will cover it, and leave you nothing to live on, nothing to send your mother, she thought desperately, edging towards the door.

The request seemed only to infuriate him further.

'Damn and blast it, Sara, this is ridiculous! Will you please . . .'

'I'm sorry.' She had reached the door. The handle was in her hand.

'No, you're not, you're delighted. Why pretend? This is the chance you've been waiting for, isn't it, Sara? Well, I can tell you . . .'

At that moment the telephone on his desk shrilled, and he broke off with a muttered swear word.

He snatched up the receiver.

'Beverley? I thought I told you . . . Oh. Delia . . .'

Sara saw her chance and took it. Before he could turn back to her she slipped through the door. So Delia *was* still in the building. And she wouldn't leave it, Sara thought grimly, even if it meant missing her flight. Not until she had given some kind of explanation.

Ignoring the buzz of voices that rose up from the secretaries behind her, she sped along the corridor. Delia wouldn't be in the editorial offices, she was sure of that. She'd be downstairs, in the main fashion department. Not bothering to wait for the lift, she raced down the stairs. She reached the fashion floor and flung the door back, just as Delia was replacing her phone. Susie and Jacinth,

her assistants, were both with her. They took one look at
Sara's white face and tight lips, and fled. Sara shut the
door firmly and stood in front of it, cutting off all retreat.
She and Delia stared at each other for a moment in
silence, and Delia's face crimsoned. Clearly she had not
expected this. She was the first to speak.

'Sara,' she said awkwardly, 'I told you I have a plane
to catch.'

'It can wait. Or you can catch a later flight.' Sara kept
her voice low. 'You're not going near this door until
you've explained.'

To her surprise, Delia put up no fight. She didn't even
argue. She just gave a sigh of resignation and put down
her bags. Very deliberately she reached for her cigarettes,
lit one, and sat down with insolent slowness.

'All right,' she said eventually, 'fair enough. You can
stop guarding the door. I shan't make a bolt for it.'

Feeling suddenly foolish and melodramatic, Sara left
the door and crossed the room to Delia's desk. Delia's
small blue eyes met hers unswervingly, but her hand shook
a little, Sara noted, as she drew deeply on the cigarette.

'Well?'

Delia gave a nervous laugh. 'O.K,' she said, 'I'll admit
it. I arranged the whole thing.'

'You did *what*?' Sara stared at her in disbelief. Whatever
she had expected—evasions, tears, explanations—it was
not this calm admittance.

Delia shrugged. 'I stage-managed it. Fixed it. Whatever
you like. If it makes it any better, I'm sorry.'

'You're *sorry*?'

Delia leaned forward impulsively. 'Yes, Sara, believe
me, I *am*! When I first had the idea—well, I hardly knew
you then, and we'd never got on . . . but now, I *like* you,
Sara, really I do. I'm ashamed of myself.'

Weakly Sara sat down and stared at her. Delia gave
every appearance of sincerity. Her eyes were wide, her
expression intent and earnest, her voice little more than a
whisper.

Sara shrugged. She felt completely at a loss, bewildered,
all her anger defused. 'You've a funny way of showing

your liking,' she said finally. 'Why would you do such a thing, Delia? I mean, even if I were your worst enemy . . .'

'But you see, you were,' Delia cut in. She saw surprise register on Sara's face, and rushed on before she could reply. 'I was *jealous*. Can't you see? I *hated* you!'

'Jealous?' Sara stared at her in confusion. 'Of me? But why—I don't understand . . .'

'You wouldn't!' Tears welled in Delia's eyes.

'But jealous of what?'

'Of Max, you idiot!'

'Of Max?'

'Don't sound so surprised! Honestly, Sara, sometimes I think you must be blind! A so-called reporter and you can't see what's going on under your own eyes!'

'There was nothing to see.' Sara stared in horror as the tears welled, ran down Delia's sun-tanned cheeks and fell with a plop on the desk before her.

'There was plenty to see!' Delia snapped. 'He never stops making excuses to see you. You're closeted in his office for hours. If he comes into our room he makes straight for your desk. He asked you out to lunch. He took you to that party of his the very first night! He thinks you're beautiful, that's why he suggested the modelling . . .'

'But, Delia . . .' Sara gazed at her, fighting off the odd sudden surge of emotion that went through her at Delia's words. 'There were explanations for all that. You know we've never got on . . .'

'Oh, I know you *say* that!' Delia wailed. 'I don't believe you! No woman in her right senses would turn Max down. And besides, whatever *you* felt, it was obvious he was interested. Any fool could see that.'

'I don't see it,' Sara said quietly. She looked away, thinking quickly of that scene in his office, in the car last night . . . Could it be true what Delia was saying?

'You wouldn't! Sara, can't you understand what I'm talking about? I love him!'

Sara felt her hands clench involuntarily; she could not meet Delia's gaze.

'You see?' Delia cried. 'You don't understand. You're so cold, Sara. I think there's something wrong with you. You're not like a normal woman at all. *You've* never been in love in your life, anyone can see that. It's the standing joke in the office, don't you *know*? Sara the ice-maiden, Harry calls you. Deirdre thinks you're frigid . . .'

She broke off, and Sara felt a shaft of pain go through her. She was used to office bitchery, but she had never realised it went that far. She coloured, and forced herself to meet Delia's tearful gaze.

'Delia, please,' she said quietly, 'all this has nothing to do with it. I still don't understand . . .'

'It has everything to do with it! Can't you see, I wanted to finish you in Max's eyes, make sure he never looked at you again. Like that. The way he does look at you sometimes, and I could kill you when he does!'

'You mean you thought you'd discredit me?'

'Yes. Anything! I don't know what I thought. I wasn't acting rationally at all. I was desperate. Jealousy makes you like that. You wouldn't understand, of course . . .'

'I might.'

'Might you?' Delia's eyes narrowed. She hesitated, stubbed out her cigarette, and at once lit another. She drew a deep breath, as if she had suddenly made up her mind to something.

'Well,' she went on, her voice calmer, 'I had to do something, you see. Just recently, the situation had become a bit more complicated.'

Something in her voice, in the sly innuendo of her tone, made Sara's blood freeze.

'Recently?' she prompted quickly. Delia gave a little smile and lowered her eyes.

'Since I went to bed with him,' she said softly.

'*What?*' Sara stared at her in disbelief, her mind instantly racing. Delia gave a sharp little laugh and stood up.

'Don't look so shocked, Sara,' she said lightly. 'Not everyone shares your Victorian attitudes, you know.' She stopped, sat down again, and leaned towards Sara, her eyes wide with honesty. Then she sighed. 'It's no good,' she said, 'I can't treat it lightly. It happened about two weeks ago, after I went out to lunch with him. He invited me out that evening, and then . . .' She hesitated. 'He's a wonderful lover, Sara. I haven't much experience, actually, but after that, I was lost, Sara, can't you understand? I want to marry him. He's the only man, I know that now. I'll never look at anyone else. And so, you see, I was desperate. You know his reputation with women. I felt so insecure . . . Sara, please say you'll forgive me. Say there's nothing between you, please!'

'There's nothing between us,' Sara said dully.

Impulsively Delia reached across and hugged her.

'Oh,' she cried, 'you darling! You don't know how happy you make me. Honestly, Sara, I am sorry about all this, I'll make it up to you, I promise.'

'It doesn't matter now, Delia. I've resigned.'

'*Resigned?*' There was a pause. 'Did you tell Max the truth?'

Sara shook her head. Her eyes met Delia's.

'I thought you might do that,' she said steadily.

Delia crimsoned. 'But I *can't!*' she wailed. 'Don't you see? Anything but that! I was counting on you, I knew you wouldn't tell him. But if I do—don't you see? That'll be it. Finish. He's so ruthless, puritanical, almost. He'd never understand. It would all be over. Please, Sara, promise me you won't tell him. It can't matter now, not if you're leaving anyway . . .'

Sara stood up. Suddenly she felt absolutely exhausted.

'Don't worry, Delia,' she said quietly, 'I shan't tell tales. As you say, it's too late now. Why should it matter?'

'I can get you another job!' Delia put her arm around her. 'I'd just have to say the word to Daddy, you know. Nothing could be easier—a better job than you have here. And you've always said you didn't want to work with Max, so really I haven't done anything so bad, have I? I've just precipitated things.'

In spite of herself, Sara smiled. Delia's selfishness and capacity for self-excuse were so extreme you could only laugh at them. And she was right in a way. It didn't matter now.

'You've certainly done that,' she said drily. 'Now you'd better go and catch your plane.'

'Sara, you're an *angel!*' Again Delia kissed her impulsively; she held Sara at arm's length, her own face now radiant. 'And do you think he *might* love me, Sara? If I work at it?'

Sara forced herself to smile; she felt almost suffocated by Delia's perfume, and felt suddenly sick. Her heart twisted with pain, but she spoke lightly. Delia looked so vulnerable, so easily hurt, that she could not find it in herself to be angry, or to disillusion her. She tried not to think of that chain of ex-mistresses, of the sad girl near Sloane Square. Fire and ice.

'How can I know, Delia?' she said gently. 'After all, as you say, I'm hardly the best judge. But if you love him as much as you say . . .'

'Oh, I do!' said Delia defiantly. 'He'll marry me, Sara, you'll see! After all, someone's got to take over Daddy's newspapers, and it doesn't look as if it'll be Piers. And besides . . .' she had reached the door, her face set stubbornly, 'I always get what I want, and I want Max very badly indeed.'

Then she was gone, and wearily Sara sank back down in her chair. She looked at her watch. No more than fifteen minutes had passed since she left Max Christian's office, but it felt like a century. In fifteen minutes, everything had changed. She'd thrown in her job, and she couldn't go back on that now, not after what Delia had told her. Max had been only too quick to accept that she was a liar, a cheap flirt, someone who would discredit the magazine to get her own way . . . and he was Delia's lover. She forced her mind to speak the word, and pain swelled in her heart like a blow from a fist. The pain was inexplicable, stupid, she thought angrily. It was not her affair. Hideous images swam into her mind, of Max and Delia in bed together, of Delia wrapped in his arms, of that dark hair mingled with her blonde on some pillow . . . She fought them off, and stood up abruptly. This was no good; she would have to go back to the office and face everyone. The news would be all over the building by now, but she had the next two months to get through somehow. She would have to work.

Tiredly she made for the door, trying to shake off the feeling of lassitude and despair that enveloped her. As she opened it she could hear voices, low and urgent, in the corridor outside. In the doorway, she froze; she could not make out what was being said, but she knew those voices. Cautiously she looked out. At the far end of the corridor were Delia and Max. He had her cornered against the wall, his arms on either side of her, his face a few inches from hers. Delia's head was bowed, a strand of her long fair hair lay stretched over the dark sleeve of his jacket.

'Damn it to hell, Delia, I want . . .' Even though his voice was so low, Sara could hear the words. Quickly she shrank back inside the room, and pushed the door to.

The conversation seemed to go on for ever. Once Delia laughed, a low sensual laugh, quite unlike the artificial laugh she affected on social occasions. The laugh broke off abruptly and there was silence, as if something, someone, had stopped Delia's lips. Sara closed her eyes and rested her hot forehead against the cold walls. Would they never go?

Suddenly she heard Delia's voice, quite clearly.

'Oh, will you, Max? *Please* . . . Then I . . .'

Her voice sank again, and Sara covered her ears against it.

When she took them away she found, to her relief, that the conversation was over. Delia laughed once more, then Sara heard the click of her heels going down the stone stairs to the lobby. She shrank back against the wall, and heard Max's footsteps along the corridor, that quick light pace she knew so well. He passed within three feet of her, not slowing, and then he too was gone.

Suddenly Sara felt overwhelmed with a flood of desperation. Oh, why hadn't she left the room then, why hadn't she stopped him, tried to explain? Panic welled up inside her. It was the old story, she thought quickly. Max was right; she was proud and obstinate, and now she had thrown away everything, her job, her financial security. If she left the magazine, she'd never work with Max again, wouldn't see him . . . A sudden vision of weeks, of months passing by without hearing his voice, seeing that dark head bent intently over his desk, came to her, and her heart contracted. Was that what she wanted? After all, whatever he thought of her, whatever his relationship with Delia, she could still *work* with him, learn from him. She drew in a deep shuddering breath, trying to calm herself, but her mind whirled with conflicting emotions. Out of them she plucked one; all she knew was that she had to see him, had to speak to him. After all, it wasn't too late. She hadn't put anything in writing; she could retract her resignation.

Suddenly, on impulse, she flung back the door and raced along the corridor to the stairs, words and sentences and excuses jumbled in her mind. She couldn't tell him the truth, of course, not after what Delia had said. But that didn't matter; she needn't explain, she could just say she'd changed her mind . . . but she must do it at once, quickly . . .

As she reached Max's outer office she ran slap into Mark Shand, she cannoned into his arms, and a sheaf of papers he was holding cascaded to the floor. Hardly seeing him, Sara tried to brush past, but he reached out an arm, and stayed her.

'Sara——' He drew her to him. 'For God's sake, what's happened? You look as white as a ghost. Jennifer says you've resigned—but that can't be true . . .'

'No—I don't know. Mark—I must talk to Max. I can't . . .'

She broke off as she heard the door of Max Christian's office slam violently. His secretaries, she realised, were watching this scene open-mouthed. Carefully, firmly, she disengaged herself, trying to stop the trembling that shook her body.

'I must see him now.'

She turned and crossed to Beverley's desk, oblivious to the stares, to the fact that Mark Shand still hovered uncertainly in the doorway. Fighting back the tears, she cleared her throat.

'Will he see me, just briefly, Beverley?'

Beverley dropped her gaze; the other secretaries exchanged glances.

'Well. I . . .' Beverley glanced at the door of Max's office doubtfully. From inside came the sound of a drawer being slammed violently shut.

'Please.'

Still Beverley hesitated, her hand on the intercom switch.

'It—er—it might not be a very good moment, Sara,' she said gently. Her eyes met Sara's with a look of sympathy. 'You see, he's just leaving.'

'*Leaving?*'

'I've just this moment made the arrangements. He's—er—going to Montreux.'

Her finger depressed the switch on the intercom; gently Sara reached across and flicked it back into place. Suddenly all emotion, all confusion, all adrenalin, had gone. She forced herself to smile.

'In that case, let's leave it,' she said.

'Are you sure?' Beverley was clearly relieved.

'Quite sure. It was nothing important.'

'Can I give him a message?'

'No. No message.'

Feeling now quite calm, icy almost, Sara turned on her heel. Mark Shand still hovered in the doorway, an expression of concern on his narrow face, but Sara hardly saw him. She moved towards the corridor.

'I've a message for you, Sara—it's on your desk,' Beverley called after her.

'Oh?' she said dully.

'Yes, Piers Waterlow has been trying to get you all morning. When we couldn't find you, he wanted your home number. He spoke to Max about it. I think he . . .'

'Fine. O.K. Thanks, Beverley . . .'

Hardly hearing her, Sara brushed past Mark, and he hastened after her.

'Come and have a drink. Sara, please, I . . .'

She stopped. 'No,' she said gently. 'Thanks, Mark. But I'm fine really. There's something I must do.'

To her relief he didn't argue, and Sara walked stiffly

back to her office. She sat down at her desk, oblivious to the stares and whispers, to the frantic signals from Jennifer at the other end of the room.

Very deliberately she sat down at her typewriter and inserted a clean sheet of paper.

Montreux. Less than an hour ago she had resigned, and now he was dropping everything to go off on a trip with Delia. Well, it was only to be expected, she thought dully. And at least that piece of information had saved her from making a fool of herself. She had been right in the first place; she must trust her instincts. She was allowing herself to be swayed by feeling, she was getting far too caught up in a web of emotions she did not understand in the least, but which all had their root and being in this strange, distant man. So, she thought coldly. It was better to finish it there and then, to disengage, to go somewhere else where she could work impersonally, coolly, the way she was used to. No more scenes; no more upheavals. She began typing: *Dear Mr Christian, I should like formally to* . . . It took her no more than five minutes to type the letter of resignation.

When she dropped it into his in-tray shortly after, Max Christian had already left.

CHAPTER SIX

'WELL, what *are* you going to do, Sara?'

It was Friday, and Jennifer sat perched on her desk, her brow furrowed with concern. They were early, the office was still empty, and Sara was making some cups of watery Nescafé. She sighed, and kept her back firmly turned so that Jennifer should not see the expression on her face. So far she had managed to dodge all Jennifer's questions, just giving her a brief, edited explanation; but she had known that her friend would not be put off much longer. She tipped some milk into the two cups.

'Well?'

Sara shrugged. 'I don't know,' she said finally. 'Look for another job, I suppose.'

'You realise you've been ridiculously hasty, as usual, I suppose?'

Sara passed her the cup, and Jennifer gave her a shrewd glance.

'And you're regretting it, that's obvious. You've been as miserable as sin all week. So why not swallow your pride, and tell Max you've changed your mind?'

'He's not here to tell,' Sara said evasively.

'*That's* true.' Jennifer sipped her coffee meditatively. 'Have you ever known a simple photo session last so long? Beverley says he won't be back before next week at the earliest. It looks as if Deirdre was right about those two all along.'

Sara looked away. Every time she thought of Montreux a shaft of pain shot through her that she was powerless to control, and could not explain.

'I suppose so,' she said lightly.

'Still, you could tell him then. Why not? He'd take you back like a shot, I know it.'

Sara sighed. 'Jennifer, I can't,' she said gently. 'I may have made the decision on the spur of the moment, but I'm sure I was right. I'd be better off working somewhere totally different, away from all this.'

'Away from Max, you mean.'

'I suppose so.'

'He's not an easy man to escape. Have you asked yourself what you're running away from, Sara?'

Sara looked up quickly, her cheeks colouring. It wasn't running away, she thought defensively. That was what *he* had said she did, that day in his office, when he . . . She forced the memory of his touch from her mind, pushed it down, away, tried to smother it, but still it surged back, as fiercely as if he were in the room, the touch of his hands, the demands of his mouth . . . She closed her eyes. Oh, *why* had he ever touched her? If only that hadn't happened, then maybe she could have followed Jennifer's advice, maybe she could have dealt with all this reasonably, coolly, as a business affair. But now . . .

Impatiently she put down her cup and picked up the day's mail which lay on her desk. Jennifer sat calmly, watching her.

'Have you talked to Geoffrey about it? At least you could do that. He might make you see sense.'

Sara shook her head miserably.

'I did try to talk to Geoffrey,' she said stiffly, 'but he's very ill again. I spoke to his wife yesterday. He's in hospital. I'm going to see him when he's a bit stronger. Maybe next week.'

Jennifer sighed. 'Well, talk to me, then,' she said. 'The trouble with you, Sara, is you cut yourself off. You close up. You won't talk to anyone. Mark has tried, I've tried . . . Someone's got to make you see sense. I mean, if you ask me—*which* you don't—the whole thing is fishy. That business of the dress, and Delia. Honestly, I'd trust that woman as far as the door, and yet you let her maneouvre you into resigning!'

'That had nothing to do with Delia,' Sara said quickly.

'Then why did you do it?'

Sara sighed. Jennifer knew her too well, she thought. She would pose the one question she did not want to answer, even to herself.

'Well, at the time . . .' she began miserably.

'It had nothing to do with Max going off to Montreux?'

'No, certainly not. Well, perhaps a bit. I don't know,' she sighed desperately.

Jennifer eased herself off the desk and glanced at her watch.

'Well, I think you ought to ask yourself that question, anyway,' she said gently. 'I mean, anyone could see that you were getting more and more emotionally involved with Max. It started the moment he came here. And after all, he's a terribly attractive man. Though how he can put up with Delia beats me. But if you were jealous, or something . . .'

'Jealous?' Sara stared at her. Jennifer laughed.

'Quite a common emotion, I believe,' she said lightly.

'Even you aren't immune to it, you know.'

'Of course I wasn't jealous! Why on earth should I be?'

Jennifer said nothing, but her eyes never left Sara's face. Sara was the first to turn away. There was a moment's silence, and then Jennifer sighed.

'Yes, well,' she said. 'Maybe you've done the right thing. I don't know. Max is a heartbreaker by all accounts. Maybe you are better off out of it. But in that case——' she flicked a pile of messages, and a letter that lay on the corner of Sara's desk. 'In that case, why don't you take pity on poor Piers Waterlow? He's called the flat five times, and there's a mountain of messages here from him, not to mention that little billet-doux you're trying to conceal—so, why not give the son and heir a whirl? The state you're in, being wined and dined by Piers Waterlow might be just what you need!'

In spite of herself, Sara smiled.

'Not my type,' she said lightly.

'Who is?' said Jennifer mockingly.

'I don't know.'

'Then don't you think you ought to find out?'

Both girls looked up quickly as they heard the door open, and Jennifer's face broke into a wide grin.

'Well, there you are,' she whispered. 'What perfect timing! You have a visitor, dear, unless I'm mistaken.'

Giving Sara a broad wink, she made for the door; standing there, wearing a leather jacket, his eyes masked by dark glasses, was a man Sara did not at first recognise. Jennifer gave him a wide smile.

'It's Clive Paget, isn't it?' she said cheerily. 'If you took the glasses off you might find her. She's over there in the corner, behind the Xerox machine. The desk with the wilting rubber plant. See you, Sara!'

And without a backward glance she swung out.

Embarrassed, Sara got quickly to her feet, but Clive gave her a wide smile.

' 'Allo, darlin'. Remember me? The wizard of the lens. I want you up in the art department. The light box is thick with transparencies of a very lovely young lady. Come and take a look.'

'The fashion pictures?' Sara groaned. 'I'm not sure I want to.'

'Well, you're comin'.' He looked at her critically as she came towards him. 'You look a lot better in those than you do now, *if* I may say so.'

Sara smiled wanly. 'Thanks, very gallant. No make-up today, you see.'

'Never mind.' He planted a kiss on her cheek and put his arm round her. 'Today there's an air of mystery about you—pale and interesting—a bit languid, know what I mean? I quite like it.'

When they reached it, the art department was deserted. Clive switched on the light box and indicated the rows of pictures laid out.

'Good, eh? There's a cover in these. Max'll go for them, I know. What do you think, love?'

In disbelief Sara stared at the transparencies. A beautiful woman stared back at her—poised, apparently confident, apparently radiant with happiness. For some reason she could not explain, the image so contrasted with her present feelings that it hurt; it was like looking at a picture of what she might have been, she thought suddenly.

She turned away, and Clive's face fell.

'You don't like them?'

'Yes, of course I do. They're amazing.' She gave him a watery smile. 'I can't believe it's me, that's all. I don't know how you did it, Clive.'

' 'Ad a good little model,' he said drily. 'Maybe that 'elped. Plus my well-known ability to bring out a woman's 'idden mystery and sensuality ... Not so 'idden in your case, of course.'

'That's not what most people say,' she said flatly.

'Then most people's fools. The lens don't lie. 'Ere.' To her surprise he put an arm around her, and tilted her face up to his; his expression, in contrast to his words, quite serious and intent. 'What's bin 'appenin' to you then, duchess?'

Sara smiled. 'Nothing much. I'm leaving the magazine.'

'So I 'ear. News gets about, y'know. Bit sudden, weren't it?'

'Sort of.'

'Miserable?'

'Sort of.' She smiled.

'Come and work with me, then.' He grinned. 'I told you, you're a natural. You know this business, always ravin' after the new. Nothin' they like better than a new face. I could get you any number of assignments. Just say the word.'

'Be a model, you mean?' Sara pulled a wry face.

'Sort of.' He winked. 'More than that, if you like. Quite fancy you, Sara, I do. Given me a few sleepless nights, you ' ave.'

'I'm sorry about that,' she said demurely.

'Like 'ell,' Clive dropped a kiss on her forehead, then held her at arm's length. 'So, 'ow about it, duchess?'

Sara sighed and shook her head.

'Thank you, Clive, but no,' she said. 'I wouldn't be any good, and besides . . .'

'Good at what?'

'At modelling,' she said firmly, disengaging herself with a smile. Clive sighed theatrically.

'Charmin',' he said dramatically. 'You realise what you're turnin' down, I suppose? Fame. Riches. Me.'

'Even so.'

' 'Ow about a trip to the Seychelles?' he said wickedly.

'The Seychelles?' Sara stared at him, wide-eyed.

'Certainly. Off any minute. Palm trees, deserted beaches, moonlight . . . doin' it for some American magazine. They'd be wild about you. Showed them these pictures in fact——' he lowered his voice conspiratorially, 'I think it's fate. You leavin' 'ere and all. It's a sign—Kismet! Wouldn't you rather be on a beach in the Seychelles than sittin' 'ere nursin' a broken 'eart?'

'What makes you think I'm broken hearted?' she asked quickly.

Clive grinned. 'Intuition. Famous for it, see?'

For a moment Sara hesitated, tempted. Then she shook her head.

'No, Clive,' she said finally. 'It sounds wonderful, but I can't.'

'Think about it.'

'All right.' She smiled. 'But I shan't change my mind.'

'You never know. 'Ere.' He gave her a small pasteboard card. 'There's me name, there's me number. Ring me any time in the next ten days if you change your mind. O.K., duchess?'

'O.K.'

He turned to the door.

'Oh—and Sara. No strings—promise. All right?'

She laughed.

'I don't believe you, but all right.'

Clive gave her an injured expression.

'I may not look it,' he said, 'but I am a gent. Very good at mendin' broken 'earts too—but that's by the way. Remember, just ring. 'Bye, duchess.'

He was gone before Sara could answer. She looked down at the card in her hand in bewilderment. All it said was *Clive Paget*, with the number of the Chelsea studio and another number for an answering service. She hesitated, glanced at the photographs on the light box, and then put the card in her bag. The Seychelles—however tempting, that really would be running away, she thought wryly. And besides, it would be breaking her contract. No. She couldn't go; somehow she would just have to get through the next two months, though if it were all as bad as the past week, she didn't know how she would bear it. Feeling on edge and miserable, she went back downstairs.

There was the daily editorial meeting at ten-thirty, when the staff went over articles received, and planned the next issue. Usually she looked forward to them; today there would be Harry, self-important and fussy in Max's absence, chairing the meeting. They would waste time, she thought impatiently. Deirdre Neal would argue about trivia and there would be no quick clipped voice to cut her off; no stimulus; no sudden darts of dry, unexpected humour; no life. However could she have resented Max's presence as editor? she thought miserably. Without him, the whole place seemed dead. How much he must have wanted to go to Montreux, she thought, he who never took time off, whose working hours were already legendary. And that realisation, sour and black, lodged in her heart; all day nothing would shift it. She typed, she telephoned, she wrote, she went to the meeting. Max was said to be returning the next week; Beverley's desk was piled high with telexes from him. From a thousand miles away he issued directives and Harry obsequiously, fussily, put them into effect. Sara was assigned a story; dully she agreed to do it. She was to go the next week to interview Asian immigrants in the East End, for a long article. Where had Max been, she thought miserably, when he made that decision? In some smart hotel in Montreux; perhaps with Delia; perhaps in Delia's room . . . No! She slammed the brakes on her mind as the painful images began to accelerate in her head. No!

For the rest of the day she worked like an automaton. At about six-thirty, just when she was finally, reluctantly, getting ready to leave, her telephone rang. She hesitated. Beverley had just come into the room, looking exhausted, with a sheaf of folders under her arm, and was making for her desk. She made a sign, and wearily Sara picked up the receiver.

'So, you're not going to evade me after all.' The voice was light, she did not immediately recognise it. Tiredness swept over her in waves.

'Who is that?'

There was an exaggerated sigh. 'Forgotten so soon? Or do you deliberately ignore messages?'

'Piers?'

'The one and only. Are you avoiding me, by any chance?'

Beverley had stationed herself by Sara's desk, and was watching this interchange with a smile. Sara felt miserable, inexplicably let down; why couldn't they all just leave her alone? She didn't want to talk to Piers. She didn't want to talk to anybody, she realised.

'Draw your own deductions,' she said crisply. But Piers was not easily repressed. He laughed.

'Well, you're not going to be able to avoid me much longer,' he told her. 'I shall woo you in the conservatory, among the potted palms. Very suitable.'

'What are you talking about?'

'You'll be in the East Wing, of course, and I'll be in the West. But a little detail like *that* won't deter me.'

'Piers, I don't know what you're talking about, I . . .'

'You'll find out.' He laughed again. 'See you next weekend, Sara.'

'*What?*'

But he had hung up. The dialling tone buzzed in her ears.

Beverley leaned across and placed a pink folder in front of her.

'Piers Waterlow?'

Sara nodded.

'He's quick off the mark. He's beaten me to it.' She grinned. 'You'll find the details in here, complete with schedule and map.'

'Map?' Sara stared at her stupidly.

'An editorial conference, on the prospects of the Waterlow empire in general, and this magazine in particular. In the Cotswolds, at Sir Andrew's, next weekend. Harry's going; Deirdre's going. You're going.'

Sara flipped open the folder and stared at the contents in disbelief.

'I've spent most of the last two days fixing it all.' Beverley sighed. 'I'm finished. Typically Max sprang it on me at the last moment. There's a telex from him in there that explains it all.'

Sara felt her hands begin to tremble; she looked up at Beverley.

'But why do I need to go? I mean, I'm leaving the magazine, there's absolutely no point in my . . .'

Beverley shrugged. 'Max wants you there. Who's to argue?'

'I see. And he'll be there?'

'Naturally.'

Sara felt an odd lurch of excitement, immediately succeeded by a dull ache of nervousness.

'I can't go,' she said flatly. 'I've arranged to go and see my mother that weekend. I must see her; it's all fixed.'

'You'll have to unfix it,' Beverley said unsympathetically. 'Max insists you be there. Come on, Sara, don't be daft. It'll be fun—and interesting. Sir Andrew has a lot of plans for the magazine.'

Sara kept her eyes fixed on the folder before her. The telex was on the top, and the words of its print-out danced before her eyes.

'Max arranged all this from Montreux?' she said slowly.

'Montreux?' Beverley looked surprised. 'He's not in Montreux, he's in Frankfurt.'

'But I thought . . .'

Beverley smiled. There was an expression on her face that Sara could not quite fathom, but she knew questions would be useless. Beverley was legendarily discreet. She stood up now, smoothing down her skirt.

'He was only in Montreux one night, I think,' she said casually. 'Since then he's been jetting around all over the place. I think Sir Andrew has plans for expansion into Europe. But you'll find out next weekend—won't you, Sara?'

She left quickly, before Sara could reply, leaving her staring down at the papers in front of her. Suddenly Sara felt as if all her tiredness had evaporated into the air; she wanted to laugh, to shout, to dance—she felt suddenly vibrantly alive again. The Cotswolds! And he had not been in Montreux—or there only briefly. The telex, she realised suddenly, was addressed to her personally. Rapidly her eyes scanned the print; the language was the usual formal telex shorthand, *presence requested . . . Canst arrive 10:00 am . . .* She read on to the end; all was as she would have expected, except for the final coda: *Dress formal. Max.* Sara felt the corners of her lips curl into a smile; somehow she felt certain that those words would not be included on anybody else's telex. It was like a private message, a private joke, a challenge. His presence was suddenly so overwhelmingly strong to her that it was as if he were in the room, by her side, speaking to her directly, and beside the force of that feeling nothing else mattered, none of the past muddle, argument and un-certainty. She would go, she thought, her heart filled with gaiety. And she would buy some new clothes, even though she was broke, even though she was worried about money. For once she would be frivolous and irresponsible and damn the consequences. She would have to explain the change of plan to her mother, of course, and for a moment that thought checked her. But the gaiety was so strong, it drowned all guilt, all worry, all doubt. Without pausing for thought, she dialled the number of her flat.

'Jennifer?' she said. 'Quick—think! It's Monday. Where is there late-night shopping?'

'Round the corner at the Indian take-away.'

'Not that. Clothes.'

There was a stunned silence on the other end of the line, and Sara laughed. She felt almost drunk with a mad kind of exhilaration.

'Never mind,' she said, 'I'll find somewhere.'

'I think there's that place in Kensington where . . .'

Kensington. Where he lived.

'Then I'm off to Kensington,' she said quickly.

'But . . .'

'I'll see you later,' she said, and rang off. She replaced the phone so quickly that the pile of messages and the note from Piers Waterlow tumbled to the floor. Sara did not stop to pick them up, but just grabbed her bag and her coat and made for the door. At the door she stopped, went back to her desk, and carefully took Max's telex from the pink folder. She folded it quickly, mocking herself as she did so, but knowing she had to keep it with her, like a talisman. She put it into her bag and hurried out of the building.

The park had been laid out by Capability Brown, at the end of the eighteenth century. From the formal terrace in front of Sir Andrew's house the eye was led, apparently naturally, but really with consummate artifice, to the horizon. A great avenue of oak trees hid the long drive to the front of the house, but on this side the grass swept away from the West Wing in one gentle, uninterrupted curve to the lake below. Its water was a dull flat gold in the later afternoon sun, and one swan, perfectly still, as if posed, waited by the sedge at its borders. The air was cold and clear; a smell of woodsmoke drifted.

Sara glanced quickly and covertly behind her, up at the great windows of the house, and ducked down a path that led to the Victorian shrubbery. She wound her scarf tighter around her throat, and thrust her gloved hands into her pockets. No one had seen her leave, she thought; with any luck she had managed to evade even the persistent Piers, who had been following her around like a spaniel ever since she arrived that morning.

Gratefully she found herself under cover; the gravelled path led between tall banks of funereal dripping rhododendrons. Here she was completely sheltered from view. There was a maze, Sir Andrew had said; perhaps she would go there. She found it quickly, and turned in through the high yew hedges. A memory came back to her; a childhood visit to Hampton Court with her parents, to the maze there, the excitement and the terror mixed with it; running between the hedges, calling to her father. She had found her way to the centre, but had lost him.

She shivered, and hesitated. What was the classic route? Always left, she thought, and tried that, but it led nowhere. To her annoyance, she found herself back at the entrance; she tried again, this time trying no fixed pattern, but just letting the paths lead her, turning on impulse. And suddenly, just when she thought herself totally lost, she found herself in the centre. There was a wooden seat, and a round pond, its lilies blackened with frost; under the brown water were darts of gold: carp.

She sighed, and drawing her coat round her, sat down on the seat. For the first time that day she felt at peace, secure in her isolation. There had been a preliminary meeting that afternoon, with the main discussions reserved for the next day, but it had been desultory, ineffective, and Sir Andrew had impatiently curtailed it. Max had not been there; he had still not returned, his flight was delayed. A week, she thought. Another week, and still she had not seen him.

He was probably arriving now, she thought, he had been expected at any moment. Was that why she had hurried out, taking the side door, making sure no one saw her? Was that it, was she still running away? She sighed, her breath making little ghostly puffs in the cold air, as she idly watched the carp circling, doubling back, circling again, silent under the water.

She knew now. She had known—for how long? Perhaps from the first, she couldn't be certain. Perhaps when she let herself take that message home with her . . . But no; earlier than that. She closed her eyes. Since you met him, her mind said. Since he first touched you. What did it matter when? I love him, she thought, letting herself say the words for the first time openly. I love him. And the knowledge, the admission, eased her heart a little.

It was hopeless, of course, and she would tell no one. Not Jennifer, not her mother, not Geoffrey, no one. She would just store that knowledge inside her, hidden away, a secret joy and a secret sadness. And she would have to leave the magazine, there could be no going back now. The pain of seeing him every day, of thinking of him going home each night to Delia, would be more than she could bear. For he would marry Delia, she now felt certain of it. Piers had hinted as much that morning; his mother was furious at the prospect, he had said gleefully; *she* had wanted Delia to hook a title. And Delia herself, deeply tanned from the ski slopes, radiating confidence and happiness. At the first opportunity she had led Sara away from the others.

'I think Max is going to talk to Daddy about it tonight,' she had said. 'It'll probably have to be unofficial for a bit, of course, till they've talked Mummy round. But since Montreux . . .' She had kissed Sara's cheek. 'How can I ever thank you enough, you darling? Now tell me, when exactly are you leaving the magazine?'

In six weeks, Sara thought. And the brevity of the time cut her. Just six more weeks of this quiet covert happiness; of seeing him, and hearing his voice, if nothing more. Six weeks; she would have to store the memories, she thought; of his quick angers and unexpected gentleness, of his frequent arrogance and well-hidden vulnerability. And then nothing but memories; the future stretched before her like a wasteland . . .

'Sara.'

She started and swung round; it was as if she were dreaming.

He was standing a few feet from her, between the high dark walls of yew, motionless, watching. His face looked tired and drawn; he was wearing a long black overcoat, his hands thrust deep into the pockets, and his eyes did not leave her face. Quickly she rose to her feet; her thoughts had been so intense, so powerful, that she felt as if he must read them, and she knew the blood rushed to her cheeks.

'Max! I . . .'

The impulse to run to him, to feel those strong arms come round her, was so strong that she took a step forward involuntarily. He must have moved as swiftly; the next second he held her. For a moment she felt his arms, his breath against her skin, and looked directly into those perturbing dark eyes. As quickly, fighting herself, she stepped back, and he let his hands fall. They stood, looking at each other, and she saw his mouth twist with an odd pained smile. Then he turned away and sat down, and when he looked at her again it was with the old, slightly mocking expression, his editorial face. She stood awkwardly by the edge of the pool, uncertain whether to make some excuse and go, or to stay and speak to him.

'In hiding?' he smiled.

She shrugged, forcing herself to behave naturally.

'In a way.'

'I don't blame you.'

He looked away, as if suddenly bored, letting his gaze travel over the surface of the pond, to the hedges, the trees beyond.

'Did you have a good flight?' Sara asked nervously, unwilling to let the silence lengthen. 'You were delayed, I think.'

His eyes met hers.

'Oh yes,' he said, 'I was considerably delayed. Two weeks, almost.'

'No,' she said quickly, 'I didn't mean that. I meant . . .'

'I know what you meant.'

He was going to talk about her resignation, suddenly she felt certain of it. She looked quickly towards the exit from the maze, wondering how she could get away, and as if he read her thoughts, Max smiled mockingly.

'If you're thinking of running away,' he said, 'I wouldn't advise it. You're quite likely to get lost. It'll be dark soon, and it's harder finding the way out. If you wait, I'll show you. Now. Why don't you sit down?'

He gestured to the seat beside him, and reluctantly, hesitantly, she did as he bade her, keeping a distance between them which she knew he noted, for his mouth tightened. He said nothing, however, but just sat there, his face averted, his eyes shadowed.

'Are you sure you know the way out?' she asked finally.

'Oh yes.' He spoke calmly, distantly, as if his thoughts were far away, his eyes still on the horizon. 'I've known this place since I was a child, you see.'

He spoke lightly, casually, but there was something odd, and dark, in his tone, and Sara stiffened.

'I lived about a mile away from here once, for a time. Then this place belonged to a . . . friend . . . of my mother's.'

'Oh.'

'Her lover, actually. So we visited it often.' Now there was no mistaking the pain and the angry bitterness in his voice, and Sara felt her heart turn over with pity.

'I know about all that,' she said awkwardly. 'About your father and . . . I'm so sorry.'

She broke off, suddenly terrified that she had said too much, had stepped over that invisible boundary of privacy he kept around himself, but to her surprise he did not react, either at her knowledge or at her words.

Instead he shrugged. 'The past,' he said flatly. 'You think you can escape from it, and then, when you least expect it . . .' He broke off and turned to her, his eyes so cold and hard that she had to force herself not to drop her gaze.

'I want your advice,' he said abruptly.

'*My* advice?' she stared at him.

'Yes, yours. I'm thinking of getting married.'

The pain was so intense, so sudden, it was like a blow to her heart. She felt the blood drain from her face, and her mouth go dry. To hear it from Delia, or Piers, was one thing. But from Max . . . it was too hard, she thought; she could not bear it.

'So, tell me, do you think that a very foolish decision?'

'I don't know why you should ask me,' she said defensively. 'As you know, I'm not much of an expert.'

'But I do ask you.'

She clasped her gloved hands together tightly in her lap, and lowered her eyes to them.

'Are you surprised?'

'Yes. No.' She hesitated, but there seemed no point now in not speaking the truth, so, taking a deep breath, she let the words tumble out. 'Of course. If you love someone then . . . it would be natural. Inevitable.' Unbidden, a ghostly voice rose up in her mind, *fire and ice*. How much he could hurt someone! 'If you were totally certain, that is,' she ran on. 'If you thought you would never change your mind. And I would have thought that maybe . . .'

She stopped abruptly, and Max smiled.

'You don't think I'm the marrying kind?'

'No. Yes,' she faltered. 'It's just that such a commitment . . .'

'You don't sound very certain.'

'I don't know!' she cried wildly, thinking only that somehow she must bring this conversation to an end. 'I don't know you very well. I can't judge. I . . .'

'I want to be married very much.' He spoke drily, turning away from her once more, cutting off her protestations. 'I want to live with my wife, and have children, and make something together that would last. Always.' He paused. 'You don't believe in that, of course. I can tell from your face.'

Sara stood up quickly.

'I've never encountered it,' she said stiffly. 'But I . . . I wish you every happiness.' She turned towards the exit. 'I'm sorry, I'm very cold. I think I must go back.'

'But of course,' he said smoothly, his tone totally altered. He stood up. 'I have no right to turn up after two weeks in the wilderness and bore you with this kind of sentimental discussion. We should be talking about work, shouldn't we, Sara? Or your resignation?'

He took her arm, urgently, just above the elbow, and steered her towards one of the passages through the hedges.

'I would have gone the wrong way,' she said, trying to make her voice light, hearing it come out all wrong, forced and artificial.

'As usual,' he said grimly.

Without hesitation, looking neither to right nor left, he propelled her along the narrow pathways in a harsh grip, never allowing her to slow up, even when once she stumbled. The hedges passed before her, a dark blur; she saw nothing, felt only the numb edge of pain.

It was darkening rapidly, above them on the slope the lights of the house's upper windows shone out over the empty parkland. As they reached the edge of the maze, and Sara saw the gap of the entrance in the yew hedges before them, Max suddenly stopped.

'Damn it to hell!'

With one swift movement he twisted her back so she was pressed between the hedges and his body. He half lifted her, half pulled her, with an easy strength, wrenching her head back. Hard and savagely, before she could move or react, his mouth came down on hers, forcing her lips apart under the sudden fierce pressure. For a second, a minute, there was no sense of time, everything was blotted out; her blood stirred under his touch, her lips burned with a fever of desire, pent up, suddenly full in her.

'Dear God, Sara, I want you so much . . .' His voice was thick with desire, his lips against her neck.

'No!'

From somewhere she found the strength to fight off her own feelings, to push him back. She stood there for a second, rooted to the spot, her heart pounding, pain and want surging inside her. For a moment those dark eyes, blazing in his pale face, held her, mesmerised. Then he reached for her again, his hand moving to her face, as if to cradle it, to stroke it, with a gesture so tender, so gentle, that the pain and regret was like a whiplash.

'How could you!' She backed away, like a frightened animal. 'Leave me alone!'

And then, without pausing, she began to run. Out of the maze, stumbling in the shadows, across the grass towards the house. Her breath caught in her throat, the cold air seared her lungs, but she did not stop running until she reached the terrace. There, for a second, she looked back. Darkness had fallen; he had not followed her.

CHAPTER SEVEN

In her room a fire had been lit. The curtains were drawn, the dress she had bought with such care and excitement had been laid out on her bed, in readiness for the dinner that evening. Sara stood before the fire, still shaking, her breath coming in gasps, letting the warmth of the room, the deep silence quieten her. When she was calmer, she went into the bathroom next door and ran a bath. Slowly, methodically, she undressed. She washed her hair, then bathed, lying a long while in the scented water. Her first impulse when she got back to the house had been to leave, but as the agitation subsided she decided against it. She was here; it was better to go through with it.

After all, she told herself, Max was famous for his womanising, for that succession of decorative women, taken up and then dropped so carelessly, so heartlessly. Yet how could he talk to her about marrying Delia one moment, and then the next . . . She shut her mind to the memory. After all, he was impatient in all things, always. If he wanted something at work, then he pursued it at once, until he got it. And so, if momentarily he had

wanted her—had he wanted her?—he would no more
hesitate . . . Yet in other things he could be so rigorous, so
unswervingly truthful, so contemptuous of hypocrisy or
lies . . . for him, of all men, to behave to dishonourably,
so uncaringly—to Delia and herself.

Slowly she got out of the cooling water, dried herself,
and began to dress carefully. Whatever happened, she
thought, he must never suspect her feelings, never guess
the response he awoke in her. She must be cool, distant,
as if nothing had happened, as if she didn't care. And
perhaps, if she stayed close to Piers, avoided Max, he
would lose whatever passing interest he felt. If it was anything at all, she told her reflection, it was her apparent
coldness that could sometimes attract him. Perhaps it was
a challenge to him: certainly it sometimes seemed that
way, as if he were determined that he should be the one
to crack that frigid reserve. The office ice-maiden. Colour
came to her cheeks as she looked at herself in the glass.
The dress she had bought was black, it bared her shoulders
and was startlingly dark against the whiteness of her skin.
She looked at herself coldly, appraisingly. She had put on
a little make-up; her hair curled softly around her face
and neck; she looked a little like the girl in the fashion
photographs, but stiff, brittle, a piece of porcelain. Her
face looked unmarked, unaffected; her heart, heavy with
hurt and incomprehension, felt as if it would break.

Downstairs, to her relief, she found only Piers and his
father, seated before a huge fire in the drawing room, and
as soon as she entered, Piers was at her side.

'Sara—darling! You look wonderful. Now, come over
by the fire. I'm going to mix you one of my special cocktails.'

Piers disappeared to the other end of the room where
he made a great deal of fuss with glasses, measures, different bottles, and a silver cocktail shaker. Sir Andrew
smiled, and motioned Sara to sit beside him.

'You may regret this, m'dear,' he said. 'Piers's cocktails
are pure poison. You sure you wouldn't rather have a
whisky, like me?'

Sara laughed. She liked Sir Andrew and judged him

shrewd, though she noticed it pleased him to affect a kind of heartiness and bluffness which was initially deceptive. She shook her head.

'I'll risk a cocktail,' she said.

'Well, I'm glad you're the first down, m'dear, anyway. Gives me a chance to have a bit of a word with you.' Sir Andrew looked at her appraisingly. 'What's all this about your leaving us, then? I told Max, we can't have it. The magazine needs people like you.'

Sara coloured.

'So, what's the reason then? Not gettin' married, I hope?'

Sara shook her head, as Piers returned. He produced a shallow glass containing an evil-looking green mixture, and gave Sara what he obviously imagined was a languorous look from beneath his long lashes.

'Sara doesn't believe in marriage, Pa.' He seated himself firmly beside her. 'She's a dedicated career woman.'

Sir Andrew glanced from one to the other, and Sara saw him repress a smile.

'Bit of a Women's Libber, what we used to call a New Woman. That it?'

'Very much so.' The words were spoken coolly, cuttingly; Sara nearly dropped her glass. She swung round to see Max standing in the doorway. He was wearing immaculate evening clothes and lolling elegantly against the door-frame; it was obvious he had been listening to their conversation. Instantly she felt herself tense, and saw that Piers did also. Ostentatiously he moved a little closer to her on the sofa, and draped his arm protectively along its back, just by her bare shoulders. Sir Andrew got up with an exclamation of pleasure.

'Max! So you're here—when did you arrive? Come and have a drink . . .'

'Piers. Sara.' Max crossed to them, and to Sara's horror bent forward, lifted her hand, and give it a perfunctory but gracefully executed kiss. Piers glared at him.

'How lovely to see you both,' Max said gravely, his eyes not leaving Sara's face. He turned back to Sir Andrew. 'I arrived this afternoon, actually. I was exhausted, so I went for a bit of a walk. I felt I needed some fresh air.'

He drifted away, following Sir Andrew to the cupboard where the drinks were kept, and the two men began an intent conversation. Piers turned to Sara, his face sulky and suspicious.

'*You* went for a walk this afternoon, Sara. Where did you go? I was looking everywhere for you.'

'Nowhere special. I was exploring a bit, that's all. I found your maze, and went and watched the fish.'

'She was lost, as a matter of fact. I had to rescue her.'

Max was back, Sara realised, standing right in front of them, so he appeared even taller than usual. There was an expression of infuriating insolence on his face, and she felt herself crimson.

'Oh, so you two have met up already, then?' Sir Andrew had joined them, glancing quizzically from one to the other, and Sara knew that the undercurrent of tension that had entered the room with Max did not escape his notice.

'Yes, we did,' she muttered.

'Briefly.' With cool aplomb Max allowed his gaze to slip to the neckline of her dress, and back to her mouth. Sara felt just as if he had reached across and touched her, in front of the others, as if her lips were branded with his kisses.

'Well, I think that old maze is very boring.' Piers made no attempt to disguise the pettishness in his voice. He turned to Sara, laying his hand possessively on her bare arm. 'If we got up early tomorrow, Sara, we could go out and I could give you a proper guided tour, before you start all this conference business. You can't have seen half of it yet, there's the rose garden . . .'

'Particularly spectacular in December,' said Max gravely, giving them both a radiant smile. Piers ignored him.

'Then there's the Japanese garden, and the Gothic temple, and . . .'

Sara smiled as warmly as she could. 'How lovely!' she said. 'I should like that very much, Piers.'

To her surprise Piers blushed like a girl at her words, and settled back on the sofa with an expression of undisguised triumph on his face. Max gave her a look of utter contempt, and at once turned away to Sir Andrew. Piers obviously saw his chance, and promptly took it; his arm curled around her shoulders, and Sara stiffened. If she was to play *that* game she had better be careful, she realised; Piers, on his home ground, seemed a lot less sure of himself, a lot more vulnerable than he had been at Delia's. He might be an incorrigible flirt, but it would not be fair to lead him on. Gracefully but firmly she removed the arm, and Piers sighed.

'Now, Sara darling, you're not going to be cruel and cold and horrid?'

'I might be, if you don't behave.'

Piers smiled; he leaned closer so his lips were almost against her ear, and their conversation was inaudible except to themselves.

'Why didn't you answer my messages?'

'I was very busy, Piers.'

'Too busy to take pity on me? Sara, I think I've fallen madly in love with you. *La belle dame sans merci . . .*'

He gave her his Peter Pan look, and Sara suppressed her laughter: 'That's nonsense, Piers, and you know it.'

He had the grace to smile sheepishly, but was not to be easily put off.

'Well, possibly. But I feel as if I *might* fall madly in love with you—at any moment. If I were given some encouragement.'

'Well, you're not going to get any, so I should give up if I were you.'

'No, I shan't. It's enormous fun, and besides, it makes dear old Max absolutely furious, haven't you noticed? He keeps giving me the most deadly looks. There! He gave me one right then. If I were more sensitive, I'd shrivel up and die on the spot!'

Before she could dodge him, he placed the lightest, the sweetest of kisses, on her cheek. Sara got up hastily to find that not just Max, but also Lady Waterlow, who had just come in with Delia, was fixing them with a glacial stare.

Sir Andrew was quick to come to her rescue; Piers was totally unabashed; but Lady Waterlow, Sara noticed, kept a firm eye on her. Clearly a penniless journalist was not at all the kind of woman she had in mind for her only son. Piers was swiftly shepherded away to entertain a couple of giggling debutantes and when everyone went in to dinner, it was obvious that Lady Waterlow had given considerable thought to the *placements*. To Delia's obvious rage, she was placed at the far end, between a couple of young Guards officers; Piers was firmly flanked by the debs, and both Max and Sara had been banished to the opposite end of the long polished mahogany table. Sara had Sir Andrew on her left, and—she saw to her dismay—Max on her right. On the other side of Sir Andrew was Deirdre Neal, decked out in peach chiffon from head to foot, and clearly hell-bent on monopolising her chairman for as long as possible. Without being overtly rude, there was clearly to be little escape from Max.

With slightly mocking courtesy he drew out her chair for her, and then settled himself close—too close—by her side.

It was a beautiful room, with deep lacquered red walls which reflected the gleam of the table silver, the soft flickering light of the candles; the walls were adorned with large oil paintings—of Lady Waterlow's obviously fecund ancestors. Nervously Sara arranged her napkin, crumbled the tiny bread roll on her plate, kept her eyes fixed on those paintings—anything to avoid the eyes of the man sitting next to her.

Max had turned towards her, she could sense it without looking, his eyes travelling over her hair and face to the long line of her neck and pale shoulders.

'You understood my message, then,' he said finally.

In spite of herself, Sara smiled. So she had been right.

'Dress formal?' she said lightly.

'That's right.'

'Were you worried I'd disgrace everybody by turning up in trousers?'

He smiled. 'No,' he said slowly. 'I wanted to see you

look exactly the way you do. Very beautiful. It was a purely selfish request.'

The compliment, on his lips, only increased her nervousness; her hand trembling slightly, she reached for her wine glass, almost knocking it over.

'Careful! We don't want another accident.' Briefly, momentarily his hand came down on hers, steadying it. The glancing touch seemed to burn into her skin, and she flinched. Max noted her reaction; so did Deirdre Neal.

'*Doesn't* Sara look lovely tonight?' she said sweetly, breaking off for a moment her conversation with Sir Andrew. 'I said to dear Delia earlier, what a transformation! Quite like Cinderella.'

A sharp retort rose to Sara's lips, but she managed to bite it back. The last thing she wanted was to provoke Deirdre, she thought, or to allow the conversation to take any turn other than the innocuous. She turned back to Max, meeting his eyes for the first time.

'How was your visit to Europe?' she asked politely.

He shrugged; she knew he detested small talk.

'All right. Exhausting. I missed the magazine.'

'We missed you,' she said quickly, and then coloured deeply, for his eyes had become instantly alert. 'It—er—wasn't the same without you,' she went on lamely, 'at the morning meetings and so on . . .'

'You missed my abrasive wit, you mean?' he said sarcastically. 'Or perhaps my endless capacity to interfere?'

Sara dropped her eyes. 'No,' she said steadily, 'I don't think that any more, in any case.'

It was the nearest she had ever come to giving him a direct apology for all the things she had said and done in the past, and he seemed to note it, for his expression softened.

'Well, you seem to have got on very well without me in any case.' He paused. 'When I came back this afternoon from my walk I read your last article—the one about the Asian families in the East End.' He hesitated. 'It's very fine, Sara. But you must know that.'

He had never praised her work in such a way before, and Sara felt her heartbeat quicken. She *was* pleased with the piece; it was the best she had yet written. The poverty and the dignity of the people she had interviewed had moved her; it had been easy to write—had almost written itself. An image of the last woman she had spoken to came into her mind: a thin woman, draped in a scarlet sari, a clutch of tiny children peeping shyly out from behind her skirt. All living in one room; the husband out of work. As Sara was leaving, the husband had returned—from the labour exchange. The woman's face had quite simply lit up, become irradiated with happiness. Her English was poor. 'My man,' she had said to Sara proudly, 'my man.'

What she would give to be able to say that, Sara thought, to be able to show the joy Max's presence awoke in her, the glow his words now lit in her heart. But she must not.

'Thank you,' she said awkwardly. 'But it was an extraordinary assignment. Anyone could have written it.'

'I think not,' Max said drily. 'They couldn't. You couldn't have written it three months ago either.'

Sara stared at him; she might have known, she thought, that there would be a sting in the tail.

'You've changed, Sara,' he said softly, before she could speak again. 'You may not think so, but you have. Oh, you were always a good journalist—but sharp. There was no heart there. Now there is. It's as simple as that, and it makes all the difference.'

He had turned right round to face her, and there was a curious intensity in his words, as if he very much wanted her to understand something. At the gentleness in his voice Sara felt overwhelmed with guilt.

'That's not quite true,' she said falteringly. 'I was hard, but worse than that, I made mistakes—stupid elementary mistakes. I allowed my prejudices to influence what I wrote. I wasn't always truthful . . . enough.' She paused. 'I was wrong in what I wrote about you, I realise that now. I should have apologised, long ago.'

He smiled. 'Is this a peace-making? I told you once before, I think, one should never apologise, never explain. Leave the past where it is, in the past. You weren't altogether wrong in what you wrote, you know.'

Sara looked away. Was this *his* way of apologising? she

wondered. Was he admitting that at least what she had written about his private life was true, the endless affairs, the endless succession of lovely women? Perhaps, she thought.

'In any case——' she saw him make a conscious effort to alter the tone of their conversation, which had been so hushed it was attracting the attention of Deirdre Neal, 'what interests me is what's happened to you in the last few months to effect such a change.'

He let his eyes travel along the table until they rested on Piers, who had been trying, without success, to attract Sara's attention for some while.

'I have a good editor,' Sara said lightly.

'Just that?'

'That and other things.'

'I see.' He frowned. 'Well, in that case, perhaps you'll reconsider that resignation of yours. I can't afford to lose you, you know.'

Sara felt her heart contract with pain at his words, but she allowed nothing to show on her face.

'I'm afraid I can't change my mind now,' she said gently.

'Then I shall have to change it for you.' He touched her hand lightly, and Sara quickly removed it.

'You know how stubborn I am,' she said lightly, trying to make a joke of it.

'Not as stubborn as I am.'

He said it curtly, and at once turned away abruptly to talk to the woman who sat to his right. So, Sara thought, her audience was over. He had said what he wanted to say, and—typically—had then lost interest. How impossible it seemed ever to hold his attention for long! The woman next to him was slightly older than he, perhaps forty, Sara guessed, looking at her jealously. But she was vivacious, attractive, her tanned arms ringed with heavy diamond bracelets. As Sara looked, Max picked up the woman's arm, touched one of the bracelets, said something to her Sara could not catch; the woman laughed, took Max's hand flirtatiously; he bent his dark head closer towards her. What was it his mother had said of him, all those weeks before, at his party? *Max always had a weakness for beautiful women.* It was true, Sara thought; he was one of those men who needed women, needed perhaps the constant thrill of chase and consummation. Delia, she saw, was also watching his flirtation, her lips narrow, her face a mask of angry displeasure.

In spite of everything she had done, Sara felt a wave of pity for her, a kindred sympathy. She knew what Delia was feeling, the very same emotions tugged now at her own heart; Delia might marry Max, she thought suddenly, with total certainty, but she would never hold him. In pursuing him, she was pursuing unhappiness. No woman could hold Max long, she thought, turning her face sadly from the whispered conversation at her side. He was too animal, too predatory, too dangerous. It was that that made him so attractive, of course; his mouth, his kisses, promised such abandon; his cold eyes such destruction. Even now, watching him touch another woman, she felt a sudden surge of want for him, utterly physical, flood through her body. She must never let him touch her again, she vowed silently; it hurt enough to love him; even if it were not for Delia, for his impending marriage, she would risk nothing more. He would break her, she knew it; first her resistance, and then her heart. Instinctively she drew back from the dark figure at her side, making stupid jumbled plans—never to be alone with him, never to let him suspect, never to let him see . . . after all, she thought miserably, it shouldn't be hard—for six short weeks.

The rest of the dinner passed quickly. Sara talked gratefully to Sir Andrew; Max seemed to have forgotten her presence altogether. When the women withdrew, she sat in the drawing room trying to cheer a hostile, tearful Delia. The men were a long time over the port and cigars; after half an hour, she felt she could safely leave, and so, pleading a headache, she said goodnight to a frosty Lady Waterlow, and slipped from the room. The woman with the diamond bracelets settled herself on the sofa beside Delia as she left; *Tell me more about Max, darling*, Sara heard her say as she left; *I had no idea he was so charming* . . .

She went back to her bedroom. The sheets were turned

back, the heavy silk curtains were drawn. She put on her nightdress and lay on the covers, staring up at the canopy above the bed, willing the tears to stay away, fighting her memories, odd snatches of conversations, of things Max had said, whirling in and out of her mind. She knew she would not sleep, that if she did the old dreams of loss would haunt her; compulsively she pleated the silk bed-covers between her fingers, willing the man out of her mind. At twelve she heard footsteps in the corridor out-side, a burst of laughter. The other guests were retiring. She heard taps run, a few muffled creaks as people went to bed. Then silence. An owl hooted in the garden outside; the longcase clock in the corner whirred and clicked. One o'clock passed, and she knew sleep would not come.

She got up finally, furious with herself. Perhaps she would read, perhaps that would lull her. Then, as she reached for the book, she heard a sound in the corridor outside. She tensed, but there was silence. Then she thought she heard a soft tap on her door. She sat up on the bed, startled. It must be Delia, she thought, perhaps unable to sleep either, and seeking someone to pour out her thoughts to. Or Piers. Surely it could not be Piers?

The tap came again, louder. Then the handle turned, and the door opened. Max stood in the doorway, still in his evening clothes.

'I hoped you'd still be awake,' he said calmly, walked into the room, and shut the door.

Sara stared at him, numb with outrage and astonish-ment. Did he think her so cheap, such a pushover, was that it? He smiled at her with total composure, and she found her voice.

'What . . . what are you *doing*?'

'I'd have thought it was fairly obvious,' he said sweetly, mockingly. 'I've come to visit you.'

'You *can't*! It's the middle of the night. Everybody is in bed . . .' She broke off. She was sounding ridiculous, she thought bitterly.

'You're not.' He smiled. 'Neither am I.'

'Will you please leave at once!'

'No, I won't.'

There was an armchair by the fireplace, the remains of a log fire smouldering in the grate. He proceeded to throw some logs on the fire, so the flames shot up, sending flickering shadows dancing on the walls. Then he sat down in the armchair, as if it were the most normal thing in the world.

'Are you drunk, or something?'

He considered the question maddeningly.

'No,' he said finally. 'I don't think I get drunk on one whisky, two glasses of wine and one glass of port. Not in the space of——' he looked at his watch—'some six hours. And I don't think I've come to play the role of the seducer, either, so you can stop looking so outraged. I took considerable risks to get here, you know. Lady Waterlow's notions of propriety are so Victorian that the men are in the East Wing, and the women in the West. I've had a long walk, and avoiding all the creaking floorboards was hell.'

In spite of herself, Sara was amused; she almost relented, but as quickly forced herself to be stern. Hadn't she been vowing to avoid just this kind of situation only a short while before? In spite of what he said, she didn't trust him not to touch her; another man, maybe, but not Max. She looked at him coldly.

'Well, my notions of propriety are fairly Victorian too,' she said. 'So you'd better walk right back. Deirdre Neal is in the next room, and I don't want to start a scandal.'

'Deirdre is fast asleep and snoring loudly,' he said imperturbably. 'You can hear her quite clearly from the corridor. And on the other side of you there's a boxroom, so we're quite safe. I checked this afternoon.'

'You did what?'

'I checked. After all, I didn't want to go blundering into the wrong room, did I?'

Sara stared at him in dismay. 'So!' She drew in a deep breath. 'You planned this little expedition, did you?'

'Of course I did,' he said mildly. 'It was the best way of ensuring that I could talk to you without interruption. And without your running away.'

'How did you know it was my room?'

He smiled. 'Not difficult. Simone de Beauvoir novels by the bedside, the inevitable jeans in the wardrobe. I wasn't likely to make a mistake, was I? And I do know this house quite well.'

Of course you do, she thought, feeling sick, and not just from your childhood, either. Delia's room was at the far end of the same corridor. How many times had he made the journey from the East Wing to the West before? she wondered. Delia's voice sang in her mind: *He's a wonderful lover, Sara.* She was sure he was, she thought bitterly, looking at the tall powerful man in the chair, who watched her with such composure. He was strong, she thought. He would be as demanding in bed as he was everywhere else. She remembered the expert touch of his hands, the thrust of his body against her, the hard, warm pressure of his mouth on hers, in the garden. The memory shot through her body like a flame, and she shivered.

'Are you warm enough?' Max asked sardonically, and she saw his eyes travel up over the lines of her body under the thin nightdress.

'I'm not dressed for conversation,' she said sharply, 'I'm dressed for bed,' and the words were no sooner spoken than she could have bitten off her tongue. His eyebrows lifted, and he smiled.

'Is that an invitation?'

'You know quite well it isn't,' she said fiercely.

'A pity.' He looked away, threw another log on the fire.

Sara hesitated. Short of making a loud scene, there was no way of getting rid of him. If she kept well out of his reach . . . she sighed.

'Very well,' she said, more calmly than she felt, 'you'd better say whatever it was you came to say, then perhaps you would go.'

'Very well. I came to talk about your resignation. And don't sound so angry. I thought we made some kind of truce at dinner.'

'That was work. That was different.'

'Work—work!' He leaned back in his chair, and crossed

his legs, watching her every movement. 'Do you ever think of anything else, Sara?'

'Not often,' she said quickly. 'I'm like you in that respect.'

He gave her a lazy mocking smile, the kind that left his eyes cold and watchful.

'Oh, I wouldn't say I thought about work all the time,' he said lightly.

'Well, no, perhaps not.' Sara made her voice as sarcastic as she could. 'Not when you're at the opera, or the theatre, or one of your glossy parties, or with one of your . . .' She broke off.

'Do go on, Sara,' he said with an icy politeness. 'This is fascinating. With one of my women, is that what you were going to say?'

Sara blushed, furious with herself that she should be so crude, so unguarded.

'Well, was it?'

She tilted her chin defiantly. 'Yes, it was, as a matter of fact.'

'You're quite wrong.' He looked away. 'In the past, maybe, but for the last few months . . .'

'And this afternoon?' she said sharply.

He shrugged and looked away. There was a moment's silence, and when he turned back to her his face had changed.

'Would you like to know what I usually do when I'm not working?' he said flatly. 'When, as you imagine, I'm indulging in an endless round of parties and seductions? No, don't interrupt me, Sara, I'll tell you. I'm usually at home, by myself.'

'How touching! I suppose you'll tell me next that you're lonely.'

'No,' he said seriously, ignoring the angry antagonism in her voice, 'I'm not lonely—exactly. I work sometimes. I read. I listen to music.' He paused. 'And I think about you.'

Whatever she had been going to say next, the words froze on her lips, the reply was so unexpected. She stared at him.

'You think about me?' she said finally, her voice little

more than a whisper. 'Why should you do that?'

'Because you . . . interest me,' he said calmly, as if they were discussing another person. 'Because you intrigue me. Because I feel we're very alike, and that sometimes I understand you while at others you mystify me completely. Because I care what happens to you. All those things. Also . . .' He paused, and she saw his eyes move languorously once more over her body, 'because you attract me. Very much.'

Sara froze. She wanted to wrap the folds of the thin nightdress tighter around her body, to shield it from his eyes, but she knew that kind of prudishness would only amuse him. So, she thought, she had been right. That *was* why he had come here. All this talk was nothing more than some protracted preliminary to a seduction routine. And Delia was asleep just a few rooms away. It was horrible, she thought, horrible. But even as her mind said all those things, her body stirred; she could feel the insidious pulse of attraction beginning, growing . . . oh, why wouldn't he leave?

'Come here.'

She hesitated. If she refused, he would only come to her, and there would be a struggle, and then . . . Summoning all her courage, she walked slowly towards him, out of the shadows, until she stood a few feet from him, in front of the fire. She forced herself to meet his eyes, and spoke calmly.

'Max,' she said, her voice low and urgent, 'will you believe me when I say I would prefer you to go? Please.'

'I don't believe you. You can't.'

He reached for her hand, and she quickly drew back.

His mouth tightened, and she saw that dangerous angry glint come into his eyes that she dreaded.

'I see,' he said coldly. 'You're going to play the old games.'

Sara stared at him in bewilderment.

'I'm not playing any games! I . . .'

'Oh, come on, Sara. You're dealing with a man, not a boy. You're happy to flirt with Piers Waterlow, I notice, because he doesn't offer any real threat, does he?'

'Maybe I like Piers,' she began defiantly.

'Like him?' Max stood up, his face white with anger. 'I'm not talking about liking someone, Sara. Don't come out with your schoolmarm phrases to me! I'm talking about wanting someone, really wanting them, the way a man wants a woman, and a real woman wants a man ... But you wouldn't know about that, would you? All you care about is your precious virginity, isn't it? Because you are a virgin, aren't you, Sara? And not for any good reason, any real reason, but just because you're too goddamned terrified of what might happen if you lost it ...'

'That's not true!' she cried hotly, the pain starting up again inside her. 'That's not true at all. It's none of your business anyway, but if I wanted to go to bed with a man then ...'

She broke off, her mind whirling.

'Then what?'

'Then I should!' she cried defiantly, not caring what she said any longer, wanting only to hurt him as much as he hurt her.

'Oh, you would?' His voice was low, dangerous, but she was beyond caring.

'Yes, I should! Why should you imagine that it's only men who can indulge in casual affairs the way you do?'

The taunt stopped him dead.

'Is that what you think?'

'Yes, it is! I ...'

'Then come here.'

Suddenly he was beside her, and before she could move, he had pulled her roughly into his arms, holding her so tightly that her arms were pinned behind her. With a cold brutality he wrenched her face up to him, bent his head, and kissed her roughly on the mouth.

A shudder went through her whole body. Max pressed himself against her, so that through the thin nightdress she could feel the pulsing hardness of his body, the strength of his muscles. His skin was rough against her face, and his lips forced hers apart. She struggled helplessly, but he held her until he had finished the kiss, until she could feel his body's arousal. Then he pulled back, just a fraction, still holding her tightly, so his face was a few inches from her own. His eyes blazed at her.

'Now,' he said roughly, forcing her to look at him. 'Now, Sara, come to bed with me.'

Her whole body was shaking; her mouth and her arms felt bruised, and her blood seemed to be pounding in her head. Shame and anger fought for possession of her.

'So,' she said bitterly 'that *is* why you came here. Why didn't you say so? Why lie? You're usually more direct in your demands!'

'You want me to be more direct?' he asked harshly.

'No, I don't!' She tried to push him away, but he held her too tightly. 'I want you to go, to let go of me . . .'

'I'm not going. Not until you stop telling lies. Damn it, Sara, you think I'm the liar?'

'I don't care! Leave me alone!'

'When I've finished. And I haven't finished. You're going to learn a few things, Sara, if it kills me. A few things about yourself, about your body. Now, come to bed with me.' And he twisted her arm so sharply that she cried out in pain.

'I will *not*,' she hissed at him. 'I don't want to. I . . .'

'Again, then.'

And he bent her head back, found her mouth as she desperately tried to turn her head away, and he kissed her again, this time less roughly but expertly, deeply, so that she could feel a deep pleasure start to throb through her whole body. Still he held her arms behind her, effortlessly, with a contemptuous ease, so she could not move. With his other hand he began to caress her, bending her body back, so that he could run his hand up the side of her thigh, across the curve of her stomach, and up to the swell of her breasts. A long shudder of desire shook her, and she heard her breath catch in her throat. He groaned, and easily, urgently, his hand slid under the thin cotton and found her naked skin. His fingers stroked and caressed her breasts, and she felt her nipples go hard under his hands. She swayed against him, and he lifted his head. She saw again, through a haze of mounting desire, that fierce dangerous look in his eyes.

'Come to bed, Sara. I want to . . .'

She summoned all her will, and tried to wrest herself from his arms, but his grip on her tightened.

'I want you, Sara, can't you feel it?'

He caught her hand and forced her to touch him, so that she could not doubt him, and she felt her lips part with desire. The light from the fire flickered on his face, shadowing those cold blue eyes, giving all the hard lines of his face a mask of pain mixed with desire, so that she longed to reach up, to kiss his lips, his eyes, but she forced herself not to respond, to keep her hand cold and lifeless against the pulsing of his body. She made herself speak.

'I don't want you, Max I've never . . .'

'Liar.'

He stopped her reply with his mouth, softer this time, gently as if with the same agony of longing she herself felt. He released her hand, so she could have pushed him away, struggled to free herself, but the freedom bound her as compulsion could not. She was going under in a swell of pleasure such as she had never known, would not have believed possible, and Max seemed to sense her response; his body relaxed, the aggression left it; he cradled her in his arms and she let him mould her body to his, as gently at first, timorously, she let herself return his kisses. Slowly she let her hand move over the strong arms, the wide shoulders, she held his hand, and then pressed it against the wild beating of her heart. Her breath came fast, painfully fast, but she loved him so, and it was so good, so sweet . . .

Suddenly he pulled away from her, with a harsh cry like desperation. He held her from him, would not let her touch him, and they were silent. Sara drew in a long shuddering breath; memory came back, and she felt the tears start to her eyes. Gently he bent and kissed them away. He took her hand, and held it against his lips. When he spoke his voice was quite changed; it was broken, ragged with emotion.

'Sara.' He drew her to him. 'Forgive me, please. I didn't mean . . .'

'Max, stop!' She knew she must not let him speak, that

she had to tell him what she felt, make him understand, otherwise she would give in to him, she knew it.

'I can't, Max,' she said shakily. 'You make me want to. But I can't. You're right, you see.' She looked up at him pleadingly, careless of the tears that spilled over on to her cheeks. 'I am old-fashioned, stupid. That was all bravado, before, not true. I'm not a modern woman at all. I'm . . . if I went to bed with someone, it would have to be because . . . because I loved them, and they . . . we . . .' Her voice broke, and he gathered her into his arms.

'No, wait.' She stopped his lips gently with her hand. 'I know it's different for you. I know you want to prove a point, show me I don't have to be so cold, wake me up in a sense. But please, Max, I beg you. Don't do it. Leave me in peace . . .'

'You little fool!' He pressed his lips against her cheek. 'You don't understand. I don't want to do any such thing. What do you take me for, Sara, for God's sake? You think I'm the kind of man who'd force himself into your room at night just out of some cheap desire—or to win some stupid senseless argument? I don't think you're cold, I've known you for what you are from the first moment I touched you, that day in my office. A woman, Sara, with a woman's heart and a woman's body and a woman's mind. A very beautiful woman, Sara, who can drive a man wild with desire. Sara, can't you understand, I'm serious, I . . .'

'Max—no, please!' she cried brokenly. 'I can't bear it! You don't understand. You have no right . . .'

'I have every right.' He tilted her face up to him, and she saw in his eyes something she had never glimpsed before, a deep tenderness, an urgency. Her heart turned over with pain.

'Listen, Sara, I want to tell you something. Today, when I was late—my flight wasn't delayed. That was just an excuse. I had to go somewhere before I came here. Before I saw you again.' He hesitated. 'Sara, I went to see your mother.'

The shock was like icy water; she recoiled. Going behind her back, just as her father had deceived her mother ... she felt blank, unbelieving. She stared at him as if he were a stranger.

'You did *what?*'

'I went to see your mother,' he said steadily. He dropped his gaze. 'I felt I had to talk to someone who really knew you, Sara. I wanted her to persuade you to stay on at work. I wanted to ask her ...'

'How *could* you!' She stared at him in horror. 'You had no right! How dare you go prying into my personal life, talking about me behind my back, you ...'

'Sara, you don't understand. Please.'

'I understand only too well.' She drew herself up, fighting back the tears, icy with shock and anger. 'You can't resist it, can you, Max, playing the amateur therapist? First you trick me into telling you about ... about my parents. Then you take my work apart. Then you try a little sexual therapy—because that's what all this is, Max, isn't it? Why don't you admit it? Or was it just an irresistible challenge, the office ice-maiden, being the one who finally cracked that famous frigid reserve! And now this! Going behind my back ... not even telling me. My mother didn't even know I was leaving. I hadn't told her! That hadn't occurred to you, I suppose?' She backed away from him, her breath coming quickly, her own voice sounding odd and high with emotion, ringing in her ears. He stepped towards her, apparently bewildered, and she pushed him violently away.

'I hate you, Max!' she cried. 'I hate you for this! I'll never forgive you!'

'Will you listen to me a minute, damn you?'

'No,' she cried impetuously, 'I won't! I've listened to you too much already. I listened tonight, and I almost believed you, because you're so ... so plausible, and I'm such a fool. But it's never going to happen again.' She stared at him defiantly, hardly knowing what she said, the hot tears spilling down her cheeks. 'I'm leaving the magazine, Max. As of now. Sue me if you like, I don't care. Do what you like, but I never want to see you again!'

He stared at her for a long moment, his face pale as if

she had struck him, his eyes blazing with pain and anger.

'God damn you, Sara,' he said finally. 'If that's what you want, have it your way. Live with your lies. Run away! For the rest of your life if you like. Why the hell should I care?'

He strode to the door; then he stopped and turned to her, his features contorted with anger.

'And just remember, Sara. When you finally decide to grow up, don't come running to me. As far as I'm concerned, you're finished!'

He half shouted the words. Then he slammed the door violently behind him. The noise was like a pistol shot; it reverberated right through the house.

When he had gone, Sara could not stop shaking. Uncontrollable trembling shook her body; her forehead burned, her head ached, her body felt icy cold. A wave of nausea hit her, and for a while she knelt on the cold tiles of the bathroom floor, waiting wretchedly, thinking she would be sick. But gradually the nausea passed, the trembling lessened. The room was bitterly cold, but the coldness seemed to help to calm her. She got up, and began pacing up and down, back and forth. Time passed, and eventually a thin grey light pierced the windows. She went back into the bedroom, and drew back the curtains there. The first birds were beginning to sing; beyond the metallic waters of the lake there was a thin rose line on the horizon. From here she could just see the path she had taken that afternoon; it disappeared behind shrubs and trees; she thought of the maze, of the cold acrid scent of the yew as he had pushed her back against it, of the warmth of his mouth and skin.

She would have to leave; now she could not possibly stay. She felt betrayed, used, but worse than that, curiously violated; no one knew about her father, no one. But her mother would have told Max, she was sure of it; he knew now, and she feared him for it.

Quickly she dragged out her suitcase, packed her clothes, dressed. For an hour she fell asleep, sitting awkwardly in the chair by the cold ashes of the fire. At seven she woke, aching and stiff. Carefully, not making a sound,

she opened her door and crept along the landing, down
the wide galleried stairs to the hallway. No one was in
sight. Hastily she tried the front doors, but they were
locked; she could not open them. She paused, listening:
there was no sound in the house. Perhaps there was a
back way out? As quietly as she could, glancing over her
shoulder, she took the passageway that led to the back of
the house and the kitchens. Just as she passed the dining
room, the door was flung back. Sara froze.

'I don't believe it!'

Standing framed in the doorway were Deirdre Neal and
Delia. Delia had obviously been weeping; her eyes were
red and swollen, Deirdre's plump arm was around her
shoulders.

Before Sara could speak, Delia gave a muffled cry.

'You . . . you *bitch*!'

She burst into loud sobs, and ran for the stairway.

Deirdre Neal gave Sara a look of vindictiveness mixed
with obvious satisfaction.

'Well, dear,' she said, 'you have turned out to be a
dark horse and no mistake, haven't you? *Not* the way
you're inclined, I'd have said—but then still waters run
deep, so they say. Even so . . . I'd have thought in Sir
Andrew's own house that you might have had the
decency . . .'

'Deirdre.' Piers had come up behind her, his handsome
face troubled and embarrassed. 'For God's sake, go and
calm Delia down, can't you?'

Deirdre gave Sara a scornful look, and disappeared.
Piers glanced quickly along the corridor, drew Sara into
the dining room and shut the door. Sara leaned against it
and dropped her case to the floor. She couldn't take much
more of this, she thought wretchedly. Piers looked at her,
and to her relief obviously decided to ask no questions.
He smiled at her wryly.

'Well,' he sighed, 'You look the way I feel. *That* little
scene's been going on for a good hour. I gather Deirdre's
a very light sleeper. So, what are you proposing to do?
Walk the three miles to the station?'

Sara shook her head wearily.

'Come on,' Piers took her hand, 'I'll take you back to London.'

'No, Piers, please! You mustn't . . . I've caused enough trouble already.'

'Quite a bit,' he said drily. 'I shouldn't worry too much if I were you. Delia's got an incredible sense of survival. But I'm not too keen to stay here myself, never was that fond of thundery atmospheres. So, you wait here, I'll bring the car round to the front. No arguing. There's a side door, just down the passage. Take that.'

Before she could say a word he was gone, and a few minutes later Sara heard the crunch of his sports car's tyres on the gravel. She hurried out to the car, Piers helped her in, and revved the engine. It took only minutes before he was accelerating away down the drive. As the car reached the bend at the head of the avenue, Sara turned to look back at the house. Lights were blazing from upstairs windows; at one of them was a tall dark figure, silhouetted against the panes, watching their departure. Quickly she turned away.

When she returned, the flat was cold, deserted; there was no sign of Jennifer. A film of dust lay over all the furniture, wan light from the grey streets outside came through the grimy windows; the sink was piled with dirty coffee cups and glasses. Sara went straight to the telephone. She dialled the number of Geoffrey's house, and sat there, her address book on her knees, perched awkwardly on the arm of a chair, gazing sightlessly at the windows. The line rang and rang and rang. She put down the phone and re-dialled, the ringing tone echoing in the silence around her. No answer. Tiredly she put down the receiver, and as she did so the address book tumbled to the floor.

Absently she bent to pick it up, and then stopped. A small white card had fallen out of it, and lay, face up, on the carpet. She stared at it for a moment, then, not pausing to think, picked it up and dialled a number.

It rang three times, then a bleary voice answered.

'Bloomin' 'eck, whoever you are, it is Sunday, y'know . . .'

'Clive, it's Sara.'

There was a moment's silence. When it spoke again, the voice sounded more awake.

''Allo, duchess! This *is* a surprise. Fancy comin' over for breakfast?'

She smiled; suddenly she felt better, she felt harder, more resolved, clear what she must do.

'I won't come to breakfast,' she said, 'But I will come to the Seychelles. If you still want me to.'

'Want you to!' A whoop of triumph came down the line. ' 'Course I want you to.'

'No strings, the way you said?'

He laughed. 'No strings, duchess. Just get your bags packed, right? We go Wednesday, all right?' His voice broke into song. '*Leavin' on a jet plane . . .*'

'*Don't know when I'll be back again,*' Sara finished dully, a sudden feeling of fear gripping her stomach.

'Right, duchess!' He paused. 'You won't change yer mind, now?'

Sara shook her head, and let the thin pasteboard card slip from her fingers.

'No, Clive,' she said quietly, 'I shan't change my mind.'

CHAPTER EIGHT

'IN a minute, when the plane banks, you'll see the beach. 'Ang on . . .' Clive leaned across her towards the window. He pointed. 'There you are, see?'

Sara looked; the sea below was a deep impossible blue, endless, without limit. Then suddenly she saw it, just below them, a wide scimitar of silver sand, behind it hills, thick lush forest.

'You'll see the 'otel in a minute. Little thatched roofs— the Almirante. Came here five years ago for *Vogue*, I did. You're goin' to love it, Sara. The best cocktails in the world bar none; grilled lobster on a moonlit terrace, the soft waters of the Orient, lullin' you to slumbers. And me, givin' you 'ell with the cameras.'

He grinned, and refilled her glass with champagne. Sara sighed.

'I can't believe it,' she said. She turned to him. 'I think it's all a dream, I'm going to have to wake up in a minute.'

He patted her hand. 'No dream, duchess.'

'But it seems so far away. Such miles from ... from London.'

'S'not far—six hours. Over the dark continent of Africa, turn left at Madagascar, aim for the blob in the middle of the Indian Ocean, and bob's yer uncle! Several weeks, all expenses paid, at the beautiful people's number one 'ide-away. Can't be bad, can it, Sara?'

'The beautiful people?'

'Certainly. Place is stiff with 'em. Jet-setters every one. It'll be just us, them, an' the turtles ...'

'Well, I just hope I'm going to be able to manage, that's all.' She sighed. 'Just because it worked once, in the studio ...'

'Shut up!' Clive grinned. 'You're a right Jonah, you are, Sara. I know what I'm doin', even if you don't ... it'll be fine, trust me. Coupla days to get a bit of colour back in yer cheeks—you look a bit peaky, as my old mum used to say—then off we go. You wait till you see the clothes they got for you!'

The airport was tiny; just a couple of runways, and a new little white building, shaded by palms and banana trees. The airport staff were all blacks, clad in brilliant white starched uniforms. There seemed no tiresome formalities, or if there were, Clive managed to get round them. In minutes they were through Customs, and outside. Three little jeeps, painted pink and white, with canopies, were drawn up waiting for them, sent specially to meet their flight by the hotel.

They were such a retinue, Sara thought with amusement, as Clive marshalled everyone into the jeeps. So many people, just to take a few pictures! There was Clive and herself; his assistant; Francine, who had come along to do the make-up; Vincent, who would do her hair, and find the locations; and Carla, an American girl from the magazine who was in charge of the clothes. God knew what she would be wearing, Sara thought, as she watched the trunks being loaded on to one of the jeeps; there looked enough clothes to last someone a lifetime!

She felt her heart lift with excitement and apprehension, as she stood in the shade, waiting. She had done the right thing, she was sure of it. It was best to get away, to cut all ties, to put as much distance as she could between herself and all that had happened. To come somewhere strange, with strangers, to do something different, something she'd never done in her life ... surely that would kill all the memories?

She fanned her skin against the warmth of the sun, and looked back towards the runway. London wasn't six hours away, she told herself firmly; it was a lifetime.

'Come on, duchess, quit dreamin'!'

Hurriedly she climbed into the seat of the ridiculous little jeep next to Clive. The driver set off at a lick, steering the vehicle expertly round the bumps and cracks in the narrow dirt road.

'Is it far?' She craned her neck, trying to glimpse the hotel through the thick tangle of palms and undergrowth.

'Five minutes.' Clive winked. 'Then you've got 'alf an hour to unpack, then it's cocktails on the sea terrace, O.K.? The sun's over the yard-arm, not that that matters. But you ought to see a tropical sunset, just for starters.'

The hotel turned out to be every bit as beautiful as Clive had claimed. Long and low, thatched with palm fronds, it consisted of a central complex, with a restaurant and bar and discotheque, surrounded by tiny chalets, each with its own little wooden terrace and garden. A porter took Sara's bags, and her excitement mounting, she followed him down a narrow path through the trees.

''Alf an hour, duchess, right?' Clive called after her, and Sara waved her assent.

Her chalet was on the very edge of the hotel enclosure. Suddenly they came out through the trees, and she saw the sea. She caught her breath at the beauty of it. The sand, pale with millions of tiny crushed shells, reached almost to the little wooden house where she would sleep. That was perched on stilts, backed by palms, its windows looking straight out across the still water. Inside it was simple but luxurious; the floors polished wood, the bed deep and comfortable, the bathroom modern. Iced water was in a flask; there was a huge bowl of fruits, none of which she recognised; by the bed was a vase of pale green and white orchids.

When the porter had gone she unpacked quickly, and then, impatient to be outside, took one of the fruits from the basket and went out on to the raised wooden terrace. She leaned against its pillars and bit into the fruit. It tasted strange, mysterious, very sweet, like nectar, and its pale apricot skin smelled of honey. She breathed deeply, languorously, catching the smell of salt, listening to the ebb and suck of the waters on the sand. How still it was, she thought, how peaceful! No ghost of the past would trouble her here; no dark dreams would come to her in the night. It was perfect.

That evening, just as Clive had promised, they sat on the hotel terrace, drinking an iced punch laden with fresh fruit, and watched the sun go down on the horizon. It went suddenly, with amazing rapidity, for they were close to the Equator. One moment the sky was stained brilliant purples and heavy gold; the next it was black, studded with a myriad stars.

They ate a delicious meal; the chef was Creole, Clive said, the food a bizarre and wonderful mixture of French, New Orleans, and native cooking. There was thick gumbo soup to begin with, brought in a huge pot, smelling intoxicatingly of beans, prawns, and some sharp hot spice Sara did not recognise. Then there was iced mango, tiny grilled slices of swordfish, and the lobsters, caught that afternoon, grilled on a charcoal fire, their shells blackened, their flesh dripping with butter, tasting of the sea. Sara ate ravenously; with the punch her spirits lifted. At the end of the meal, they sipped tiny cups of black coffee, and glasses of Armagnac.

'Good, duchess?' Clive leaned across and touched her

arm lightly. Carla had brought her guitar, and now she was singing, a soft low song that mingled with the sound of the waves.

Sara smiled. 'I've never eaten so much in my life,' she sighed ruefully.

Clive grinned. 'Well, don't get fat, that's all. In the stuff you'll be wearing . . .'

'When do we start?' Sara yawned.

'Day after tomorrow. Need a day to get over the flight. Vincent's got to find the right locations. Then off we go. If you're good, I'll take yer swimmin' tomorrow.'

'Are there sharks?'

Clive laughed. 'Only two-legged ones.' He gestured to a large party across the other side of the terrace. 'Recognise 'im?' Sara shook her head. There were several beautiful women at the table, two older men, and another about forty. His hair was sleeked back, shiny with brilliantine. His white shirt, open to the waist, revealed several gold chains nestling in the thick matted hair of his tanned muscular chest. As if he sensed Sara's glance, he turned and looked at her for a moment; a heavy face, slightly dissolute, dominated by piercing black eyes.

'Ricardo Monti.' Clive winked. 'That's his yacht down by the beach. South American playboy, old style. A string of polo ponies and a string of ex-wives. Stay out of 'is way, Sara.'

Sara shivered. She didn't need that piece of advice, she thought; the man looked hateful, and so did the party with him. Their loud orders for more champagne, their bursts of laughter were all that spoiled the quiet and peace of the place.

She stood up.

'I'm going to bed now,' she said. 'I'll see you all in the morning.'

Clive kissed her cheek, Carla blew her a kiss and went on strumming her guitar. Quickly Sara left them. She wound her way through the paths, heavy with the scent of bougainvillea, and went out on to the beach. She took off her shoes and stood there a while in the moonlight, letting the dry cool sand run through her toes. Gently the sea lapped the shore; out in the bay, at anchor, was the yacht Clive had mentioned. How odd! This afternoon she hadn't even noticed it.

She looked at it for a moment, her brow wrinkling with displeasure. Lights blazed over the water from its windows, across the still air came the blare of a transistor. For some reason, the yacht's presence disturbed her, unsettled her.

Max! she thought, and suddenly the need for him was acute, agonising, like a stab in the side. She remembered the pain, the confusion on his face that night in her bedroom, the odd broken reaching gesture he had made towards her, the truth in those dark watchful eyes. She had said she hated him; her skin burned with self-hatred at the memory. How could she have told such a lie?

Sadly she turned back towards her chalet. If only she could begin again, she thought miserably, wipe out all the past, unravel it. But you couldn't do that anyway, she thought. Nothing could change the fact that Max didn't love her, however much he might have once wanted her. Why, by now he might be engaged to Delia.

She went inside, but the room now felt hot and stuffy. Not even five thousand miles would lay Max's ghost, she thought, as slowly she began to undress. Distance wouldn't do it, neither would time. Nothing would ever change.

She climbed into bed. The pale orchids were already dying.

After the first day, the time seemed to go by very quickly. They worked in the early mornings, before it became too hot, had a siesta after lunch, and then usually went swimming in the evenings. The pictures went well, and Clive was pleased, she could see that. Sometimes she grew impatient, it all took so long—holding a pose, keeping looking natural, or sultry, or bored, or haughty, or whatever act Clive deemed suitable for the clothes, the location. But she enjoyed herself; it was a good group, she thought, warm and friendly, hard-working, everyone good at their jobs, patient with her, helping her learn.

Ricardo Monti's yacht had disappeared the day after

they arrived, and for some reason that had made her feel better, lighter hearted. But still nothing could quite ease the ache in her heart; it stayed there always, a dull pain, sometimes flaring up suddenly, without warning. One night she tried to write Max a letter; she sat in her room late into the night, covering the pages with writing. In the morning she tore them all into tiny pieces and threw them into the sea. What could she say? She heard his voice in her dreams, clear and harsh. *It's finished, Sara. Finished.*

They had been there a week. Ten days. She had posed in bikinis, in silk shirts with bare legs, the silk carefully wetted so it clung to her skin; in the mountains, with a group of village children; by the turtle rocks; in the sea; on the beach in a long taffeta ballgown, her arms dripping diamonds, the dawn just rising . . . After that shot, which took hours to set up because of the difficult lighting, they all went back to the hotel for breakfast. Clive looked tired, restless.

'Nearly in the bag, duchess,' he said, over the coffee. 'There's a couple more shots I want tomorrow, then that's it. Back to 'orrible old London.' He sighed. '*And* I 'aven't got much further with you, 'ave I? I dunno, I must be losin' me form.'

Sara smiled. 'You said you were a gent, and you've been a gent. I'm very grateful.'

'So.' He looked at her keenly. 'Was it worth it, then?'

'Of course.'

He grinned. ''Aven't mended that broken 'eart of yours, though, 'ave I?'

Sara looked away.

'Absence makes the 'eart grow fonder, that it, Sara?'

She felt the familiar dart of pain. No, she thought, that wasn't it. It didn't even feel like absence; Max felt close, all the time, locked in her heart; so near and so impossibly distant. What difference did it make, London or the Indian Ocean? Nothing changed.

'Well,' Clive stood up, 'I'm not goin' to work you today, Vincent an' me are goin' off to find these last locations. Francine's got a touch of sunstroke, silly cow, or an 'angover or somethin', and Carla's got a date with some bloke in the next chalet. So you're on yer own today, duchess. That all right with you?'

'Fine.' She stood up. 'I'm going to look for shells. I might go swimming.'

Clive was just going; he turned.

'Watch out for sharks!' He winked, and gestured to the bay. Sara had her back to it, and she swung round. Anchored a little way out, its pennants fluttering, was a white yacht. She recognised it at once. Ricardo Monti's.

She went for a walk that morning, going deliberately in the opposite direction to the yacht. She told herself it was foolish, but still she felt much better when it was out of sight around the curve of the headland. She found a beautiful conch shell, watched the native fishermen drag in their nets laden with tiny silver fishes.

For a long while she sat in the cool shade of the palms, listening to the rustle of their dry leaves, to the lap of the water. She tried to force herself to be practical, for the idyll was nearly over. She had to plan, she thought, decide what she would do when she went back to London. But her thoughts would not settle; they circled and re-circled, and under them always was one thought, Max. She saw him again as she had first seen him at work, his head bent over his papers, his long thin fingers tapping irritably with a silver knife against a list on which her own name was circled. She saw him standing, tall and dark against the hedges of a maze. She thought of his childhood, so like and so unlike her own, of a distrustful little boy, a quick, unpredictable, frightening man.

Hugging the memories to her, she went back to her cabin to change for lunch. Just as she was getting ready there was a tap on the door, and one of the porters brought in a letter on a silver salver. Sara took it up eagerly, a sudden wild hope rising up unbidden; but it died, as she recognised her mother's writing.

That was odd, she thought, quickly slitting the envelope open. Her mother rarely wrote; she had the address of the hotel only in case of some emergency ... and it was a long letter, written over a week before, its pages closely covered in her mother's small back-sloping writing. She took it out on to the terrace to read, peering at the words in the brilliant light that danced on the paper. There was her mother's usual local news; what the neighbours were doing, her cousins . . . Suddenly she went numb, a name leapt at her from the page. *Now, Sara dear, I want to tell you about Max.*

Suddenly she felt cold, afraid, but she forced herself to read on, her eyes skimming the pages impatiently. A long description of his visit, how much her mother had taken to him, such charm, such gentleness . . . She stopped, read on with mounting disbelief, to the end, then turned back again to the last page.

Sara dear, this isn't very easy for me to write. We're not as close as we should be—I don't know why, probably my fault, though I tried and it wasn't easy. But you know, Sara, sometimes you frighten me, you're so cold, so hard, and it isn't right in a young girl like you. I know you judge your father harshly, and feel he let us down and so on, and maybe that's made you wary of men, I don't know. But the fault wasn't all on his side, you know, though I wouldn't have admitted that once. Still, a lot of water's gone under the bridge, and maybe now I see things a bit clearer than I did.

You see, we were very happy once, laughed a lot, even when there was no money. Things were fine until I had you, and then— well, there were all those months in the hospital, and when I came back I wasn't the same, I see that now. Something had gone wrong with me, Sara, and I couldn't be a proper wife to him. I wanted to, but I couldn't. And then—well, he was patient at first, but eventually the inevitable happened. He found someone else, as you know, and they've a family, they're very happy, I hear. I don't see him, of course, not since the divorce, and the lawyers being so vicious about everything. I think he had to do that, Sara, cut himself off from the past, pretend it didn't happen, and maybe it's for the best in the end.

But I can't bear to think that you might let that blight your life. I don't want to see you making the mistakes I did, Sara. And I thought your Max was such a good man, with all your best interests at heart. Seeing him out of the blue like that quite made my week, I can tell you. Of course he said he'd come about that silly resignation business, but I wasn't taken in by that, oh no!

All those questions he asked, and I answered him straight out, because I just **knew***, Sara, straight off, he was the man for you. So, I don't know why you've gone off now, and of course you wouldn't say much on the phone, but I hope it's given you time to think. He* **cares** *about you, that's why he came, I'm sure of it, and he looked so tired and worried my heart quite went out to him. So, all I'll say now is give him a chance, Sara; don't cut him out, the way you do people, and close up and go into that shell of yours. Don't make my mistake, and then spend rest of your life regretting it—will you promise me you'll give it a try?*

Sara put the letter down in her lap. The pages fluttered in the breeze. She closed her eyes, feeling the hot sun burning down on her face, and she felt as if she would choke. Her mother wrote exactly as she spoke, she thought, and for her to have written such a letter, after all these years, after all that bitterness . . . what must it have cost her? Her heart turned over with pity, thinking of her, so many thousands of miles away, so hopeful, and so deluded! It wasn't true, of course, any of it. Her mother was reading into Max's visit all the things she would like to see happen; what she had lost she wanted now for her daughter.

She felt the hot tears start to her eyes and spill over on to her cheeks as remorselessly it all came back; her father and Max, the only two men she had even wanted, and both of them lost to her. The pain of it racked her; how stupid, how blind, to think she could escape it on some island, however enchanted. An awful doubt stole into her mind; could her mother be right? *Could* Max have cared for her—just a little? If he had, if he might have done, it only made the pain worse; she covered her face with her hands. No, her mind cried, it wasn't true, he had not, but even that certain knowledge could not ease the agony of being without him. All those lies she had told herself, all that compulsive working. What was it he had said, in the garden, when he spoke of marriage? To be with someone one loved, to share children. Always. That was what she really wanted, had always wanted. And now it would never happen.

Blindly, hardly knowing where she was going, leaving

the letter behind, she raced down to the beach. It was noon, and the sun was oppressively hot, it burned her bare skin above the scanty swimsuit, but she didn't care. The beach was deserted; she walked along it, seeing nothing, hearing nothing, the tears still flowing hot against her cheeks. She walked for a long time, leaving the hotel far behind her, going away from the village, the fishermen, wanting only somewhere silent, deserted, where she would meet no one. At last she stopped, and flung herself down on the hot sand near some palms, her back to the sea. Then she let herself cry, awful racking sobs that seemed dredged up from the soul of her being, all the tears she never cried for her childhood, all the tears for the years of loneliness, all the tears for Max. When it was finished, she went into the sea and let it wash salt tears with salt water, let it saturate her hair, flow over her body, until she felt cleansed, calmer. Then she went back to the beach and sat in the shade, staring out to sea. She was facing west, she thought, across Africa, towards England, towards London, towards Max.

'Very beautiful.'

She had been so absorbed in her thoughts she had heard no one approach. She started and swung round, as a man stepped between her and the sun, throwing her face into shadow.

She recognised him at once; he was wearing only brief swimming trunks, hitched low on his hips, but his neck was still festooned with gold chains, the brilliantined hair glistened in the sun. Ricardo Monti.

'Don't get up, my sweet, you'll ruin the picture.'

He smiled, showing a flash of even white teeth, and before she could move, he sat down beside her. She saw his eyes run over her appraisingly, with a cold sensuality, lingering on the curve of her breasts and her thighs.

'You look a little more composed now.' Another flash of the white teeth. 'Earlier you were a little *triste*, were you not?'

He had a deep voice, an accent she couldn't quite place, not English in intonation but with an imposed correctness.

She stared at him, and he spread his hands in a gesture of mock contrition.

'I was watching—you will forgive me, but it is not every day one sees a beautiful lady in distress. So I waited a little—I know these women's moods, they pass eventually, do they not? And then, I thought, perhaps now I could be of assistance.' He held out his hand. 'I must introduce myself. Ricardo Monti.'

Sara ignored the hand, and he raised his eyebrows a fraction.

'You would rather be alone, perhaps?'

'Yes, I'm afraid I would.'

He made no attempt to move. To her horror he inched a little closer.

'You are English, I think? It is you who is here doing the modelling, is it not?'

'Yes.' She turned her face away.

'For *Vogue*, perhaps? My cousin, she is the editor of Paris *Vogue*. I know many people in the world of fashion. But none so lovely.'

Sara turned to him with a look of disgust. Did he really imagine she would respond to that kind of remark, such insincere flattery? Obviously he did, because he stretched out his hand, and touched her hair lightly.

'So beautiful, the English girls,' he murmured. 'Such hair, like silk, such eyes, such skin. But you have not English eyes.' He attempted to look deeply into them as Sara fixed him with a haughty stare. 'You have Latin eyes,' he murmured, 'they speak of much, your eyes—of love and sadness. Is that why you cry, little one?'

'Please.' She attempted to stand up, but he caught her arm and stayed her. 'This is ridiculous. If you won't go I shall go back to the hotel.'

'Don't do that.' He favoured her with another flashing smile. 'Stay and talk to me. You interest me, little one.'

'Well, you don't interest me,' Sara said hotly. 'Now will you please leave me alone?'

'So haughty!' His hand began to caress her arm. 'I like that. I like a woman of spirit. We could be friends, you and I, I feel it—here.' He pressed his free hand to his heart with a gesture so theatrical, so reminiscent of a bad film, that Sara almost laughed.

'Would you please let go of me?' she said. 'This is getting absurd. I . . .'

His grip on her arm tightened, and she saw suddenly something in his eyes that frightened her, a viciousness and a vanity, just the hint of a threat. Quickly she looked back down the beach; it was deserted.

'Just one little kiss, eh, before we part. Where's the harm in that? We're quite alone, you and I . . .' He leaned towards her, sweat and oil gleaming on his tanned skin; his breath smelled sweet and unpleasant, his mouth was close to her skin, as if he meant to press it against her neck.

'Please——' she recoiled violently.

As she did so she realised to her relief that they were not, after all alone. Someone, a woman, wearing a loose silk dress, a vivid scarf and a wide-brimmed hat that shielded her face from the sun, was coming down a path through the palms behind them. As she saw them, she stopped.

'Ricardo!' Her voice was crisp, light, unmistakably English. 'Really, you are impossible!'

He moved so fast it was comical, Sara thought. In one swift movement he dropped Sara's arm like a hot coal, was on his feet, and had put a respectable distance between them.

'My darling, I . . .'

'Oh, honestly, Ricardo, don't make it any worse.' The woman laughed and the laugh tugged at Sara's memory. She had heard that laugh somewhere before, she could not place it . . .

'When will you learn?' The woman advanced towards them, moving gracefully through the trees, her face still in shadow. 'Now go away and sulk or whatever it is you do when your vanity's wounded. I'm not going to say one word to you for the rest of today.'

'*Carissima* . . .' He hesitated, fixing her with an expression of wounded, spaniel-like adoration.

'Don't *carissima* me, it won't cut any ice whatsoever.

And don't try and apologise either—I'll do that for you. I'll see you back at the hotel, later.'

He hesitated a moment longer, and then turned sulkily, and began to walk back up the beach. The woman laughed again, and turned to Sara.

'Did he frighten you? I'm so sorry. He simply *cannot* resist women, and he *won't* believe they can resist him. It's all that Latin lover nonsense; too many Rossano Brazzi films, *I* think. Very unhealthy—but quite endearing if you know how to handle it. So will you accept my apologies? I do hope he hasn't spoiled your afternoon. Would you . . .'

She stopped suddenly, peering at Sara.

'I don't believe it. It's Sara, isn't it? Sara Ford?'

Sara stared back; the sun was dazzling her eyes, she still could not see the woman's face under the wide hat. She stood up.

'I'm sorry . . .'

The woman laughed. 'You've forgotten me. Yet we always seem to meet under the oddest circumstances. I'm Ishbel, Max's mother.' She smiled wryly. 'Fitzherbert that was. Soon, I'm afraid, Monti.'

Sara stared at her in horror and disbelief. Ishbel, unconcerned, came across and sat down beside her, kicking off her sandals and stretching luxuriously. She fumbled in her bag and brought out her cigarettes and holder.

'Isn't it *beautiful* here?' She looked out across the bay to where the white yacht was anchored. 'I come every year, first to St. Moritz, where I'm fearfully energetic, and then here—wonderful. Nothing but lotus-eating.' She turned to Sara. 'But I must say, my dear, it's an enormous surprise to find you here—oh, I don't mean Ricardo, that goes on all the time—but the Seychelles. The last place I'd have expected to see you.' She paused. 'Max told me you'd left, of course. Are you drowning memories?'

Sara looked down. She hesitated. 'I'm here to do some modelling,' she said finally. 'Just a one-off thing. We're leaving soon.'

Ishbel looked surprised. 'Modelling? But I thought you were a writer.'

'I am, but this came up, and at the time it seemed a good idea . . .' Sara heard her own voice trail away; Ishbel looked at her sharply. She seemed about to say something, hesitated, and stopped. There was a long silence, while Ishbel sat quite still smoking her cigarette, looking out to the great white yacht in the bay. She seemed to be calculating something.

'Have you been here long?' she asked finally.

'About ten days.'

'I see.' She paused. 'You were at Andrew Waterlow's, weren't you? That must have been just before you left, then.' She smiled impishly. 'He'd invited me, as a matter of fact. I quite wanted to go, but—well, I had to keep an eye on Ricardo, and that house has rather a lot of painful memories for me. Did Max tell you?'

Sara felt embarrassed. 'He mentioned something, yes,' she said reluctantly.

Ishbel sighed. 'I thought he might have done. Look, my dear,' she turned impulsively, and put her hand on Sara's arm, 'do you mind if I say something? I don't know what went on between you and Max, of course, and he would never tell me. But I regret it very much if something's gone wrong between you. Such a waste!'

She looked closely into Sara's face, those odd blue eyes, so like her son's, searching her reaction.

'Tell me, my dear,' she said abruptly, 'do you like Max?'

Sara knew it would be useless to lie; it would be detected immediately. She felt the blood rush to her cheeks, and dropped her gaze.

'Yes,' she said softly, 'I do.'

'Well then, don't you think you ought to do something about it?' Ishbel said crisply. 'He's devoted to you, you know. All that business at Andrew's—it nearly broke him. I've been terribly worried about him. He's drinking far too much, which isn't like him at all. Not getting any sleep—miserable, angry, impossible.' She smiled. 'That's why I delayed my arrival here—Ricardo's only just picked me up at Madagascar—I should have been here a week ago, but I was so worried about Max . . .' She broke off.

Sara stared at her in bewilderment.

'But I thought . . .' she faltered 'I thought that he—that he and Delia . . .'

'Delia!' Ishbel gave a snort of derision. 'Oh, come on, Sara. Max may have played the field in his time, but Delia! Don't be ridiculous, my dear.'

She stood up, brushing the sand from her dress.

'Walk back to the hotel with me,' she said warmly. 'Come on. And stop looking so miserable. Life isn't such a tragedy, you know.'

She took Sara's arm, and slowly they began to walk back down the beach.

Sara's mind was racing. Could this be true? she thought. She felt that old fierce hope start up in her heart again, and at once tried to quash it. Ishbel couldn't be right, she thought. After all, she herself admitted she didn't know Max very well, that he didn't confide in her . . .

'You know what I think is the most important thing for a woman, Sara?' Ishbel stopped suddenly. 'Knowing her own mind. You have to know what you want, and who you want, and never be too proud or too blind to admit it to yourself. It's not always easy, of course.' She smiled, a sad amused smile, and gestured out to the yacht in the bay. 'You must think I'm mad, of course. Why should you listen to me? Advice, from a fifty-five-year-old woman who's about to marry Ricardo—it is a bit absurd, isn't it?' She gave a light laugh tinged with bitterness. 'But you see, Sara, I know what's best for me. Ricardo can give me all the things I need—for a while. He's rich, he can be more amusing than you might expect. He makes his protestations of undying love, of course, and we both know quite well he doesn't mean a word of it. Any more than I do.' She sighed, her beautiful face quite clear and calm. 'So,' she said, beginning to walk again, her face turned away from Sara, 'I settle for second best. I forfeited the right to anything better than that long ago—before Max was born perhaps. And now——' she shrugged. 'This suits me well enough. But it wouldn't suit you, Sara, I knew that the first time I laid eyes on you. And it wouldn't suit

Max. With him, it has to be all or nothing. He was always that way.'

They had reached the hotel, and Ishbel turned to her with a warm smile, taking her hand.

'So think about what I've said. For Max's sake—and your own.' She paused. 'I love Max very much,' she said softly, 'in my own way. And I would like to see him .. happy.'

She glanced away for a second, up at the hotel terrace. Ricardo was there; he waved, and she turned and waved back at him, gaily.

She turned back to Sara, her face serious, her voice light.

'*What* was that line from that poem? The one about the swimmer?' Her brow furrowed, then cleared. 'Oh, I remember. *Not waving but drowning.*'

She kissed Sara lightly on the cheek. Above them the palm fronds rattled drily.

'I shan't see you again here,' she said. 'We're sailing this afternoon. Call Max when you get home, won't you? When is it you're leaving?'

'The day after tomorrow.'

Ishbel smiled. 'Remember what I said. Don't leave it too late, Sara.'

She turned and hastened up the wooden steps to the terrace, with the grace of a much younger woman. Sara stood and stared after her, quiet, listening to the silence. Ricardo took her in his arms, whispered something into her ear; Ishbel laughed, a clear light laugh that carried down to the beach. She tossed her scarf over her shoulder, a clear flash of kingfisher blue in the brilliant air, a dart of colour, like a bird's wing passing. She turned and waved to Sara, then they disappeared from view.

Slowly Sara walked back to her chalet. Her mother's letter was still there, but the maids must have been in to clean, for someone had picked it up, placed it carefully on a table, and weighted it with a smooth round white pebble from the beach, so it would not be blown away.

Sara put the letter safely away; she did not need to look at it again, already she almost knew it by heart. She stood on the terrace, looking out to the sea, holding the smooth piece of stone in the palm of her hand. She admired them, and she pitied them both, she thought, Ishbel and her mother. Her mother with her sad candour, Ishbel with her brave carelessness. Compared to them, she was a coward, a timorous fool.

She would telephone Max, she thought suddenly. When she returned to London.

CHAPTER NINE

THERE was only one flight out of the island each day, in the early morning. They took it, just as Clive had planned, the little retinue, the camera cases, the trunks of clothes, all winding their way through the trees in the soft rose light of the morning. In the jeep behind Carla strummed her guitar.

'*Leavin' on a jet plane* . . .'

'*Don't know when I'll be back again* . . .' chorused Francine and the others. Their laughter echoed through the trees.

Clive turned to her and gave her a wink. 'Sorry it's all over, duchess?'

'A bit.'

'Glad you came, though?'

Sara nodded, and turned her face away. A parakeet flew through the branches, the low sun catching the flame green and yellow of its wing.

'Yes, very glad,' she said softly.

It was a British Airways flight. As they boarded the plane the air hostesses, in their red, white and blue uniforms, plied them with English newspapers and magazines, a sleeping mask, earphones, airplane slippers.

'*Good* morning, sir. I hope you have a nice flight.'

Clive grinned as they settled into their seats in the forward section of the plane; muzak was playing, slightly out of sync, on edge, supposedly calming, in fact irritating. Clive grinned.

'Heigh-ho,' he sighed. 'Might as well be back in borin' old London already. I just 'ope there's a good movie. I'm whacked!'

Before they took off the stewardess came round, demonstrated the safety precautions, checked the seat-belts.

'If you wouldn't mind keeping your seat-belts fastened during the flight, sir? Madam?' She gave them a cool professional smile. 'We're expecting some turbulence.'

'Bleedin' 'eck?' Clive gave the girl a flirtatious look. 'Get the champagne to us quick, love. I've got a bad 'ead for heights.'

The girl smiled.

'Immediately after take-off, sir. There's nothing to worry about.'

Suddenly the engines roared into life, the muzak increased in volume. Sara leaned back in her seat, gripping the arms. She was not nervous of flying, but for some reason she felt tense, on edge. They were cleared for take-off immediately, and the 707 mounted fast, with a roar of power. It banked, turning over the island, and Sara, leaning against the window, had a brief glimpse of the hotel, the shimmering blue diamond sea, the long crescent of white sand. There was no yacht in the bay; the beach was deserted.

The stewardess brought the champagne promptly, and a tray of tiny canapés. Sara took one, but left half of it. The champagne tasted sour, acid; the pastry dry and stale.

'Want to watch the movie, duchess?'

Sara shook her head, and Clive shrugged, and plugged in his own earphones, settled back in his seat. Sara sat quietly by him, gazing dully at the huge screen in front of them. The film was a musical; without sound the images seemed overblown, garish, absurd. The images flickered before her eyes; she hardly saw them.

Since Ishbel had spoken to her, she had thought of nothing but Max. He was with her, waking and sleeping, as powerful in her thoughts as in her dreams. Her resolve to contact him, so firm at first, had become fitful. From minute to minute she alternated between hope and despair, between courage and cowardice. She gripped her palms tightly, digging her nails painfully into her skin. If she could just see him briefly, she thought. Just so that she could explain, tell him the truth—well, not all the truth, perhaps, but some of it, enough for him to understand. He would never contact *her*, not after what had happened. And if she didn't see him, speak to him, he would think she had spoken the truth, that she did hate him . . .

Without warning, the plane suddenly dropped, then lifted again. Her stomach turned over; from behind her she heard Francine give a squeal of alarm. The plane steadied once more; the captain's voice came over the intercom, calm, soothing; they were experiencing light turbulence, as expected. If passengers would remain in their seats . . .

Sara rested her head back against the seat. She felt curiously uncaring, willing to go with the fates. The plane gave another sickening lurch, and even Clive registered momentary alarm. Sara felt cold, icy; if it crashed, so be it. Except then that Max would never know . . .

They had lost a lot of height; the plane was in thick cloud now, wisps of white coiled and drifted past the windows. On the screen in front of her the bright images leapt and danced silently, madly. Sara reached for the newspapers the stewardess had brought, and began to leaf through them absently. The news on the front pages, of strikes, protests, meant nothing to her, seemed like news of a foreign country, was distant, supremely unimportant.

Then suddenly something caught her eye as she turned the page. Quickly she turned back. The rest of the page— the gossip column—was blurred, indistinct. She saw only one photograph, one item. The occasion was some film award ceremony, and the party afterwards. In the centre of the photograph was Delia Waterlow; she had had her hair cut in a new short style; she was wearing an off-the-shoulder dress and smiling at the camera. By her side, dark, attentive, was Max. *Max Christian*, ran the heavy black copy, *long one of London's most eligible bachelors, whose name in the past has been linked with* . . . there followed a long list of names and titles, with inset headshots of some of the more celebrated . . . *has been seen three times this week with Delia Waterlow, only daughter of . . . friends of Delia's tell me the engagement announcement is imminent* . . .

The words jumped and jumbled themselves on the page before her. Sara closed her eyes. In the blackness images swam before her like ghosts, Max and Delia, Delia and Max; a strand of long fair hair on a dark shoulder . . . *Let go*, she thought in agony; *let go*. His mother had been wrong; her mother had been wrong, all the hopes, all the uncertainties of the last two days had been pointless, barren.

She opened her eyes again and looked down again at the paper, and this time another item, in smaller print, swam before her eyes.

'The funeral was held yesterday, at Golders Green, of Geoffrey Fletcher, former editor of *London Now*, and numerous other publications. His death came suddenly, after a long illness; the Memorial Service will be held at St. Bride's Church, Fleet Street, next Wednesday . . .'

'Oh no!' Sara covered her face with her hands, feeling the tears start to her eyes. Quickly she stood up; Clive looked at her in surprise, and lifted his headphones.

'You all right, duchess? Feelin' sick?'

The plane gave another abrupt lurch as he spoke.

'Yes. Please, Clive, can you let me out . . .'

He stood up, and helped her pass between the narrow gap, taking her hand.

' 'Ang on, Sara. You look white as a sheet. I'll get the stewardess. Wait a minute . . .'

Without hesitating she pushed past him, and moved as quickly as she could down the gangway, unsteady on her feet, lurching from side to side as the plane lifted and sank. Pale nervous faces looked up at her as she passed, but she was oblivious to them. She knew only that she had to be on her own, had to hide . . .

'Excuse me, madam, are you feeling unwell?'

The young stewardess was blocking her path.

She had reached the back of the plane now, where the turbulence was most acutely felt; the tail section tipped and swung, the noise of the engines drummed in her ears.

'Please, if I could just . . .'

'You would be better in your seat, madam. Can I help you back to your place?' The young woman put an arm around her. 'If you feel sick, madam, I can . . .'

'Please, let me go past.'

The plane felt stiflingly hot, suffocating, suddenly the air felt thick with fear. Several passengers farther down the plane reached up and pressed their call buttons. The plane lurched again, and dropped sickeningly, throwing the stewardess against Sara heavily. Sara felt the blood rush to her head; she felt very hot, then suddenly icy cold. The plane was still dropping, she could feel it, the air seemed filled with a grey mist. The lights had gone out. She could feel something wet on her face, and there was an acrid smell, like the smell of the yew hedges in the garden. Faces swam before her eyes; she must find the way out, she thought; she swayed.

'Max!' she heard her own voice cry out, as if from a great distance. A deep grey void had opened up, it seemed to suck her into its vortex. She was falling.

' 'Ere, Sara. Duchess. You O.K. now?'

She opened her eyes, but the lights blinded her. She closed them again.

'Come on, love. Nearly give me an 'eart-attack, you did!'

He was patting her hand; then someone lifted her head, there were rustling movements, then something cold against her face, a biting pungent smell that jolted her into awareness.

'Bloomin' 'eck! Smellin' salts. They work.'

She heard Carla's voice. 'I told you they would. You should have tried them earlier. Never fails. Honey, are you all right now? You gave us quite a fright, let me tell you.'

'Where am I? What happened? The plane . . .' She looked around her in bewilderment. She was wrapped in a scarlet woolen blanket, lying on a narrow bed in a small room. Clive and Carla were hovering over her; a St. John

Ambulance nurse was in the doorway.

Clive knelt down and took her hand.

'You fainted, duchess. Just like that—out like a light. Gawd! I thought you was never comin' round . . .'

'But where am I?'

'London, darlin'. 'Eathrow, where else?'

'But the plane . . . I thought the plane . . .'

'The plane was fine. A few minutes more and we was out of it. That was the worst bit, when you did yer Victorian maiden stuff—it was all right after that.'

She struggled with the blanket and sat up; as she did so the memory came back; she looked at Clive unseeingly.

'Listen, Carla an' me are goin' to take you 'ome, right?'

'The quicker the better, I'd say.' Carla looked at her critically. 'You think it was something she ate, not just the flight? She's as white as a ghost.'

'Can you walk, duchess? We can get a chair if you need it . . .'

'No, no, I'm fine.'

She swung her legs on to the floor, and tried to stand up. But they would hardly support her, they gave, and Clive caught her.

' 'Ere,' he said, 'lean on me, Carla'll go ahead with the passports, we'll get you through in no time, love. 'Ang on now.'

He draped Sara's arm over his shoulders and put his own arm firmly around her, so that he supported almost all her weight.

'Now, easy does it. The luggage 'as gone on ahead. Think you can make it?'

Sara nodded. The nurse opened the door for them, and slowly they made their way through Immigration, through Customs. They were waved through without any formalities; it took only a few moments.

Sara hardly registered what was going on. Her legs still refused to obey her, and gratefully she leaned on Clive. The rooms swayed and tilted oddly, the floor surged like the sea.

'Nearly there, duchess. 'Ang on.'

Carla pushed open the doors into the concourse, and the noise of the airport hit them. Behind the barriers people crowded, pushing and jostling. Clive cursed.

'Christmas rush,' he said. 'All gettin' the 'ell out of it for the 'olidays. Carla love, try and get us a taxi for Sara, will you?'

'There's no need. I'm taking her.'

Clive stopped dead as the voice cut across their path. Sara swayed against him. Slowly she lifted her head, to meet a pair of cold dark blue eyes.

'Max!' She stumbled and almost fell, his arms shot out, before Clive could move, and caught her. She felt the strength of his arms, the soft cloth of his coat against her skin.

'What the hell's happened? Is she ill?'

'She's O.K., I think.' It was Carla who spoke. 'We had a ghastly flight, Sara fainted. She's just come round.'

'Oh God!' He swore, and his arms tightened around her. He bent his head so that he could look down into her face. 'Sara, I have my car. Can you walk?'

'Yes,' she stammered. 'I'm fine, Max, really. You don't need to . . .'

'You're patently not fine. Here.' With one easy movement he swept her off her feet and into his arms, cradling her like a child against his heart. He turned back to Clive, who had been watching this scene closely. Clive gave Sara a wry, lopsided grin.

'Right,' he said lightly, 'that's you taken care of, isn't it, duchess?' He winked. 'Told yer I was off me form, didn't I?' He gave Max a mock salute. 'Look after 'er, Max, won't yer? She's got a big future, that one.'

'I know that.' Max was looking at him coldly, suspiciously. He struggled to be polite. 'Thank you for all you've done, Clive. I'll ring you in the morning.'

'Right, squire. 'Bye, Sara.'

He blew her a kiss, and Max's mouth tightened. Then he and Carla turned, and disappeared into the crowd.

'Right, come on,' said Max, his voice grim. Carrying her effortlessly, he began to shoulder his way through the crowd.

Weakly Sara protested. 'Please, Max, put me down, I'm all right really . . .'

The blue eyes flashed. 'Be quiet,' he said abruptly. 'From now on, you listen to me.'

When they reached his car he lifted her into it with great gentleness, and tucked a rug around her. Then he got in and started the engine, accelerating away without another word.

He drove for some miles along the motorway into London without speaking, his eyes intent on the road. Sara was grateful for the silence, for the time to collect her thoughts. Gradually the warmth of the car revived her. She still felt curiously numb, exhausted, fatalistic. But at least her mind was beginning to work again. As they approached the outskirts of the city, he turned to her.

'Were there newspapers on the plane?'

She nodded dumbly. His mouth set in a hard line.

'I thought so.' He paused. 'So you know about Geoffrey?' he said in a gentler tone.

'Yes.'

He glanced at her, his face kind.

'I'm sorry, Sara. I knew you would take it hard. But it was better this way, believe me. It's what he would have wanted. He was very ill, you know. That last operation . . . it didn't work.'

She sighed. 'I know,' she said softly. 'It was a shock, that's all. And I hadn't seen him, you see. I tried to, but he was too ill. So I hadn't seen him since . . .' She broke off.

Max looked away. For a moment she wondered if he would refer to the other item in the same paper; he must have known she would have seen it. But he said nothing; he pulled into the fast lane and accelerated.

'How . . .' She hesitated. 'How did you know we should be on that flight?'

'*You* on that flight,' he corrected her, his eyes never leaving the road. He smiled dourly. 'Well, you'd covered your tracks quite successfully, but not successfully enough. My mother wired me.'

'I see.'

'I wonder if you do, Sara.'

He glanced in his rear mirror and swung the car across to the exit. Sara looked up in surprise; they were still in West London.

'Where are we going?' she said hesitantly, giving him a nervous look.

'To my house. Where else?'

'But . . .' He cut off her weak protest with a glance. For a moment she saw the fire in his eyes, then he turned away again. From deep inside her, she felt begin again that familiar fluttering of hope mixed with desire. But she cut it off. She must not let herself feel that, she thought desperately. It hurt too much. After all, it was there, in black and white in the newspaper. Perhaps that was why he had come to meet her. Perhaps he wanted to break the news to her himself, perhaps he thought, after all that had happened, that he owed it to her in some way.

As if he sensed her thoughts, Max suddenly reached across. He was wearing leather gloves; gently he took her cold hand, lifted it, then replaced it on her lap.

'We're nearly there.'

At his house he helped her out of the car, supported her as she walked up the pathway and steps. In the hall he paused.

'Can you manage the stairs? We'll go up to my study. There's a fire there, and some brandy.'

Before she could protest or demur, he led her up the wide curving staircase and into a room she had never seen before. Books lined the walls from floor to ceiling; there was a desk covered with papers; racks of gramophone records.

'Sit down by the fire. I'll take your coat.'

He helped her out of it, every light touch of his hands burning her skin like a flame. Then he turned away to find the brandy, glasses. Sara looked around her curiously; the room was much more his room than those downstairs she had seen at the party. It bore the stamp of his personality. Was this where he spent those evenings alone? she thought suddenly. The evenings when he said he read, or listened to music. Or thought about her.

The memory brought colour back into her cheeks, and Max turned and looked at her approvingly.

'You're reviving,' he said. 'Here, have a little brandy.'

He held the glass to her lips and she sipped it slowly; the golden liquid hit the pit of her stomach like fire. Max smiled.

'We seem to have played this scene before,' he said drily. 'You're improving. As I recall, last time you choked.'

Sara smiled wanly, and he stood for a while looking down at her.

'Do you feel better?'

She nodded.

'I hope you do, because in a minute or two—when I'm quite sure you're not likely to faint, when I can't be accused of taking advantage of your delicate condition— well then, I think I shall kiss you.'

'*What?*' Her eyes widened, moving instinctively to the door.

'No,' he said firmly. 'Perhaps you didn't notice when we came in, but I locked it. The key's in my pocket. This time, Sara, you don't run away.'

Calmly he crossed to the chair opposite her and sat down, his eyes never leaving her face.

'You have some explaining to do,' he said, 'don't you think, Sara?'

'*I* have some explaining to do?' She felt the brandy beginning to give her a little more courage, and with a quick nervous gesture she drained the glass.

'Certainly. Just a few things, you understand. Such as why you left Andrew Waterlow's with Piers; why you went off to the Seychelles without a word, a message.' He paused. 'Why you left me.'

Sara hesitated. 'Max, I . . .'

'Don't prevaricate.'

'All right.' She looked at him defiantly. 'I . . . I could hardly stay at Sir Andrew's, could I, after what had happened? And Piers said he'd drive me.'

'I'm sure he did.'

'And then, when I came back to London—Clive had

asked me to go to the Seychelles before, to model, and I wanted to get away, to have time to think, before I began looking for a new job. That was all.'

'What a remarkable number of obliging young men you seem to have dancing at your disposal,' he said coldly. 'And now perhaps you'll answer the last part of my question.'

'The last part?'

He leaned forward intently. 'Why did you leave me?'

She felt the blood rush to her cheeks and quickly looked away.

'Leave you?' she echoed, unable to keep the edge of bitterness out of her voice. 'I wasn't leaving you. There . . . there was nothing to leave.'

'There was everything to leave.'

He said the words quietly, but with force, and Sara met his eyes reluctantly. She bit her lip, clenched her hands, a chaos of thoughts and memories crowding in on her. She hesitated, but still she could not bring herself to tell him, to admit it all. She was still afraid, she realised, even now.

'Look, Max, please.' She stood up, her voice ragged with tiredness and emotion. 'I don't understand why you brought me here today—why you behave as you do, why you went to my mother—any of it. I'm sorry, very sorry for all the things I said before. I didn't mean them. But it's over now. Can't we forget it? Can't I go?'

He did not move from the chair, but just sat there, watching her for a moment, as if trying to decide whether she were telling him the truth.

'You don't understand why I brought you here?'

She shook her head. 'No!'

'For the same reason I did all the other things you mentioned.' A smile lifted the corners of his lips. 'And a few others beside.'

'And that was?'

He sighed. 'Well, it's really quite simple, Sara. I'm surprised it hasn't occurred to you before.' He paused. 'I love you.'

She stared at him silently. The words were spoken flatly,

as if he were stating the most obvious of facts, as if they were discussing work. They seemed to hang in the air between them as they reverberated through her whole being. She felt again that constriction around her heart, as if something powerful were imprisoned there and were struggling to free itself. He stood up, and came towards her. He had to make an effort to speak.

'I love you, Sara. And I've never said that to another woman in my life.'

Suddenly she felt as if something had broken in her— all the restraint, all the evasions; they fell away unheeded. A wild rush of joy that nothing could stem flooded her heart and her body, lit her face and her eyes.

Max saw the joy there, and hesitated, his eyes still unsure, pained, questioning, as if he were uncertain of her response.

'Sara! My . . . darling.' His voice sounded choked, and he put out his hand with that odd awkward gesture he had made before, as if half afraid that she would knock his hand aside, turn away, reject him.

With one swift movement she was in his arms; they tightened around her, and he let out a low groan of pain and happiness. Quickly, urgently, she reached up to him, seeking his mouth, the kisses she had craved so long, thinking only that she must obliterate that pain, that doubt from his eyes for ever. Their lips met, her eyes closed, and all else was blotted out, erased, unimportant. She cared about nothing any more, about the past, about Delia . . . nothing mattered except this moment and this man in her arms. He held her so tightly she could hardly breathe, but she wanted him to hold her like that forever, never to let her go. Her lips parted sweetly under his, as gently, oh, so gently, he rained kisses on her face, her eyes, her hair. He cradled her in his arms, their hearts seeming to beat as one, peace edged with want seemed to pulse through her veins like blood.

After a little while he drew her head down, so it rested against him just above his heart, and as she listened, felt that wild hammering, keeping time with her own, she knew with great clarity what she must say. No pride now.

'Max.' Her own voice sounded strange to her, changed, a woman's voice she hardly knew.

'Yes?'

He tried to tilt her face up to him, so that he could look into her eyes, but she kept them obstinately lowered, pressed her face against his chest.

The words she wanted to say were pounding in her head, but somehow she could not force her lips to say them. Max reached his hands down, locking them under her hips, pressing her tight against him so that she could feel the fierceness of his want, the same urgency that she felt rising in her own body.

'Max.' She forced herself to speak, for she knew if she delayed any longer she would be beyond words.

'Max,' she said softly. 'I want you so much. I always wanted you, only you, from the very first. If you want, I ... I will go to bed with you. I love you, Max, I love you so much it hurts ...'

'Then look at me.'

Slowly she raised her face and met his eyes.

'Now. Say it again.'

'I want to ...'

'Not that—the other.'

'I love you.'

And she saw at last a joy that answered her own come into those watchful eyes. He pressed her against him, murmuring her name.

'My own darling,' he said softly, his voice roughened. 'Is it so hard to say?'

She looked up at him. 'It was,' she said slowly. 'I can think it, I have thought it, day in day out, for months now. Perhaps I could have written it. But I couldn't speak it.' She looked away. 'I was ashamed, proud—I don't know. It hurt so much, you see, knowing I loved you, and thinking ... thinking that you ...' She broke off.

'That I what?' he prompted her, mock stern.

'That you didn't care for me,' she said softly.

'Oh, my God, my darling, my dear one!' His arms tightened around her. 'What fools we've been! All these months ... if only you'd known!'

He drew away a little and looked down into her upturned face, and she saw his lips lift mockingly.

'Of course,' he said wickedly, 'it's all your fault. You've lost me nearly three months now, Sara. I intend to make up for that!'

'*My* fault?' She looked at him indignantly, and he laughed softly.

'But certainly your fault. If what you say is true,' his eyes mocked her, 'you could have—er—made an appointment to see me at any point in the last three months. You could have walked into my office, like the modern woman you are, and leaned across my desk, and said firmly, "Max, I love you". So, why didn't you? It would have avoided a lot of misunderstandings.'

'I could have *what*?' She knew he was teasing her, and she made her face as stern as she could, though she knew the happiness she felt still blazed in her eyes. 'I most certainly could not have done any such thing. That's the man's prerogative. I couldn't . . .'

'What nonsense! You should have sensed immediately that I was a timorous creature . . .'

'Timorous? You?'

'Certainly timorous. Beset with masculine insecurities. Unaware that my own feelings were reciprocated, etc., etc. It was your duty as a—er—modern woman, Sara. I'm disappointed in you.'

'I apologise,' she said demurely. 'But I think we did establish on one occasion that I'm far from a New Woman—I'm an old-fashioned girl. Who uses schoolmarm phrases . . .'

'Ah yes.' He gave her a look that showed he remembered the occasion only too well, and she blushed. 'Now on that occasion . . .' He too tried to look stern, and failed lamentably, Sara thought happily. 'On *that* occasion, I did come very near to declaring myself. In fact I thought I had.' He paused, suddenly serious. 'In the garden. In your room. Dammit, Sara, what did you think I was doing? But then you threw me out. And I was so tormented by jealousy I could hardly think.'

'Jealous?' She stared at him. 'Jealous of whom?'

'Of Piers Waterlow, of course.'

'Of Piers? But that's impossible! You couldn't have thought . . .'

'Well, I did.' He paused, and for a moment she saw doubt come back into his eyes, and she reached up quickly and kissed him. He caught her hands and stayed her, reluctantly.

'You're not going to get out of it that easily,' he said firmly. 'Just put yourself in my shoes for once. Begin at the beginning.' He sighed. 'Now, let me see. Ah yes. I become editor of a magazine which happens to employ a certain young woman who has publicly savaged me in the past. A young woman possessed of an acid pen, with an obvious dislike of men in general, and of me in particular. I haven't forgotten that young woman. Not in two years.' He looked at her intently. 'I encounter her again, and what do I find? I find myself obsessed with her. I think of her constantly. I have constantly to see her. I invent excuses in order to do so. I harass her. I then overhear a conversation in which she makes it extremely clear that if possible, she detests me even more than she did two years previously. The young woman concerned comes to my office. Uncharacteristically, she appears faint. I assist her, I give her brandy, I'm kind and sympathetic—yes, I am, don't interrupt! I sit beside her and look at some damned bad article she's written, and while she's coolly going over every pencil mark I've made on it, all I can think is that if I don't touch her, if I don't kiss her, I shall go mad. She starts some ludicrous argument with me, and I find that when she gets angry—something I never do, of course—she looks, if possible, even more beautiful. Even more icy. So—I kiss her. I feel that she responds . . .'

'I did respond!' Sara said quickly. 'I felt—I felt something I'd never known before. But I was frightened, and I was angry, and I didn't want you to know that . . .'

'Well, you succeeded very well,' he said drily. 'I find myself coldly and severely repulsed. Clearly everything I'd overheard was true. My pride—I have a little pride, or did have—is wounded. I take comfort in the fact that it's not just me, it's men in general that she hates, that something has happened to her . . . in the past. As perhaps something once happened to me.' He paused, for his voice had grown dark again, and she saw him make a conscious effort to lighten it. He slipped his hand under her hair, and cradled her face up to him. 'And what happens next? I meet her, unexpectedly, at an extremely tedious dinner party, at which she not only looks very beautiful but also womanly. Soft, fragile, slightly wicked. And extremely sexy. What's more, she knows it. She flirts shamelessly with the only other unattached man in the room: Piers Waterlow.'

'I did not!' Sara said hotly and, she knew, not altogether truthfully.

He smiled dangerously. 'Oh yes, you did, and I shall find ways of punishing you for that. During this dinner party, when I'm sitting opposite her, and an extremely predictable conversation about the rights of women is taking place, it suddenly comes to me what's wrong. I love this woman! Who happens, at that moment, to be staring into another man's eyes with every appearance of complete happiness. It wasn't a very pleasant discovery. I should have liked to kill them both. But her first.'

Sara stared at him. 'You felt that, then?'

'Certainly I did. I wasn't entirely displeased when, by a curious and unfortunate accident, that same young woman had a plate of raspberries tipped over her dress and retired in confusion. Though—and I must admit it—my feelings were not so engaged that the accident didn't strike me as odd. Even suspicious.'

Sara looked away. *Delia*, she thought. They were coming to Delia. Why, by the time he was describing, he and Delia were already lovers. She felt a cold icy fear start to rise inside her, and she wanted to stop him. She didn't want to know, she realised, about all that, about Montreux, about how and why he had become Delia's lover. Pain knifed viciously into her heart. His face was serious now, intent, and she knew he was watching her closely, that no evasion would be possible.

She sighed miserably, then tried.

'You kissed me, that night, in your car,' she said softly.

'Yes, I did,' he said. 'Because I had to, because I was nearly driven out of my mind with jealousy. And you know what I did afterwards, when I'd behaved with such gallantry, and taken you home when all I wanted to do was take you back to my bed and force you into it, and damn the consequences? You know what I did?'

'No,' she said quietly, 'but I know what I did. I went home and lay in bed and thought of you. Not of Piers—of *you*.'

He gave a little twisted smile. 'You see? It was then we went so wrong. I'd decided then, whatever happened, the next day I'd make you see me, make you understand how much I cared for you. And then . . .' He broke off. Sara could not look at him.

'And then you lied to me,' he said fiercely. 'You stupid little fool! You lied—and I let you get away with it.'

'I did *not* lie!' she cried hotly, fear surging up uncontrolably inside her.

'Yes, you did. There are ways of lying. You got that damned obstinate look on your face, and you stuck your chin in the air, and announced that you were resigning. Then you walked out, damn you, and all I could do then was ensure that at least for the next two months you would be there, that I should see you. Sara,' he took her hands and clasped them against him, 'why did you do it?'

She made no answer, and Max forced her face up to look at him, those harsh dark eyes raking the lines of her face.

'It wasn't true, was it?' he said roughly. 'It was a pack of lies, the whole damned thing! I knew that story of Delia's couldn't be true. I didn't believe it of you, but you wouldn't help me, you wouldn't say a word. And so all I could think of was that I had to shake the truth out of Delia somehow. I followed her down to her office—she wouldn't admit a thing. I was desperate. Don't you see? That's why I followed her to Montreux. I came out of my office, and saw you in Mark Shand's arms; bloody Piers had been telephoning for you—I felt as if I were going insane . . . I *had* to make her admit it.'

'But I was coming to see *you* then,' she cried desperately.

'I was going to stay. I couldn't bear to leave. I . . . I saw you with Delia in the corridor, and I . . .'

She broke off, and he looked at her sternly.

'That was it, wasn't it?' he said roughly. 'The idea was so absurd it had never occurred to me that you might . . .' He hesitated. 'My mother said something about it in her wire,' he said grimly. 'For God's sake, Sara, *is* that what you thought—that I . . . I cared for Delia? What kind of a man do you take me for? You think I could love a woman like that?'

'Max, please.' She put up her hand and stopped his lips. 'Please don't say any more. I did think that—but it doesn't matter. Delia told me everything. She told me about Montreux . . . everything. It doesn't matter, it's past . . .'

'Told you what about Montreux?'

'That you were lovers. That that was why you went there with her. That you were . . . going to marry . . .'

'*What?*' He pulled her fiercely to him. 'And you believed her? You can't have done!'

'I did,' she said simply, letting the words rush out without caution, past caring now. 'She told me, you see. And you were with her so often. She had your photograph on her dressing-table, with a . . . a message. And she explained everything to me, she admitted it all, the whole thing about the dress. She only did it because she was jealous, because she loves you. And it's true, Max, she does! I saw her at that dinner at Sir Andrew's when you flirted with the woman next to you . . .'

'Because I was so damned jealous of you and Piers I wanted some revenge,' he put in bitterly. Sara rushed on.

'And the next morning, after you came to my room. I saw her then. She does love you, Max, and I knew how much that hurt, and I felt sorry for her . . .'

'God damn her!' He forced Sara to look into his face. 'If I was with Delia it was because of work, because I was seeing her father. I never gave her any goddamned photograph—can you see me doing such a thing? Are you blind or something? I detest the woman! How could I be having an alleged affair with Delia, and then making love—

attempting to make love—to you?'

Sara dropped her gaze, and for a moment all her old doubts and fears rose up again unchecked. 'I thought,' she said slowly, 'I thought that was just your ... your nature. That you needed women—well, physically, constantly. I mean, I knew about your past,' she cried defensively, seeing him begin to smile, 'I knew you'd always had mistresses, lots of them, how you tired of them. And I thought ...'

'I see.' He suppressed the smile. 'A heartless philanderer, a Don Juan, a Casanova. Well now.' He sighed, and drew her body against his with a sensuality so sharp, so unexpected then, that she gave instinctively a little animal cry of pleasure and fear. 'Listen, Sara my darling.' He tilted her face up to him, and met her eyes. 'Once upon a time, I was like that. I'm thirty-five years old, you can't expect me to be a virgin. I wanted women—lots of women. And I didn't want any commitments—none. I think I was always honest with them about that. But when I was a child—well, I'd seen a lot of hurt, a lot of lies, a log of ugliness. I didn't want that for myself, and I didn't trust women. I *was* cold, suspicious—everything you once wrote about me. I thought I would never change. And then I met you, Sara, and everything changed. I wanted you, my darling, not just for a week, a few nights, but always. Not just in bed, but by my side, sharing my life and ...' He broke off, and shook her roughly. 'Sara, can't you understand? I haven't touched another woman since the first day I came to the magazine! Nothing! Not touched one, kissed one, looked at one, or thought of one—except you. Only you. God, Sara, apart from the times with you I've been living like a monk these past months ...'

Sara stared at him. 'You mean Delia *lied* to me about all that?'

'Of course she did, you fool. And you're such an innocent, so blind, you believed her!'

'But the newspaper. Today. On the plane ...'

He caught her to him savagely. 'So you did see that! I thought so. Sara, can't you understand—people tell lies,

newspapers print lies. Every day, and nobody cares. But
I've never told you a lie, Sara, and I never shall.'

'I told you a lie once,' she said softly. 'I said I hated
you ... and then, when I was on the island, I was so
ashamed, so angry with myself.' She looked up at him.
'My mother wrote,' she said. 'And your mother talked to
me, and ...'

'And what about *that*?' he demanded with mock fierceness. 'What about running off to the Seychelles with some
damn photographer the moment my back was turned?'

'I thought about you almost all the time ...'

'Almost? That's not good enough, Sara.'

He brought his mouth hard down on hers, smothering
her protestations. When he released her, she looked at
him challengingly.

'And you left too!' she accused, 'when you went to
Europe. You stayed two weeks. I've never been so miserable in my life—until I got your telex.'

Max smiled ruefully. 'That was work,' he said. 'I
couldn't get out of it. Andrew's planning to go into
Europe. I had to set up the deals for him ... However, I
didn't waste my time. I thought about you almost every
hour of the day and night ...'

'Almost?'

He laughed. 'And I planned, of course. That's why I
went to see your mother.' He looked into her eyes, his
face serious. 'Have you forgiven me for that, Sara?'

She nodded. 'Of course. It was just my stupid defences.
I ... I couldn't bear to think of your knowing all about—
well, about my father, the divorce. No one knows, you
see, and I knew my mother would tell you.'

'My darling!' he held her tightly to him. 'You mustn't
be afraid of all that, hurt by all that. Never again. After
all, look at my parents, at my poor mother.' He sighed,
his eyes almost black with anger. 'That appalling man
she's with now, some South American playboy ...'

Sara reached up timidly and kissed him. 'I think she
knows quite well what she's doing,' she said gently. 'She
talked to me about it and ...'

'My mother's made her bargain with life, long ago,' he

said grimly. 'You may be right, it may suit her. But it won't do for us.'

'For us?'

'When we're married.'

'Married?' She stared at him, her eyes widening, fear and joy constricting her throat.

'But certainly—married. What else would you suggest?' A smile tugged at the corners of his lips. 'As I recall, I did mention it to you once before.'

'In the maze? But I thought . . .'

'I know what you thought.' He drew her to him. 'Oh, Sara, I've been so blind, so foolish! My own thoughts, my own feelings, were so clear, so powerful, I thought you must understand.' He tilted her face gently up to his own. 'But you do now, don't you, my darling? I want it so much. I want you as my wife, bearing my children, with me always. Sara, I shall always love you, you know that now, don't you?'

She looked into his eyes, and saw there the same blazing certainty that burned in her own heart. She reached up to him.

'Oh, Max,' she said softly.

She saw doubt, a moment's faltering cross his face.

'You mean you will?' he said awkwardly. 'You could still work, Sara, of course, you must. But I would take care of you. I would . . . Sara, will you?'

'But of course,' she said calmly.

She saw him fight the hope that lit his face.

'I won't wait,' he said brusquely. 'We've waited too long already. It must be as soon as possible. We could do it by special licence.' He hesitated. 'I—er—I checked.' He looked so embarrassed at this admission that Sara laughed.

'Max,' she said softly, 'did you think I'd say no?'

'The possibility had occurred to me,' he said drily.

'And if I had? What would you have done then?'

'This,' he said, and his mouth sought hers fiercely. 'And some other things,' he muttered, running his lips down her throat. She kissed him back, and felt his hands blindly seeking her body, so that a sharp shudder of desire shook them both. She held him.

'Then I've changed my mind,' she said wickedly. 'I think I might need . . . persuading.'

'Now?'

'Certainly now.'

'Sara, my darling!' He cradled her in his arms tightly, and she felt the pulse of his blood rising and quickening with her own. 'Are you sure?' he said softly. 'I don't want to hurt you—I'd die rather than do that.'

She looked up into his eyes. 'You have to hurt me,' she said levelly. 'At first. And I'm not frightened of that any more. I used to be, but not now. I want it, Max, can't you feel that? Besides, there's pleasure in that pain. And I've had the worst hurt already, Max, when I thought you didn't love me.'

'You'll never think that again,' he said fiercely. 'Not as long as you live. Sara, my wife, my darling . . .'

He released her a second, and reached in his pocket. He brought out a small box, and opened it.

'It's nearly Christmas,' he said awkwardly, 'so I thought perhaps you might wear this for me . . .'

Sara caught her breath. Inside the tiny leather box was the most beautiful ring she had ever seen. It was old, a huge square ruby, the colour of heart's blood, nestling in a bed of gold and pearls. Gently he took it from the case and slipped it on her wedding finger. Then gently, firmly, he intertwined their hands together and drew her into his arms.

'I'm old-fashioned too, you see,' he said wryly, pressing her tight against him.

She laughed joyfully, and drew his head down to hers.

'But I'm a New Woman,' she said wickedly.

'Wrong adjective, Sara,' he said, in the voice he used when he corrected her copy. Then his mouth came down to meet hers, and his voice changed. '*My* woman.'

Gently, with an infinite tenderness, he kissed her lips. Desire flared through her body like a flame, and she trembled under his touch. Urgently he drew her to the door.

'Through here . . .'

'But you said it was locked.'

He smiled, his eyes dark with wanting her.

'Oh no,' he said softly. 'Don't you see, my darling? It was always open. And now we can go through.' He drew her to him. 'I won't wait any longer.'

You're invited to accept 4 books and a surprise gift Free!

Acceptance Card

Mail to: **Harlequin Reader Service®**

In the U.S.
2504 West Southern Ave.
Tempe, AZ 85282

In Canada
P.O. Box 2800, Postal Station A
5170 Yonge Street
Willowdale, Ontario M2N 6J3

YES! Please send me 4 free Harlequin Presents® novels and my free surprise gift. Then send me 8 brand new novels every month as they come off the presses. Bill me at the low price of $1.75 each ($1.95 in Canada)—an 11% saving off the retail price. There are no shipping, handling or other hidden costs. There is no minimum number of books I must purchase. I can always return a shipment and cancel at any time. Even if I never buy another book from Harlequin, the 4 free novels and the surprise gift are mine to keep forever.

108 BPP-BPGE

Name _____ (PLEASE PRINT)

Address _____ Apt. No. _____

City _____ State/Prov. _____ Zip/Postal Code _____

This offer is limited to one order per household and not valid to present subscribers. Price is subject to change.

ACP-SUB-1

You're invited to accept 4 books and a surprise gift Free!

Acceptance Card

Mail to: **Harlequin Reader Service®**

In the U.S.
2504 West Southern Ave.
Tempe, AZ 85282

In Canada
P.O. Box 2800, Postal Station A
5170 Yonge Street
Willowdale, Ontario M2N 6J3

YES! Please send me 4 free Harlequin Romance® novels and my free surprise gift. Then send me 6 brand new novels every month as they come off the presses. Bill me at the low price of $1.65 each ($1.75 in Canada)—an 11% saving off the retail price. There are no shipping, handling or other hidden costs. There is no minimum number of books I must purchase. I can always return a shipment and cancel at any time. Even if I never buy another book from Harlequin, the 4 free novels and the surprise gift are mine to keep forever.   116 BPR-BPGE

Name   (PLEASE PRINT)

Address   Apt. No.

City   State/Prov.   Zip/Postal Code

This offer is limited to one order per household and not valid to present subscribers. Price is subject to change.   ACR-SUB-1

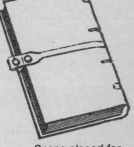